HEART
OF A
MONSTER

HEART
OF A
MONSTER

SHAIN ROSE

A
NEW REIGN
MAFIA ROMANCE

Heart of a Monster
A New Reign Mafia Romance

Copyright © 2021 by Greene Ink Publishing, LLC

This is a work of fiction and any resemblance to persons, names, characters, places, brands, media, and incidents are either the product of the author's imagination or coincidental.

Cover Design: Opium House Creatives
Print Formatting: Alt 19 Creative
Editing: https://thewordfaery.com/
Proofreading: https://www.kdproofreading.com/

Published by:
Greene Ink Publishing, LLC

To my siblings:
Kristina, Tony, Shamiah, Karah, Mari, Zetta, and Evia...
My blood is your blood.

A NOTE FROM THE AUTHOR

Please note this book touches on sensitive subjects including child sex trafficking. If you would like to learn more, please visit:

humantraffickinghotline.org/human-trafficking/
recognizing-signs

Thank you,
Shain Rose

KATIE

T HE BLOOD ON his hands turned the water red as he washed them. The white porcelain sink blurred with the pink and red ribbons of someone else's life.

"Rome," I whispered.

He jumped, the muscles in his back rippling as he tensed. His dark head of hair was dripping wet, and as it shot up, droplets of water sprayed everywhere. Those black eyes solidified into a stone-cold stare when he looked at me in the mirror. "Why are you back here?"

"I had to pee. It's not like I don't come back—"

"Get out!" He delivered the command as swiftly as a sword slicing its enemy down.

I stood my ground. We still weren't friends. We were barely acquaintances at this point. He'd ignored me too many times for that and had acted as though I didn't exist for the past couple of weeks. And in those weeks, I'd almost slept with another man, one I knew could keep me content. Yet I wanted only Rome.

"Katalina, you need to leave." His voice rumbled out low in warning.

I should have left like he asked me to. If he didn't care about me, didn't want me here, I shouldn't have cared either.

But I knew him. I knew his touch, the way his breath shook when he was with me, the way his mouth felt against mine. I knew the man under the monster.

More than anything, I knew the emptiness in his eyes. It was the same look that had marred my face over the years, time and time again.

I crossed my arms. "That's not just someone else's blood on your hands. Your face is bleeding."

He sighed and ducked his face down to splash some more water over it. "Get the fuck out of here, Katalina."

I leaned against the door frame of the bathroom for support as my full name rolled from his pillowy lips. I missed hearing his voice, missed hearing him command me. "Does the other guy look just as bad?"

I got no answer from him. The silence ping-ponged around us, ricocheting off our tension and unanswered questions. Rome wanted me to leave.

Instead, I lightened my tone. "To be honest, I might act out and fuck up one of your customers tonight. They're out of control. I just had to threaten a guy. So I'm thinking I need a good fight story." I smiled at my own joke, trying to reduce the tension. "Please tell me you killed the other guy."

He whipped around to face me. His black eyes pulled me in and tried to swallow me in their hollowness. "I did."

Those two words—he said them so seriously, goose bumps popped up over my skin. "What?"

"Don't ask a question if you aren't prepared for the answer."

"Rome, seriously? You can't...Bastian didn't say anything about kills in the past few days. If you're not following the rules...Bastian doesn't want anyone acting outside of his control."

"You still staying with him, then?" The first real emotion from him was the pain as his voice cracked with the question. It hurt me just as much as him.

"What does Bastian really have to do with any of this? You know it's all for—" I stopped. If it were all for show, I wouldn't have kissed Bastian. But Rome hadn't called; he hadn't even asked about me. He'd left me to the mob without a backward glance, even knowing I'd had my head bashed in, even knowing people were out there looking for me.

"It has everything to do with it, Katalina. You know what the family is out there doing?"

"Rome." I glanced toward the ceiling, my heart wanting to break. "They don't tell me those things. I'm not at the meetings with you all. I've never been invited. So I don't get to ask those types of questions."

"You better start. And you better be prepared for the answers."

I combed a hand through my waves as I took in his words, the way his body vibrated with a rage that was barely contained. "Are you okay?"

He crowded me against the door, looked me up and down. "Bastian's world isn't the one you want—"

"And it's the one you do? You're in just as deep as me." I grabbed the gray shirt that had splatters of blood staining it. "How are you ever going to explain this? How are you going to come back from taking lives when Bastian isn't giving you permission? He's the head of the family now, Rome. Him! Not you."

He looked away, and the breath he took in was labored, like a wounded animal struggling for life. I felt him crumbling, felt the world taking him down, felt his pain.

My hand shot out, gripping his bicep where blood lay wet over his tattoos. "Hey," I whispered and squeezed. The blood rolled down over my fingers. Warm. Still full of life. It was that vibrant red, like roses on the sunniest day after a summer rain.

"If you're hurting, if you're about to break, break me instead. I can handle it."

"Are you offering what I think you are?" His gaze ran up and down my body, searing it and branding it as his with just a look.

I swallowed and then licked my lips, knowing deep down I was his at the end of the day, that Bastian—that no man—could tie himself to me like Rome could. He'd been there for me since the beginning, and so I would be there for him until the end. "Yes."

His hand shot out so fast to wrap around my neck that I jumped and fell back into the brick wall behind me. Little fragments of the aged cement crumbled onto my shoulders as I leaned farther away from him. My body was accustomed to pain and suffering. Still, this once, I was sure this was the most danger I'd ever been in.

He squeezed, and I felt my windpipe start to close. "Kate-Bait, I will break you. And I won't put you back together."

"I'm already broken," I murmured, but it sounded far away. "And I don't expect a handout from anyone."

"At least you've learned what it's like to be in the family." He grabbed my hand and slid it under his shirt. I felt the warm liquid before it registered that he was bleeding, that he was running my hand over his wound. "My blood is your blood. I bleed, you bleed."

I whispered the family's oath. "I bleed, you bleed…" He squeezed harder so that I couldn't finish it.

Then he yanked my neck toward him so he could devour my mouth.

…Maybe this was where our end began.

ROME

I PULLED HER DOWN into the black hole. It swallowed us
up and ate us whole.
Our light was gone.

CHAPTER 1

KATIE

THE MEDS WEREN'T working. Daddy was getting worse. The glass in his hands shook so much, the water spilled over onto the worn linoleum floor. He winced and managed to set it back on the table.

Rushing to grab the towel from the sink, I did a quick wipe over the yellowed patterns, trying my best to swipe away the evidence of his disease quickly.

He sighed as I stood back up. "I'm sorry, Katalina." His voice cracked with the effort and pain of saying each word. My father had never been a man to apologize. I remember the time he took me to a baseball game just a few years ago. A man barreled into both of us. He was two times the size of my father, black tattoos of skulls covering his massive arms. He'd yelled at us to apologize for spilling his drink, told us we were clumsy.

My father stood there, composed as ever, as the man ranted on and on. I started to apologize, but my dad put his arm around

1

my shoulder to whisper in my ear, "Never let them see you cower or back down, Katalina. You are better than everyone."

Then he dropped his arm from around me, met the man eye to eye and stared him down. "Walk away or apologize for running into my daughter. And let me be clear: we will not be saying sorry."

With a crowd forming, the man's eyes bounced around. A few of my father's friends, ones I saw every now and then but never really hung out with, seemed to appear out of nowhere. They always did. Men in black suits with slicked-back hair and very nice shoes.

He stepped back from my father, eyes wide, and shook his head vigorously back and forth.

So our lives went. My father never backed down, never had to. I wasn't sure why until so much later.

Douglass King presented himself with discipline, precision, and restraint. My father had emigrated from Jamaica and followed all the immigration laws. He'd legally waited his turn, ten years of waiting on the list to come to America. He told me that when he got the call, he cried, and he wasn't sure if they were tears of joy or sadness.

He'd left his whole family—mother, brother, and sister—to come here and worked like a dog the moment he stepped foot in the United States.

Somehow, his work paid our bills. Daddy was always cutting a nice house's lawn, always fixing something in a big house that had more garages than I could count at a young age.

He'd followed the rules of the men he worked for, but one night when he called in sick, in too much pain to go in, the men in nice suits showed up at our little home's door.

"Your daddy home?" Mario's frown was genuine; I could see how his eyes creased just enough to show sympathy.

I nodded but held the door where it was, cracked just enough so the man couldn't step forward with two other men behind him. When I squinted, I saw three boys there too.

"Bellissima bambina, he's sick. I know he's sick. He needs care. We're just here to talk, heh?"

I nodded. "He didn't invite you here."

"No matter." He waved away my concern. "You know me. Look, I brought my sons and nephew to meet you. Roman, Sebastian, Caden—introduce yourselves."

All three boys stepped up on our cracked cement porch. None of them looked like boys, though. They were tall with wide shoulders that guys at my school didn't have. They filled out their dark jeans and collared shirts, none of which had a single wrinkle in them. Dark hair, dark eyebrows, and dark stares, none of them smiled at first. These weren't children. These were young men, molded by the experiences they'd already had. Not good ones either.

The night air blew cold around us, filled with a grim tension none of us could quite shake. The son that stood in the middle of them all stepped forward first, smiling at me with straight white teeth as if that would slice away at the gravity of whatever was about to happen that night. He held out his hand. "I'm Bastian." He pointed his other thumb over his shoulder. "No need to meet the others. You'll only need me."

I glanced behind him, and my eyes caught on the one who lingered back just a bit. His hair was longer, and his dark eyes stared through me like I was nothing. I tilted my head at his assessment, and he crossed his massive arms over his chest. He didn't smile; he didn't step forward to introduce himself like Caden, Bastian's brother, did.

We stared at each other like a war was beginning, a power struggle that would last decades. None of them could have been much older than me, but he seemed to be tearing apart my soul in those moments, sifting through all of me and finding every hidden part of who I was. I wanted to look away but I couldn't rip my eyes from his. They captivated me like no other person's could have.

A creak in the hardwood floors had me jumping away from the door as my father hobbled up, clearly woken from his bed. "Mario," he said from behind me. "I told you I didn't want help."

"Doug, you've worked for me for twenty years," the old man with peppered streaks in his dark hair retorted. Then he clenched a fist, his large gold ring on his pinky finger digging into his flesh.

"I cut your lawn and fixed some light bulbs, nothing more."

"Ah, you're everything more. You're family. I can get you a nurse. Just someone to help around the house, huh?"

"No." My father glared at him and then turned to me. "Katalina, go upstairs."

At fifteen, I knew my father's tone. That low, measured command meant business even if I didn't want to listen. I glanced at the boys, and one side of Bastian's mouth turned up while the boy whose name must have been Roman stared off into the darkness. "Dad, I can show them my room...so they don't get too chilled?"

He contemplated the options for a second. "Only for a minute."

I nodded and waved them all in. Slowly walking up our scuffed hardwood stairs, each step creaking beneath us, I was suddenly self-conscious. Had I cleaned my room, made my bed? Was there a bra on the floor?

I sighed and turned the rusted knob. "Sorry for any mess. I didn't expect—"

"No need to apologize. Thanks for inviting us in." Bastian glanced around the room, and his eyes fell on my laptop with papers piled next to it.

I cleared my throat. "I've just been trying to learn as much about his disease as I can."

Every paper looked crinkled, worn at the edges, and had highlights where I found ways to make my father's Parkinson's more bearable.

"You can't save him," Rome said, his voice just above a whisper, but the words pounded loudly on my heart, sending my walls flying up.

I glared at the one who was trying to crush a dream that wasn't even there. "I know I can't save him. I didn't say I'd accomplish that. I'm researching for his comfort, not a miracle."

I knew better than anyone that miracles didn't exist. I didn't need a drop-dead gorgeous guy with hollow eyes to tell me that.

Cade jumped in, trying to ease the tension in the room. "Our mother passed when we were young. I understand doing what you can to help him."

"She doesn't need to know our business." Rome's arms were still over his chest, and he stared out the window. His eyes bounced to the door when he heard a rickety squeak coming from downstairs.

"Just my dad's rocker. Doors and walls are thin here." I shrugged because I knew they probably all came from money. My father only cut lawns for people who could afford it. "Not that you're used to that."

"What's that supposed to mean?" Rome's chest puffed up like he knew it was an insult.

"It means if my dad cut your lawns," I motioned toward them all, smiling as I took in their name brand attire, their dark jeans with engineered weathering and faded spots, "you're not used to a home like mine."

"Your daddy cuts my uncle's lawn. Bastian and Cade live there." He glanced at them, and then his dark eyes fell on me like a ton of bricks. The weight of his stare crushed me, smashed my confidence, reminded me I was in a roomful of guys much bigger than me that I knew nothing about. "Not me."

"And you live where, exactly?" I raised myself up onto my tiptoes, trying to appear as big and bad as they seemed, and spun to look at myself in the mirror hanging from my door. I fluffed my black-and-pink curls. I'd dyed my hair a few weeks back, taking pleasure in the fact that I could change my look any day I wanted. "You don't go to school around here."

I would have remembered him, the way he stood there like life could pass him by and he wouldn't even raise an eyebrow. He wanted nothing to do with the world, or maybe the world wanted nothing to do with him. He had that black ink of a soul that washed over a person, that made even me feel darker.

He wasn't like the normal boys that went to my school. I walked the halls, and they turned to stare at me, at my changing hair colors, my mercurial looks, and my always-different-than-their-own skin tone. I scared the normal ones, but Rome wasn't one of them.

He picked at a few of my highlighted pages and laughed at them like I was naïve. "You don't need to know where I come from, little girl."

Cade had resorted to sitting down at my desk and fiddling on his phone, but he lifted an eyebrow at that. "Ignore him. He lives near us, about an hour from here. It's easier that way."

"Easier for what?"

"For his dad and him to be around. Family's everything, you know?" Cade replied.

Bastian walked over to tilt a photo on the wall. They hung from little clothing pins, and I'd strung lights around them to add joy to the memories. "You're close to your dad, huh? You guys look like you're always having fun."

"Of course. Who isn't close to their father?" I shrugged, baffled by the question.

They all looked at each other as if pained by my response.

"No brothers or sisters? No mother or friends?" He wiggled a picture between his forefinger and thumb as if I didn't know my own photos I had hung up.

"No brothers or sisters. No mother either. As for friends…well, you know what Cade said." I shoved a hand into my jean shorts' pocket, and my other hand caught the gold necklace hanging from my neck. "Family's everything."

Bastian hummed low as he continued studying my wall of mementos, but Rome stepped closer to me and squinted at my neck. His scrutiny had my body tightening, tingling, aching in a way I'd never quite experienced before.

"Cleopatra," he murmured as his hand shot out. His fingers touched the etchings on the front. "What a powerful being."

My breath shuddered as we stared at each other. Sure, people had commented on my necklace before. "Oh, what a pretty woman she was," they would say, or "The balls on that woman," but never had they breathed her name with such awe, like he felt what I felt about her, like he knew that whether she was a man or woman was irrelevant.

A powerful being.

I soaked up his words, his enamored stare at this woman, and thought for the first time ever that I wanted a man to look at me like that. I wanted a dark man, full of secrets and depth, to look at me just like Rome looked at my necklace.

"She's a reminder of what someone, even someone like me, can strive to be even when the odds are against them," I said.

"Or maybe of what you already are," he whispered, and his hand didn't leave my neck. It rubbed my collarbone like he knew me, like we'd met in another life and he was sure we'd be connected in this one.

We heard a loud bang from downstairs, and he yanked back his hand. I felt the loss of his skin on mine immediately but was too concerned about my father to mourn it.

I rushed to the stairs. Bastian and Cade followed. Rome showed up a minute later, like he took his time with everything in life.

We huddled at the top, quiet because we knew our fathers hadn't called us back, that they didn't want us privy to their conversation.

"Dougie, you know you can't go on like this much longer," Mario pleaded with him. "Your girl needs a dad, and she needs help. You going to let her take care of you all alone?"

Hearing the truth out loud sometimes hurts more than keeping it bottled up inside. My daddy was dying, and everyone here knew it. This disease ate at the brain and didn't give it a way out. The only dream I had now was that someone would make him more comfortable than I could. I leaned closer to the staircase, suddenly more hopeful than I had been in months.

"I don't want her involved ever," my dad responded in the soft voice he'd adopted since the disease took over. "I told you this. You respect that. You respect the one thing I got."

"I've always respected that," Mario shot back. "I'm trying to help."

"You're trying to control. You don't control my life. We made that deal long ago."

I heard a deep sigh and a string of curses before he responded again. "She'll end up in foster care. And that's a recipe for sex trafficking. I used to have deals with half the families around here."

"I'll make plans with someone." My father's voice cracked.

I hung my head and fisted one of my hands.

Rome's shoulder bumped into mine. "Easy, Cleo," he whispered. "Not time to fight yet."

At that moment, I decided I would fight Rome forever. It wasn't his right to tell me when to protect those I loved. "You all need to leave. This stress isn't good for him. And we're just fine here." I almost choked on the words, knowing how much I'd bargained with any god in existence to save my father.

"I don't doubt it," Rome grumbled under his breath.

Did he actually believe that? Did he think I'd be okay without my last parent standing? Without the man who sang me lullabies when I'd cried as a kid and had still tucked me in most nights before the pain in his body became too much?

Now, I put him to bed, sang him a lullaby just the way he'd done to me. The nights he fell asleep quickly were days I cried myself to sleep with joy that I'd given him some comfort. Most days, though, I took the pained expressions of my father and knew I wasn't much help.

The weight of the lonely world pulled my heart down into what felt like the bottom of the ocean. Without my daddy, I was nothing. Without the only person that got me, I could never, ever find a way to get myself.

His uncle's voice traveled up the stairs, reiterating what we already knew. "Dougie, you've got no one else. You and the little girl are alone. There aren't any plans to make."

"So be it," my father rasped out.

I moved to rush down the steps, but Rome grabbed my arm. "Don't."

I took a shaky breath, trying to let the conversation between the men down below come to a natural end.

Mario continued, "It's not a good life. Let me help. If her mother were around—"

I gripped the necklace, the only thing my father said she'd left behind.

"The answer is no."

I winced at the finality in my father's words. The men downstairs were right. We had no one else, and I was about to have no one at all, not even my father. Still, I trusted my father's judgment over theirs.

Bastian and Cade watched me awkwardly, like they didn't know what to say, while Rome looked me up and down.

I didn't realize a tear had escaped until Rome brushed it away. "You'll live. Because if you don't, you'll die."

My throat almost closed in fear at his callous words, but I gulped away the temptation to give into my emotion. I wouldn't show any one of them more of my weakness.

I heard footsteps coming toward the stairs.

"Boys, let's go," we heard from around the corner. They filed down the stairs.

Bastian pulled me close. "Nice to meet you, Katie. Probably best we don't meet again, even though I admit that's sort of tragic."

Cade shoved him, and he chuckled as he let me go. "Like he said, nice to meet you," Cade repeated, but I was sure he didn't care one way or the other. Both of them would forget me tomorrow. They held themselves with enough confidence, I knew that wherever they lived, they had enough attention from those around them.

Rome idled behind him for an extra second. The way he stood a whole head taller than me should have made me shrink away from him.

Instead, I shrugged and held my hands out. "What?"

He dragged one finger down my gold chain as he studied me. "Yeah, you'll live. Remember that the best of us go through the worst."

With that, he glided down the steps, and I heard the door open and close. The click of the lock was as final as a coffin lid dropping shut.

My father didn't acknowledge the conversation he'd just had when I met him at the bottom of the steps. "Go to bed, Katie. I'm on my way there, too."

"Dad, do you think we should talk—"

"Nothing to discuss that can't wait until morning." He reached over to flick off the downstairs lights and then hobbled past me to his bedroom. Normally, I'd bring him a drink or snack, but he shut his door on me and on the world.

Sighing, I made my way back to my room.

On top of one of my stacks of research was a crumpled paper with messy handwriting that wasn't mine.

> Cleopatra wasn't as pretty as she is on your necklace. It was her intelligence that allowed her to rule. She knew over a dozen languages and communicated effectively in all of them. When your dad is gone, remember that.
>
> PO Box 108
> Chicago, IL

He left his address like I was going to write him, like we could be friends, like I didn't hate the way he made me feel.

I balled it up and threw it in the trash basket next to my desk.

Late in the night, when the darkness stole away most everyone else's consciousness, my fears crept in.

I tiptoed to the bin and uncrumpled the paper. I lay awake, clutching the crinkled edges of it as tears streamed down my face.

CHAPTER 2

KATIE

MONTHS WENT BY, and Daddy got worse.
I wrote Rome every week, not sure if he was reading
my letters and not really caring at all. The outlet was
there, and I needed it.

Rome,

We celebrated my seventeenth birthday at Dad's bedside. He sang softly to me before I sang him a lullaby and tucked him in that night.

He winces in pain a lot more these days, and I'm not sure how to get better care for him.

I'll find a way,

Katie

PS Cleopatra supposedly was not beautiful but smart enough to marry some of her political allies.

PPS I'm also reading Edgar Allan Poe. He seems to know darkness and pain better than anyone else. I need a friend like that.

A daughter's love made me do what I had to do. I tracked down a suited man's son in school. Jared let me into his home. He let me into his bed, too.

Weeks of my father in pain went by, and I begged Jared's father for money. The man's slimy gaze trailed my body over and over again. I started to learn the looks, the sly brushes of his hand, and the lift in his eyebrow when I caught him looking at me in a way he shouldn't.

He gave me money for my dad's medication, got me in touch with a doctor who would take my money.

One night, I got home too late for my father to think I was doing anything a normal seventeen-year-old should be doing. I handed him the meds.

His face fell, blood draining from it until he was even grayer than his usual sickly pallor. "Where did you get these?"

"I'm working. I told you. I saved and was able—"

He grunted. "Working where? These meds cost thousands, and they're illegal to anyone—"

"I just..." I stuttered, not sure how to lie but knowing I had to. "I have a friend in the medical field."

"The high school called," he declared like I was already guilty.

I winced because I'd skipped class with Jared. "I had a headache and—"

"Jared isn't a good friend to have, Katie. Is he the one getting you the jobs?"

How could I tell him that it wasn't a job, just a gift from Jared's dad, a man he must have known of?

"I don't want you working anymore." He emphasized the word *working*. Maybe he knew I wasn't exactly working, that I'd found a clear way to make money to pay for meds but it wasn't one he would approve of.

"Dad, just relax. We need the money."

"No." He slammed his hand down on the table. "I don't want the medication. It won't help in the long run, anyway. Stop what you're doing, Katie. I don't know how you got involved, but I want it to stop now."

When his health insurance denied him again, I saw the effects immediately. Parkinson's devoured his brain function. One little pill costing thousands could make him more comfortable, and I researched tons more that I could get access to just by talking with Jared's father.

My daddy, the man who'd always made me feel comfortable, even when I had no momma to help me through anything, deserved to feel comfortable in his last days.

"I'm not selling drugs, if that's what you think," I told him.

"What are you selling, then?" He must have seen the shame in my gray eyes because his started to glisten. "Stop what you're doing now, baby. You can't come back from it if you keep on."

"We need the money, Daddy."

"I need my daughter to know she's better than anyone. Remember what I'm telling you, Katalina. You don't fit in because you were made to stand out." His calloused hand shook, but his grip was firm when he took my hand in his. "You didn't know your momma, honey, but I promise you she was just as strong."

I left him the very next night to meet Jared. When he fell asleep, I listened to the nightly calls his father made. The price to be a fly on the wall was a roll in the hay. I learned quickly that boys my age were driven by a lot of things, but the most powerful one was a girl who knew how to use her body for pleasure. I wasn't proud that I'd lost my virginity, but I was proud that it'd been for a cause.

Jared's daddy became very generous. Especially when he saw that I could leave him and his son for another boy my age. After a few months, I'd climbed over Jared to the one who could help my family monetarily. Jared's daddy didn't mind me around if I let him feel me up, didn't mind my sitting in on his important calls if I sat on his lap, if I gave him what he wanted.

The calls led back to Mario, to the men in suits who I knew had the money to help my father be comfortable.

Mario had sounded elated when Jimmy introduced me. He claimed he'd always wanted a daughter in the family, and my heart sped up at the idea of belonging. Maybe it was where I was supposed to be if my father passed away. Maybe everything would be fine.

The first letter came a few days after that call.

This will be my first and last letter.
Jared and Jimmy are not good people.
Don't surround yourself with trash or you'll start to smell just as it does.

Rome

PS Cleopatra dined with rulers, not servants.

PPS Poe's best is "The Raven." He goes mad in missing his Lenore. I find we're all missing something, and maybe that makes us all a little mad.

I did exactly the opposite of his instructions.

I solidified my role within the family by sitting in on those calls every time Jimmy invited me. They hooked me with their secrets and made sure I was aware that I could never share them.

All I shared was my body with Jimmy, more times than I could count.

Was love exchanging sex for something so necessary to my life? Jimmy saved my father. He sacrificed hundreds of thousands of dollars just for me.

I thought I loved him for that; I loved him even if I hated him for the same reason.

And the men on the phone became men I looked at as my family too. They asked about "Dougie" and wanted to make sure he was just as comfortable as I wanted him to be. When they talked business, they listened to me like a family would too. I was given a voice there; they respected my advice. I was the beautiful *ragazza* who spoke candidly, swiftly, and with just enough innocence that I was a window into many answers they couldn't have seen. I gained respect and what I thought was their love.

But I lost my father's love in the process.

He begged me to stop. We didn't discuss my job, but he knew it wasn't the respectful one he'd taught me to get.

I stuck to my reason. "We need the money."

And we did. His hands shook less. He could walk around the house. The nurse who had started to come to help him throughout the day worked wonders with physical therapy.

Still, the last night he begged me, "Stop, Katalina. You're better than what you've made yourself into."

"I'm what I need to be, Daddy." I powdered my face. "In a few more years, I'll be going to college. This will pay for it."

"Get a loan." His voice sounded strained and defeated. "I always taught you to do what you wanted, that I trusted you to make the right decision. Don't make me say you didn't."

I turned from the mirror to look him in the eyes. "You're alive. That's the right decision. No one was going to give a young girl like me—let alone a mixed one—a job, not in this neighborhood. I'm seventeen, and you're still here. We're doing fine as long as you're here, Daddy."

He stared at me for a long time. "The world should have given you every opportunity. They should have seen that different makes you beautiful."

I winced and turned away from him. "I'm not beautiful, Dad. This is life-and-death. I choose life for you. Every. Single. Time."

His stare was cavernous as he nodded, and then he disappeared down the hall.

The next morning, I found him dead in the bathtub. The note he wrote read:

You're beautiful. I choose death so you can live. I won't tell you to stop working with them. I know you're in too deep. Make me proud, Katalina. Show them you were meant to stand out or get out from under them."

CHAPTER 3

ROME

My father passed away three weeks ago, hence the new address.

Not that you care. Not that you'll write if you read this. But I had to tell someone. Is it selfish to worry that he was my last hope in connecting with this world? Ever since he passed, I only feel something when I think of him. The pain in knowing he took his own life instead of letting Parkinson's take it for him is crushing.

Did you know he did it just because of me? Because he didn't want me to see Jimmy anymore to get his meds.

I would have done anything for him.

Any. Single. Thing.

And now I have nothing to do because he's gone.

Nothing to feel either.

They placed me with a foster family, and I thought I'd care that the man who claims he wants to be my father visits me in the middle of the night.

But I don't feel a thing, Rome.

And I wonder, can you get better, can you start to feel again with nothing to live for? Or do you just continue living...for what...I don't know.

Katie

PS Cleo lived for power. Or maybe love. She died because she lost them both.

PPS I don't read much of anything anymore.

I GOT HER LETTER way too late. The date was postmarked months back, and the edges of the envelope were bent and covered with mud.

Still, I recited the address as I pounded it into my phone and drove straight there, hoping to find her, hoping to find the man who must have been taking advantage of her.

I banged on the door with the chain I took with me at times wrapped around my knuckles.

A tall skinny man with dark circles around his eyes answered. "Damn, calm down. What you want?"

"I'm looking for Katie."

"I didn't tell her she could have anyone over," he drawled.

It was all the confirmation I needed. Taking a step forward, I swung at him, and the chain links shattered his jaw. He flailed back, screaming in surprise. Clattering came from a hallway behind him.

Katie stood there, a ripped black shirt hanging from her shoulder and jeans that showed too much of her waistline hugged her hips. She'd filled out and lost weight too. Her high cheekbones were hollowed out, just like the gaze she now shot at me.

"You need to leave." Her voice was raspier than I remembered and completely devoid of emotion.

"You need to go back to your room until I'm finished with him." I pointed behind her, directing her back to safety.

Her foster parent finally recovered, and he ran toward me at full speed. My wrapped fist met his momentum head-on, and he screeched in pain while scrambling away from me into his kitchen. The man wasn't skilled in fighting, and when he pulled a knife from a drawer with a snarl on his face, I winced. Leaving a bloody mess to clean up wasn't ideal, and as I glanced at Katie, I knew I didn't really want her to see any of that.

Advancing quickly, I yanked his wrist forward fast enough to trap the weapon and twisted hard. The metal clattered on the floor as he wiggled in my grip and punched wildly through the air, hoping to land a blow.

I calculated each punch and made sure to hit him in the temple, hard in the gut, and at weak points that I knew would break bones. The chain, my training, and the fact that I'd done it all before gave me an astronomical advantage.

It didn't take him long to realize I wasn't stopping. That flight response kicked in, his body panicking and starting to flail every which way. He freed himself long enough to throw a bowl at me and yell out that his wife would be home soon.

"I'm not worried about who finds you dead." I smiled at his ridiculous warning, and my hand pulled a gun from where it was tucked into my waistband behind me.

His eyes widened despite the increasing swelling, and his hands shot up to the sky. "Is this about her? I've never touched her. She's a liar, I swear. She came messed in the head. Doesn't cry, doesn't talk, doesn't do anything."

I glanced at her. Katie was leaning against the doorframe of the hallway, watching with her arms crossed over her chest. Even though her curves had filled out, she looked tiny in that black sweater, like she was still the same kid I met who was trying to save her father.

"That true, Katie. You a liar?"

"My father was too proud to raise a girl who lied, Rome." She said the words barely above a whisper and looked down as she tucked herself deeper into that sweater. Without another word, she pushed off the wall to go back to her room.

Something twisted in my gut, snarled in anger, and unleashed in my soul.

When I looked back at the man, he was crying and stuttering over his words. "Please, man. She's beautiful and...I have a problem...we needed the money, okay?"

Bile rose fast in my throat, bitter and acrid. I shook my head once, trying to wrangle the angry beast that clawed at me to get out. The man had sold her. I knew it already, but still I whispered the question, "How did you get the money?"

A bead of perspiration formed as his eyes darted everywhere, like he'd been caught. "Look, there's only been a few guys who paid to be with her. She's asleep when they come, I swear. I got a lot of–"

I raised the gun so it pointed right at his head. "You're going to die in the next minute. Don't waste your breath, because you can't change my mind."

Changing tactics, he tried to turn the tables on me. "You're a fucking monster," he cried with his hands in the air.

"Tell me something I don't know." I motioned for him to come toward me, curling my hand up and down over the rusted metal. I carried it sometimes, when I knew I wanted to inflict real pain. My father had me use that chain to strangle the life out of my first kill. At the age of twelve, most would have cowered at the request.

24

I'd embraced it.

The man ran toward me with a loud yell, hoping to catch me off guard. I stepped to the side, raising my gun above my head so that he didn't grab for it. Muscle memory had me using his own force to yank his jaw as I moved. The loud crack signaled that his spinal cord had separated from his brain.

The sound quieted the rage in my veins, soothed the monster that wanted a life to eat. We got what we came for.

I pocketed my weapon and enjoyed the silence.

I knew how to deliver kills. I was comfortable with it, almost took pleasure in it. A man fought for his life like a fish out of water, flapping about and trying his best to flounder back to safety. He'd been no different. Normally, I called Sergio and he brought a cleanup crew right after. I was used to leaving the scene, used to washing my hands of the situation, and used to moving right on.

That day, I couldn't.

My real problem, the one that caused me extreme discomfort, was the girl in the next room.

My boots clomped on the wood floor as I peered inside two rooms that stunk of old cigarette smoke before I reached hers. She sat on a pink bedspread in the third room, legs crossed as she leaned against the wall. "Is he dead?"

"It doesn't matter." I didn't go near her but took in her dyed hair, pink tips on her dark strands. She let them fall over her face and down her shoulders like she wanted to hide behind them. "Let's pack you a bag and get you to a friend's house. Do you have a contact at CPS?"

She laughed, but her smile didn't meet her eyes. She stared out of the window, and I wondered how many times she'd contemplated running away. "I'm not calling them. They knew what Marvin was."

"Katie," I sighed. "Not all of CPS is bad. The world dealt you a fucked-up hand."

Her eyes cut to me, glistening silver like a sharpened blade. "He paid someone at CPS. They aren't all bad, sure. But that guy was. They're all getting a cut. The girl that was here before, she told me..."

She choked back a sob and brought her arm up to cover her cry. She straightened then and wiped away the tears so roughly they left red marks on her cheeks. "They get thousands for having men visit us. Over and over and over again, Rome. Before that, her own *family* before was selling her for years. The world is fucked up. I'm not calling CPS, not calling anyone I don't trust now. I've got friends. They'll come get me."

"If your friends are Jared and—"

"Rome, do you want to take me in?" She glared at me, cutting me with just a look, like it was a challenge, like she knew I'd say no.

I recoiled at her question like she'd drawn blood. She couldn't live with me. I'd just murdered someone with my bare hands in the house she lived in. I was what the mafia made me: a monster and nothing more.

"I'm no good for you, Cleo. I'd ruin you."

"Then let me go where I need to go. I'm safer wherever I land than I ever was with the dead man out there."

Maybe I was too young to make a different call, but I still wonder if I should have.

———

She didn't write to me again.

I couldn't write to her either since I didn't have her location, only snippets of information from some of the calls Mario and the guys made. I was running my bar, trying not to be a part of the meetings. When Mario needed me, he called me.

I delivered kill after kill. Tonight, I did one quick. After a couple of missed punches, he'd run at me, hoping to outmaneuver me with force.

I needed efficiency this time, even though the frustration and need to torture was there. We'd found out he'd been trafficking women through the business we helped him keep afloat. He deserved a beatdown, but I took his life fast instead.

Mario Armanelli, the boss of the family, wanted a late family meeting. My plans for torture and suffering would have to be inflicted on those that aided the trafficker.

I stepped over the obese, balding man as I pressed and held the number three on my phone. "Job is done. Take care of the mess. I made it easy for you, no red anywhere."

Sergio sighed into the phone. "Thank you, Rome."

I hung up and drove my truck through the cool night air with my window rolled down. I took the side alleys and got lost in the sea of buildings. One road led to another until the old factory our family owned came into view. The massive garage hid most of our cars, and one of the guys opened it immediately when he saw me approach.

It'd been a while since I'd taken my place at the right hand of Mario Armanelli. I was a young underboss, but I'd earned my seat. I protected his life and solved the problems he needed me to.

I nodded to a few familiar faces as I walked into the open space that must have been where they used to house the large crates. Now, we had an expensive circle of luxurious chairs on the cement slabs, and they all faced the middle one. The rusted metal of that folding chair had seen better days, and so had the people who would sit in it. One of the younger members dragged it to the center of the room, letting it scrape loudly against the ground, drawing the attention of everyone there.

These impromptu meetings always had everyone jumpy and on their toes. No one knew who the boss was going to call to the middle: the hot seat, the electric chair of the mob, the one you never wanted to be in.

Mario patted my shoulder as I sat down next to him. "My boy. Thanks for the easy cleanup. Sergio's getting old. Frankie's out of town, but we need to bring him in more to help Sergio."

I shrugged. "It's fine. Wanted to be on time. Not every day we have a meeting sprung on us. Who's in trouble?"

Mario grunted and rolled a thick gold ring on his finger. His olive skin wrinkled around it, worn from age and years of strain. Running the mob and keeping his businessmen in line kept the man busy.

And me too. I did the dirty work. The dirtiest of all. I killed the men Mario didn't need anymore, that disobeyed us, that stepped out of line.

Just a year ago, one man stepped so far out of line that Mario would have been dead had I not jumped in to save him at the exact right moment. No one saw it coming. Except his right-hand man, my father.

Mario and I cried that night. He cried like he'd lost a brother, and I cried like I'd lost my father.

Because we had.

Life within our family was a dangerous business. Irish, Russian, and Albanian families watched for a weak spot. They found one with my father but didn't expect that I'd bridge the gap. Mario Armanelli lived on as the Chicago Boss, but he'd changed after that night.

He wanted new ways for the mob, and he tightened up his team, kept me close, and started to pull the Italian families back together.

Mario squeezed my shoulder and then gave it a little shake. "It's not you." He chuckled. "Never you, son."

I rolled my eyes at him even mentioning it could be me.

No one came between us. I'd lived in the family under my father from a very young age. My mother left me to my father early on, or he took me from her—I wasn't sure which. But I wouldn't have been surprised at either.

I never asked, because he never would have told me. He didn't care about the niceties of parenting. He was ruthless, cold, and vicious. It made him good at what he did. And it taught me the same skills.

He never shielded me from his work. I'd seen a man murdered by the age of four and knew how to handle a gun by the age of six. By twelve, I'd taken a life and knew how to drown out their pleas as they begged for it.

It made me the perfect person to step into the job, to step into the lifestyle.

Except I wasn't my father. I'd made ties. I'd conquered my emotions, crushed them into nothing when I needed to for the family. And I put my trust there.

In the family.

In my father.

I believed in the mob. I indulged in my lifestyle because it was a good one. I saw enough death within the family to know it may not be a life that would last long. So I indulged in the luxuries.

If my life would be short, I intended to make the most of it.

Until we lost my father.

Questions started for me then. The little voice in my head that said I could have been wrong about everything festered and grew.

Love for the life disintegrated. The soul within me withered. I turned from a child with trust to a man with only one purpose: to fill the shoes of the underboss for the family and never be left open to deceit again.

I took life after life and felt less and less pain.

Bastian and Cade, Mario's only children, nodded at me as they strolled in. When I saved their father's life, I'd saved their family. I became one of them, another son of the mob boss. Still, they only met my eyes for a moment. Maybe because they didn't care, or maybe there was nothing there to look at.

"Today, the only person in trouble is Jimmy." Mario confirmed what I'd suspected.

I cracked my knuckles. Jimmy had been sliding through the cracks for years now, getting away with shit he shouldn't. The Armanelli family had cleaned up a massive mess for him more than once. We couldn't afford slipups, not with RICO laws as restrictive as they were now. Tonight, Mario would decide if Jimmy was worth the risk.

He walked in, black suit pressed and a swagger in his step. He wore the gold family ring, along with about nine others, and flaunted extra diamonds where he could. A Rolex weighed down his wrist; the gold chain on his neck was overkill. He wanted to make a statement, but the one he really made walked in behind him.

I sucked in a quick breath.

Katie.

She had always been a little thing, probably only five-five and skinny enough to pick up without any struggle. She had curves, but they were young ones. She was green. So was I. I realized my twenty-one years seemed unripe to most, but I'd seen the world.

On Jimmy's arm, what had she really seen?

She wore a pink sweater, her black hair pulled back in a tight bun and tipped with red now. She walked close to him like he would protect her.

Her almond eyes and smooth skin screamed innocence. It was beautiful and frightening at the same time. These men were nothing like the ones she should be around. Some of them smiled, Bastian actually catcalled, and Mario hushed him.

I leaned toward Mario. "Why is she here? Did he inform you?"

"I knew about it," was all Mario said. "Jimmy?" Mario announced, and everyone gave our boss the attention he deserved. "You brought the little Katalina finally."

She smiled and walked up to Mario. She held out her hand, no fear in her eyes as she shook his hand and he brought her in for a kiss on each cheek.

"Thank you for having me," her voice rasped out to Mario, a hair above a whisper, and it rubbed every man's dick just the right way. Her lips glistened with gloss, and the eyeliner she wore was thicker than I'd ever seen on her.

Fuck, she was a pretty little thing. She always had been. Her frosted gray eyes held your soul when she stared you down, like she could suck you in and never let you out. And tonight she'd dressed in soft pinks though she'd painted on the face of a woman.

She still wore the gold necklace. I saw it tucked under the neckline of her sweater. Didn't she know this wasn't the place to wear something like that? She had to if she was with a man like Jimmy.

What a piece of shit she'd picked to be with, too. I held back a growl just thinking about how dirty this man got. He'd trafficked buses of women. He'd tied them down, shot them up with drugs, then sold them off.

It was the old way, not something we'd ever focused on much, except that we knew it wasn't the way Mario wanted to leave the mob, and he would leave it to his son one day soon enough.

Traditions were sometimes buried so deep into the ground that it was hard to determine if the roots were toxic. And poisonous roots needed to be ripped out.

My eyes skittered up Katie's arms, but her sleeves hid any track marks I may have found. Had she fallen a victim to the temptations of the world, to what she'd been forced into so long ago in that foster home?

A jolt of realization shot through me—there were so many others like Katie, but I shoved those thoughts away.

I wondered how I'd protect those I loved, how I'd protect my own little thing now. My ex-fiancée, Sasha, had come to me just a few nights back. We'd fought again. Life of the mafia, I guess.

She didn't see this side of things. She didn't know about the drugs, the trafficking, the body counts.

Even when I'd told her, she'd held strong that she deserved more of my time. She didn't understand—family was family. Or maybe that was the real problem: I didn't see her as a part of that family.

That night she repeated it over and over, and then dropped a bomb.

She was pregnant.

My baby was in her belly.

And a baby changed everything. A baby made me reconsider what I was doing.

"You ask and you shall receive, Mario," Jimmy sneered. He grabbed the girl's elbow, and she went with him to sit down where he normally did.

Mario tsked at him. "You know you don't sit there tonight, Jimmy. You sit in the hot seat."

"I didn't do anything outside of the family," he countered.

"You didn't traffic two hundred women in just this past week by sending your crew out to lure new foster kids? They may be your crew, Jimmy, but you work for me. Those are my men, my soldiers, and my name they work under. That's *mi famiglia*, no?" He emphasized that word. It meant something to us all, and it sliced through the room. The attitude toward Jimmy shifted. I could feel the ones that had been on his side turn their backs.

Jimmy stuttered, and two of Mario's guys grabbed him to shove him into the chair. His feet dragged across the floor as he wriggled in their grip.

The metal clanked as they held him down in the chair like a jail cell closing. Jimmy sat alone in that cold, ominous chair. The blubbering erupted from deep in his gut immediately, an act for sympathy and a last-ditch effort that wouldn't sway our jury.

His show was of no entertainment to me. Instead, I watched Katalina. No fear was in her eyes. No shudder ran through her body. She picked at a piece of lint on her jeans and crossed her legs, as if ready for the night's events.

In her room the first night I met her, there had been so much more emotion in her. Marvin stole it away, and Jimmy hadn't seemed to jog even a memory of an emotion either. She'd been emptied of feelings a long time ago.

Were her eyes as dead as mine when she stared through the room?

What have you been through, Cleo?

"Admit something, Jimmy," Mario said with a sigh, rubbing the bridge of his nose. "Let me at least know you're honest. Did you bring them in or not?"

"I swear I didn't." He wiped a meaty hand over his nose and sniffled.

Mario dragged a finger back and forth over one eye as if to clear away dust irritating it. The guy on the right punched Jimmy until blood splattered. "That's enough. Admit something, Jimmy. Don't you know I'm trying to set an example for my boys?" He motioned toward Cade, Bastian, and me, as if I were his boy too.

"Katie will tell you." His pleading eyes shot to her. "I didn't do it. I've been with her all week. I only left a few times."

Mario turned to Katie, and my body tensed. Something in me instinctively wanted to tell her to run. The hot seat was dangerous, and sparks could fly from it to others very quickly.

I didn't. It wasn't my job to save her, at least not this time.

Those smoky eyes of hers scanned the room and fell on me like I could give her the answers. Maybe I should have tried.

Maybe we wouldn't have ended up where we were if I had.

"Katalina, Douglass was a good man," Mario said, and I reared back at him saying her father's name. We all knew he'd died a while back, that she'd had to go into foster care. Yet I knew more. Her letters, her words, echoed through my head. "I always relied on your father to tell me the truth," Mario said the words softly.

Her eyes narrowed; a phoenix of feeling rose in her. Suddenly, anger and fury whipped from her toward Mario. You could feel it in the air, the control she had over the room.

She nodded at our boss, and I thought I saw her chin quiver, yet the sound that rolled from her lips was steady. "Because he wasn't a liar. He never uttered anything but the truth before he died. I'm not one either."

A few of us dropped our heads at the fact that she'd lost her father. Family ties ran deep enough that some felt another's pain. Mario shouldn't have used her father for leverage. Couldn't he have used something else? Couldn't he have been less calculating?

Mario lifted an eyebrow. "You're right. Douglass was my kind of guy." He clapped his hands together as if it was decided. "Tell me where Jimmy was last night. With you? All night?"

She turned to stare at her boyfriend. He glared back at her, bullets of sweat forming as his eyes bulged silently, commanding her to back him. She hesitated, and I swear if Jimmy could have, he would have strangled the answer he wanted out of her.

She whispered, "He was with me."

Jimmy yelled, "See! I'm not making up stories. Don't pin this on me, Mario." His brow was furrowed as he pleaded with him.

The silence stretched as we all waited for Mario's decision.

Katalina spoke up before anyone else did. "He was with me," she repeated. "But after we fought some and he held his gun to my head, he left to see Sasha. He didn't return the whole night."

"You little *stronza*, do you think I give you what I do so that you can—" Mario's muscle men shoved Jimmy down in his seat just as he was rising to go at her.

She didn't cower or shrink back. She dragged her red fingernails across her lips. Her eyes shined like she enjoyed it, like a feline ready for a fight. I might have been the only one to see her brilliance in that moment, but it radiated from her. Katalina thrived in the midst of her lover's demise. I wasn't proud to admit my dick hardened watching her, and I wanted to know more about her than I should. I wanted to bottle up her radiance and study it, take her to one of the places I kept secret and hold her there long enough to slice away her layers and understand her.

She was the first enigma I'd come across that enraptured me.

But my heart jolted back as my mind registered her words.

"Sasha," I whispered. The name matched my unborn baby's mother, my ex-fiancée. The rhythm of my heart sped up, my stomach suddenly jumped into my throat.

It had to be a coincidence.

But there weren't coincidences in the mob.

Mario set a hand on my shoulder. "Not your Sasha, son. She's an untouchable. Who is this Sasha?" he asked.

Jimmy eyeballed us both. "Look…" He sighed and then ran a hand through his hair that was wet with his sweat.

The walls around me shifted at the fear in his voice. No one's voice shook like that unless they knew they were about to reveal something unredeemable.

"This morning, I went there when you were working, Rome." He groaned at his own story, as if he was disappointed in his actions. "I shouldn't have been seeing her. You know how she was though? How she looked at you with those big doe eyes, huh?"

Was.

I attempted to rise from my chair, but Mario held me down, a hand on my shoulder. "You're lying," I said, but my voice cracked and I cleared my throat. "Don't fuck with me, Jimmy. I've always wanted to kill you. Don't fuck with me and make me do it."

He shook his head. "She was going to cause problems, okay? She tried to tell me she had my baby in her belly and—"

I flew off my chair at the words. They rang too close to the truth.

The baby was mine.

No one was supposed to know about her pregnancy. We were going to wait to tell everyone.

Mario's muscle men surrounded me. They were nobodies in the grand scheme of things. They did our dirty work when we needed scapegoats.

I shoved at them, fought them, took out one guy's knee and hit the other guy in the throat. Three more jumped up, but Bastian and Cade pulled me back.

"Calm down," Bastian kept whispering.

The rage consumed me, coiled around my soul, burned deep in my tendons and pumped through my arteries and veins. When I couldn't break from my cousins' grasp, I turned to Mario. "I get him. His life is mine."

Mario nodded. "So long as it's here. Now. Those are the conditions. Everyone sees now what happens when you hit an untouchable and traffic women with my family name attached."

Our new way of life had come years ago. The Armanelli family endeavored to stop making money on drugs and women. We wove ourselves into businesses, undercut gas prices, played with the stocks.

Jimmy started crying, begging for his life.

I closed my eyes and saw Sasha. Her hair would whip in the wind so wild, she would threaten to cut it. And on our best days, I would tell her no, that it was beautiful, and she'd smile so damn big. We'd had our problems, but her light shouldn't have been extinguished by a man like him. I snapped my eyes open. "You took what was mine, Jimmy."

"I didn't. She said you weren't with her anymore. She said—"

I let the chain fall from the cuff of my long-sleeved shirt. The clank of the rusted metal on the cement revved the beast in me.

Jimmy's rapid breathing turned to a wheeze at the sight of my chain, and he recoiled in his chair. "Please, Rome. Don't do this to me. Don't turn on me when I've been family—"

Letting him finish the sentence and use our family as a negotiation card would have been criminal. You can only hold back a monster for so long. I whipped the chain forcefully enough across his face that it tore away most of his cheek.

Some men believed in waiting a few minutes to let the pain sink in, but I piled it on. Pulling a knife from my pocket, I shoved it into his thigh. His scream fed my need to torture.

"Did she beg for her life? Tell me you made it easy on her." My plea was real. I whispered the last word, "Please."

"Rome, I swear it was quick. I shot her, man. I shot her, and she was gone pretty fast. I—"

"Where?"

"Huh?"

"Where did you shoot her?" I weighed the knife in my hand. It was nice and balanced. I'd had it sharpened just a week ago. It'd cut through his flesh precisely.

"Her stomach."

"Right where she was growing my baby?" I asked so softly, some members leaned forward to hear me. "Right in the place where your stomach acid can eat away at your body for as long as an hour before you die?"

"It wasn't that long. I...the baby was mine," he blubbered as I stood over him.

I glanced around the room. Mario was shaking his head, and Cade and Bastian glared at the man in front of me. Everyone either squirmed in their seat because they normally didn't handle the killing or they looked on excitedly to see the fucker go. When I met his girlfriend's gaze, I glanced back at him. "What if your little woman over there was pregnant and I gutted her like a fucking fish?"

For a moment, he looked hopeful. "You mean like one for one? I'd be hurt, Rome." He looked at her with a love so fake I almost laughed at it. "If that's what it takes, though..."

I turned my head toward Katalina. She lifted an eyebrow at me, completely and utterly unfazed by the turn of events. Her mouth kicked up in one corner, and she looked as though she dared me to try.

"Were you part of this, Katie?" I tilted my head toward Jimmy, knowing he was dead as a doornail either way but wanting to know if I needed to kill her too. I would kill everyone to avenge my child.

"Part of my boyfriend continually cheating on me with your girlfriend?" She asked the question in disbelief. A scoff left her mouth, and her face twisted as if she were sick to her stomach before she whispered, "Seriously? Does it even matter?"

I shook my head. This was the shit no person should be a part of. The mob afforded you luxuries, but it plagued you with despondency too.

"The truth will come to light," she muttered.

"My truth is in his death," I replied.

She shrugged her shoulders like him dying didn't mean a thing to her. "No skin off my back."

"You little bitch!" he spat.

I cut into his stomach. He gasped and scrambled to cover the blood gushing out.

"You reap what you sow. Your stomach acid will kill you if the lack of blood in your veins doesn't first."

"You're fucked in the head." Tears sprang to Jimmy's eyes as they bulged at the amount of blood soaking through his shirt. "Sasha told me how you killed all those people, how you're a monster. She was fucking happy that baby had a chance of not being yours, and I bet she was thankful I killed them both, because a baby by you—"

I took his arm and yanked him off his chair. I snapped the shoulder out of place and sat on his back. I didn't give him time to recover, jamming the knife into it. "I want you to know that as you're lying facedown on the cement, you're getting stabbed in the back just like you stabbed us all in the back." I got up and let him blubber in his own blood. I walked to

Katalina and crossed my arms over my chest. "Want to kiss him goodbye?"

She unfolded her legs. She wore tight dark jeans and pink stilettos that matched her sweater. Suddenly, the stilettos looked fierce, like she'd walked in with sheep's clothing and now gave me a glimpse of the wolf beneath. Even with those heels, the top of her head barely reached my chin. Still, she went toe-to-toe with me. "I always see my men off. Haven't you heard?"

With that, she walked over to Jimmy and gripped his arm with both hands. It took the full weight of her body to roll him over.

When he faced her, he mouthed, "Help me."

She leaned in and whispered, "You got what you deserve." Then she kissed him on his bloody lips before taking out a gun someone let her bring in. Another point in her favor.

She held it to his head and asked, "Feel familiar?"

His eyes went wide, and then he begged her, "Please do it. I'm in pain, Katalina."

I almost lunged for her. That man deserved to suffer, but I saw the same posture in her that I had when I stood over someone evil while I had the upper hand. She was relaxed, not coiled to kill.

She looked around the room, everyone watching her. "I want in, Mario."

He nodded. "It's a blood oath. Family first, honey. You don't get out. You bleed, we bleed. You die, we die."

She nodded slowly as if she knew she didn't have any other option. For some reason, I almost blurted out to stop, almost tried to tell her she didn't need to be a part of this.

Yet I saw the hunger in her eyes when she looked back at her boyfriend. She wanted this. She wanted so much more than this.

"Goodbye, Jimmy." She pulled the trigger.

A few of the boys jumped, ready for the gunshot. All we got was a click. Nothing happened. No bullets were in the chamber. She looked at the gun and shrugged. Then she laughed and laughed as she walked away to sit back down. Jimmy sobbed and begged for anyone to take his life.

Some of the men, ones that had only recently made it into the inner circle, started to squirm. Watching a man turn gray and cold as he bled out wasn't easy at first. You had to get used to it. He wrenched in pain for a couple of minutes, the stomach acid starting to take effect.

Soon, most everyone lost interest. Some went about their business, talking to one another about other transactions we needed to tie up that day. Mario talked with Bastian and Cade about tomorrow's plans. Others looked at their phones, handling more affairs.

Katalina and I stared at Jimmy. Every so often, I glanced her way. I saw a new look, one with much less bravado, fall over her features when he coughed up some blood.

She'd put on an amazing act for everyone in the family. She even pulled the trigger, and she must have thought it was loaded. She'd been willing to kill him, but there was a love there too. She was a young girl, still conflicted about her life, and she was going down the wrong damn rabbit hole to figure it out.

"I want to ask the girl some questions," I whispered to Mario before I approached her.

Mario glanced at her and then me. "She's a tough little thing, but I really like her, Rome. She's good people for us. Good to have a woman among us, huh? Maybe she'll teach us a different perspective."

"She's not a woman, Mario. She's a girl," I mumbled as I stood.

"Too late now. She's known too much for too long." Mario shrugged. "She'll be like a daughter to me. I've always wanted one, and a ruthless one is even better." A laugh burst from him, and he slapped his meaty, ringed hand across his knee. "The way she pulled that trigger, even I jumped."

I shook my head, concerned for the very first time that we'd stripped someone of their last straw of innocence.

My black boots clomped across the floor to Katie. I waited for her to turn her attention my way as I stood over her, but her eyes stayed on her boyfriend like he was her world.

"You wanted him dead. What's so interesting now that he's dying?"

"I've only ever seen a person die exceptionally slowly. This is fast but painfully slow too."

"You care about him as much as the father you saw dying?"

"Not even a little," she retorted immediately, and her moon-gray eyes sliced over to me, filled with hate. "I just tried to kill him. Why would you think I cared about him?"

"I saw that. It was a nice act. Now I've seen you sitting here staring at him with, what? Is it pity? Love? You love a man who murdered a pregnant woman?"

Her cherry glossed lips pressed together. She stood up so quickly, I heard her knees crack. "I didn't know he did that."

I nodded. "I want to believe you, but when you're born into a family like mine, you remember that everyone lies."

"There's no point in lying to you." She folded her arms over her chest.

"Isn't there? I could snap you like a twig." Maybe I wanted to see her quiver under my threats, make her understand that this wasn't a place for a girl like her. She needed to be afraid. She needed to know that I held the cards here, that this was my family and one of our untouchables had just been touched.

"You could, but you won't." She glanced at Mario, who studied us as he talked with his boys. "Mario makes the rules."

"Most of the time," I corrected. "When my father was murdered, I became Mario's right-hand man. I'm the enforcer, the lone wolf of this family who gets to do as I please."

She shook her head like that wasn't fair. Yet the family operated the way it did now because Mario had to trust someone with his life and that someone was me. I'd proven my worth. The catch was, when I failed, they would kill me. The mob didn't favor anyone because of sentiment. They did it because it benefited them.

Katie stared at her dying boyfriend and bit her lip, shaking her head at what I'd told her.

"Do you want to take him to the hospital?" I asked, knowing I was rubbing salt in her wounds. I didn't care. The pain of losing my ex-fiancée fed the anger I felt toward her.

"I just don't like suffering, Rome." She sighed, and some of the confidence left her. "Where's the bathroom?"

Funny thing about someone who wasn't a part of the family: they'd ask something like that. They'd think this was a place where there were common amenities for them. Still, I entertained her. I ticked my head toward a white door in a darkened corner with a red exit sign above it. It led to the back hallway. Like a mall, this facility was big and the hallway led to other rooms where we held things no one should be going through. She took one last glance at Jimmy. He was unresponsive now, enough blood having left his body to prevent him from feeling death overtake him.

She shuddered and then stalked forward quickly on her own as if I wasn't going to lead the way for her.

"Hey!" I yelled after her as she shoved down the handle of the door and barreled through it. One motion sensor long-tube light flickered on. And just as the door closed, Katalina vomited straight into a beat-up trash can that happened to be around the corner.

CHAPTER 4

KATIE

DID I LOOK at Jimmy with love or pity? Sympathy or hate? Could I feel both in that moment? My body heaved at the thought of him on the floor, writhing in pain. Or maybe it was heaving up the idea that I would never have to share a bed with him again.

Would I have taken him to the hospital had I been given the chance? Or better yet, had it been me, would my boyfriend have driven me there?

The answer to that last one was a resounding no.

I needed to remember that, remember my place.

One flimsy door separated me from a roomful of men who would put a bullet through my head in an instant. And I stood in a hallway of cement walls and dim lighting with the man who had just stabbed my boyfriend numerous times. I was ready for fear to whip through me, make me shake in terror. Rome stood a whole head taller than me, and his shoulders were wider than I remembered. He was bigger, more muscular, more everything than I remembered. Tattoos wove over his neck and arms like they wanted to wrap him up in all their corrupt markings.

The reaction I had to him staring at me with a look of disgust wasn't fear but irritation and maybe a little heat. That annoyed me even more.

I grabbed the metal rim of the trash can to steady myself and wiped the back of my other hand across my mouth.

"Couldn't have waited until the bathroom to do all the dramatic vomiting?" he blurted out.

"Oh, I'm sorry. Is it a bother to you?" I threw back, surprised I was quick enough to toss snark at him in my state. But I was more than ready. If I stomped his foot with a heel, would he be so unemotional then? "The person I was living with for the past year is dying on the floor out there."

"Then, I guess we were a year late in killing him." He grunted and pointed to a door with black chipped paint to our right.

"You can go now. I don't need an escort to the bathroom." I flipped my hair over my shoulder, ready to leave this whole incident behind, when he grabbed my arm and shoved me into the bathroom. He followed me in and turned to lock the door behind us.

When he spun back around to find me sputtering, about to scream, his hand flew to my mouth. I clawed at his forearm where tattoos wound up to his wrist. I couldn't get him to budge an inch. When he took a step closer, I winced and covered my chest.

I'd been here before. I knew the drill. I hadn't planned for it tonight, though. Rome never looked the type to take advantage of a woman, and by now I had a pretty good understanding of the men who did. I thought tonight would be different, that Mario was protecting me now, that maybe me moving toward being a part of the family meant my body wasn't up for grabs.

I guess I'd have to fight off this man too.

His dark eyes flared with anger, and he suddenly looked ill himself. "I'm not here to hurt you, Katie. Jesus." His grip on me loosened. "I could have done that in the hallway if I wanted to. I need you to answer questions without screaming, okay?"

I nodded, probably a bit vigorously, willing to do whatever it took to get him away as soon as possible.

"Listen." He crouched so that our eyes were level with each other. "Remember, it's just me. The boy in your room. You're Cleopatra, okay?"

I squinted at him in question. I wore the necklace still, and his finger pulled at the chain. It fell from my sweater and glinted in the light.

"Remember you stood in a space full of men tonight and the night I met you. No one harmed you. You hold cards, huh? Don't fear me. I'm not here to hurt you," he repeated, but then he tilted his head as if thinking about it. "At least not yet."

I studied Rome, his strong jaw, the way the back of his hand rubbed across my collarbone as if to soothe me. It was in a single moment, us standing there in that small bathroom, that I found everything I'd been missing since I lost my father.

Suddenly, I was hopeful in another individual.

I nodded, my body warming up after a year of being as cold as ice. He lifted his hand from my mouth like a man stepping back from a wild, beaten animal. He spread his fingers and waved them in front of me, showing me he wasn't trying to pull anything over my head.

"Did you know about Sasha?" He got straight to the point.

My heart squeezed, and I wasn't sure if it was because he thought I did or because I suddenly longed for someone to care for me as he did his lover.

"No." I wiped my mouth and glanced into the tiny mirror. It was cracked, and a piece of it had fallen out, but I could still see that my hair had frizzed out. My makeup was smudged and my lip-gloss was nearly nonexistent. I turned the water on, cupped a splash of it to my mouth, and rinsed it out. Then, I splashed my face. "I only knew he went to see other women. I tracked his whereabouts sometimes. I knew he was trafficking women. Mario's guy brought me a cell and let me know that I needed to cooperate with them."

Rome pulled at his dark hair. "They shouldn't have involved you."

"I was sleeping with the enemy. Of course they involved me."

"You're a child, Katie." He eyed me with disgust and disbelief.

"Am I now?" I shot back at him. "Aren't you too? You can't be much older than me." I rubbed the mascara under my eyes and reached for a paper towel.

Of course, the metal dispenser was empty. Rome lifted the bottom of his shirt, and I saw a flash of his abs before he grabbed the back of my head and smeared his shirt all across my wet face to dry it.

"I'm old enough to know right and wrong. That man sleeping with you was wrong."

"It was consensual." I was muffled by his shirt. I hesitated and then mumbled, "Mostly."

"Your age makes it not." He paused too as he dropped his shirt back down and met my gaze again. "Entirely and completely."

I rolled my lips between my teeth, my anger rising. He had no right to judge me or who I was with. "My sex life isn't up for discussion. What other questions do you have? I don't have much information on your fiancée."

"Ex-fiancée," he corrected and sighed before he leaned against the wall. "She was only in my life because she'd told me she was having my baby. I..." He looked down at his scuffed black boots. "We were never compatible, but I'd have taken care of my baby. She didn't deserve—"

I cut him off. I didn't know much, but I knew enough to understand his guilt, the weight of a death on your hands. No one needed to bear that. "She was sleeping with Jimmy. I know that. She had been for a long time, Rome." I took a breath and stepped toward him. "Jimmy whispered in the middle of the night, but I listened. He argued about that baby, Rome. And I know you probably don't want to hear this now, but she told him he was the father too."

He nodded slowly, keeping his face angled toward the ground. His feet moved back and forth, and when my hand acted on its own accord to touch his shoulder, he flinched.

I kept it there.

Whatever burden he felt could have been mine too. I wanted to carry the weight along with him.

Then he shrugged me off. When he looked up, those chocolate eyes had turned off whatever emotion he'd felt. The connection we had was gone.

"So, you know something more about it all, then. Did you know she was with me?"

I stepped back, but the room felt smaller, more dangerous and suddenly congested with this darkened soul of a man. "I didn't know anything."

"But you just said you did. You knew she was sleeping with him. What else?"

"I only shared that with you so that you didn't—"

"Do you think you belong here with us?" He stalked forward as I cowered back. "Do you think any of us care about you here?"

"Mario does," I stuttered. The door thunked when my back hit it, leaving me nowhere to go as his chest met mine. "Mario is going to take care of me. He said I'm in. Blood oath and all."

"You'll do the blood oath, but it doesn't make you blood." His words stabbed at the only thing I longed for. "You know the first rule of the family? Act as if you don't know us. You walk out of here tonight with no one. We don't pass in public and smile at each other. It's a new way. Family isn't family. It's strangers. You'll be on your own."

"Mario will take care of me."

"Or you'll learn to take care of yourself. You better because Jimmy isn't around for you anymore, and Mario has no use for you if you don't have Jimmy to tattle on."

"That's not what I'm here for. That's not—"

"You're bait. Plain and simple."

I closed my eyes and shook my head, trying to shake away the words. My frizzed-up waves whipped around my face, and he slammed his hand into the wall next to my head.

When I jumped, his laugh was menacing. "You don't belong here. Find a friend or go back to foster care and leave this behind."

I'd already left the things he mentioned behind. Nothing else was out there for me except this. "Foster care?" I shot back as anger boiled in my blood at him mentioning it. "Back to Marvin and earning him a little cash here and there? You took that home from me, remember?"

I didn't say he saved me from it, that he risked his freedom to gain mine. I needed to thank him, not taunt him with it.

"I didn't take anything from you! That man needed to die, Katie. He should have died a long time ago. You couldn't have been the first one he did that to."

"I know," I murmured and looked down at the white tiles of the floor. "God, I know."

He lifted my chin with a soft touch. "I'll help you find somewhere to stay. Don't mix yourself up with us. You're not made for this world."

To begin again and again with not a soul I knew and a preconception of what I would be felt near impossible to bear. I wasn't just a foster kid; I wasn't just an orphan. Mario had offered me a home, a purpose, and I was going to take it. "Jimmy was trafficking girls just like Marvin. You all knew because I helped figure it out. I'm going to continue to do it and I'm going to do whatever I have to. I'm made for whatever I need to be."

His thick eyebrow lifted, mocking me. "Made to conquer us like Cleo?"

"Only if I have to. Women fight to survive. If we don't, we die," I said, the words suddenly rooting deep down into my being.

"There's life beyond just surviving and dying."

"You'd think that, right? When I wrote you after my dad died, I had hoped there would be. Only for a moment though. I still remember the blood, Rome."

His lips pursed together as he listened to me, his touch still soft on my neckline.

"I tried to pool all my daddy's blood in my hands and pour it back into his wrists before I applied pressure. Then I ran for the phone and screamed for the ambulance to come as fast as they could."

I looked toward the ceiling and tried to hold back the pain. "I figured we could use a miracle, right? We'd never gotten one. If God could give other families one, surely we deserved one too. Maybe they could revive him, and we could tell the story to all the friends we didn't have."

The memories after they showed up didn't get better. Social services dragged me away from the ambulance.

And foster care with Marvin and his wife followed suit. Marvin was sweet until the night came.

I did what I had to do.

I survived by choosing the boys I wanted to sleep with after too many nights spent with Marvin and the men who paid to sleep with me in my foster home bed. Boys at school were clumsy but nice. Jared and his father took me in most nights.

I did what I had to do.

I looked Rome dead in the eye. "I didn't get a miracle, but I fought to survive. I guess I'm doing that again or else I'll end up dead."

He murmured, "You're not dying, Katalina. You're just getting started." His eyes searched mine, consuming me, stripping me down. Somehow, I felt like he could see my fear, could see that maybe I wasn't that strong, but he shook his head and repeated, "You're just getting started."

Then, before either of us could stop one another, our lips crashed together. I tasted him and lapped up every ounce of confidence he had in me. Deep down, I knew he was the only one who thought I was strong enough.

He ripped his lips from mine and winced as if in pain. "Stay away from me, Katalina. You know too much and yet not enough to stay away. You'll ruin me or I'll ruin you."

He breezed past me, hot one second and cold as ice the next.

Still, his belief that I could survive cemented a bond between us. I couldn't shake how unsteady I felt after our kiss, how I suddenly felt tied to him. I became a part of him, and he became a part of me that night, whether he wanted to or not.

It should have been the last time I saw him or interacted with him. I didn't need a person to give me hope and then wrench it away a second later when the world had already done that again and again.

That night, the Armanelli Family told me the rules. Just like Rome said, we weren't supposed to get in each other's way—we were to distance ourselves from the family. I should have stayed far, far away from him for that very reason.

Yet we mixed ourselves up in each other like a toxic drink, one that was bound to kill us if we kept tasting it.

7 YEARS LATER

CHAPTER 5

KATIE

I NEVER SHOULD HAVE ended up at Rome's bar. My day had been long though. One of my oldest friends had stopped in at the coffee shop that I still worked at long after graduating from college. She mentioned Rome and how she worried about him.

I almost asked her what the hell for? Rome was a beast of a man and could take care of himself. Yet, the only reason she worried about him was because over the years I'd mixed up our friend groups. My self-destructive side that didn't care about a thing in the world reared its ugly head every time I thought of him ignoring me, acting as if he didn't know me.

So, I kept showing up at his place of business, goading him to disclose that we knew each other through the family.

He never did. Rome protected the family at all costs, even if he'd kissed me in a bathroom all those years ago.

We passed one another with hatred and longing in our eyes but acted like strangers in front of everyone. Over time, our friends had us down as tolerable acquaintances, but no one knew the truth.

I'd ended up at Heathen's Bar because I could have a drink, pass the time, and maybe catch a glimpse of him.

Unfortunately, Georgie found me there.

I stumbled a little more theatrically than necessary when he pushed me. Little old Georgie always liked a girl he could throw around, and so I indulged him.

Most men I dated didn't want me to tell them they were weak, that I could take a punch, or a push in this case, much harder than they were capable of giving.

See, little old Georgie had caught me flirting with one of the bartenders. He didn't want his sidepiece doing anything of the sort.

I smiled to myself when he shoved me again and flailed my arms as if he'd truly thrown me off balance.

"Why the hell do I keep you around if you're going to eye-fuck every guy you come across?" he bellowed, the sound coming from deep in his round belly.

"Georgie," I whined and tried to muster up a few tears. "I'm sorry. It's just you were out of town with your wife, and I thought maybe you wouldn't want me back this time."

He all but preened, smiling like he wanted to buy me the world. He probably could. At least enough to fill up my small part of it. He was worth millions, according to the information Mario provided. He'd been selling drugs and sex trafficking women on Armanelli ground. Even as the Armanelli family tried to clean up their business, I knew the drug selling was still a part of it. They didn't want other gangs selling on their territory, and when they caught wind, well, someone paid dearly.

I was the bait, sent to catch the wind.

I'd finally gained access to one of Georgie's bank accounts, and I'd snapped the pictures needed for evidence. He was on borrowed time. The rush I got just thinking about how he would pay for the hell he'd caused pumped through me.

Until Rome.

He towered over everyone in his bar and scanned the place like a hawk guarding his nest. When his eyes fell on us, he didn't look away. He crossed his arms as his scuffed boots came almost toe-to-toe with my shiny black stilettos. With worn dark jeans, a T-shirt, and a five-o'clock shadow so overdue it was heading towards midnight, he should have looked grungy. Instead, it all added to his grittiness, enhanced his tattooed arms and menacing stare. A sign should have hung above him flashing the word *Danger*, but women's mouths would have watered anyway.

"We got a problem here, Kate-Bait?" He tipped his chin toward Georgie.

I winced a little as Georgie's hand dug into my neck. That wasn't fake. He'd found a little of my weakness by gripping me right where Jimmy used to.

Jimmy had gotten a lot meaner during my senior year of high school. He knew my father had committed suicide, knew I didn't have a foster home to go back to, and wanted to keep better tabs on me. We fought constantly, and he usually won the fight—if not verbally, definitely physically. The man could crush a windpipe faster than I could let out a scream.

The nightly phone calls saved me from him. The men on the other line wanted to meet me, and Jimmy answered to them. That was how the Armanellis found purpose in me. They knew I didn't mind a roll in the hay, that I listened well, and, most importantly, that I enjoyed finding a weakness. I was good at that, brilliant at it really.

Georgie was just another man in the long line of men I reported back to the family about.

"No problem, Rome." I wide-eyed him and tried to steer him off with a look, but he was studying Georgie's hand on my neck.

"Look, we don't allow manhandling in our bar."

I shook my head at him, trying to get him to stop. Georgie didn't like being told what he could and couldn't do with me. It made him feel inadequate. Useless. And that led to reckless behavior.

He squeezed me a little harder. "My girl gets what she deserves."

I smiled at Rome with a plea in my eyes but bunched my shoulders. I wanted Georgie to think he had control, that he was dominating me, but that required me to play the damsel in distress. I wasn't sure Rome would be able to see through the act.

Rome straightened and brought a hand to his chin. "Your girl?"

Georgie yanked me back into his belly by my neck. "Yeah, my girl. And tell your bartenders that too."

Rome's lips lifted at the corners. It wasn't a smile, although some would mistake it for that.

I knew Rome rarely smiled. Not really. Over the years of being around him, I'd discovered he could glare, growl, stare someone down, and deliver on every threat he made.

When he stepped toward Georgie, I knew my night was going to end badly. Georgie must have known it too.

Rome got closer to us. "I'm a little confused."

Georgie stuttered as he shifted me in front of him as if he could use me as a shield to ward off Rome. "There's nothing to be confused about."

I tried to hide my eye roll at how cowardly he was. Sure, Rome was intimidating. He stood taller than everyone who came into the bar, and tattoos snaked around every one of bulging muscles.

Quite frankly, his dark features were overkill.

But no man should have been using me—who stood at a mere five and a half feet—as a shield. Especially when I'd put on a wonderful performance throughout our relationship of being a meek, terrified woman he could throw around.

Rome stepped closer until his body was inches from mine and he looked over my head. "Isn't there? Kate-Bait comes in here all the time, and I'm positive she belongs to *no* man."

I widened my eyes at Rome, trying to signal for him to stand down. Mario must have told him about Georgie, there was no doubt. Rome knew most of the ins and outs of what we were all doing. He needed to back off.

"Rome, don't you remember? I told you about Georgie." I emphasized his name, trying to jog his memory. "You know how good Georgie is to me, how he always treats me like I'm a treasure."

Rome blew out a breath and rolled his eyes. Damn, he was in a mood and wanted to take it out on someone. "And yet he grabs you like you're trash. Like I said, it's not allowed in my bar."

Georgie's temperature rose. I felt it in his grip and the way his stance against mine changed. He wanted to prove himself.

Rome ran his tongue over his teeth as if counting how many he had before he unleashed the beast that must have been bouncing around in him. He looked straight at me, and I couldn't quite tell if he was going to let it loose on me or on Georgie.

He looked lethal either way. Deadly, unhinged, and, unfortunately for me, way hotter than Mr. Georgie behind me.

Georgie thought being hot meant exerting your power, though, and I was just a bit too late in realizing it to avoid him slamming me sideways into the wall.

My head ricocheted off a stud, and I saw maybe one or two stars. Nothing to write home about, I promise.

I could have saved the night. I could have tried to calm them both down.

Really, Georgie didn't hurt me too bad, he didn't have the strength to. Flying into a wall was a piece of cake, but it pissed me off that I hadn't caught it. That I'd probably have a bruise on my head the next day because I'd been paying attention to Rome rather than him.

And maybe, just maybe, I'd come here to pay attention to Rome or get attention from him in the first place. I wasn't sure.

All of it pissed me off.

So, I couldn't be held responsible for losing my shit and turning to Georgie as Rome shoved him into the wall.

I pushed Rome off him and growled, "Oh, no. He's mine to fuck up now."

Before Rome or Georgie could respond, I kneed Georgie in the balls, and he crumpled with a look of surprise in his eyes. As he bent over, I kneed him in the nose.

He screamed as blood spouted from it.

"We're over. Obviously," I said and walked back to the bar.

He'd leave without saying another word to me. The man had a wife and what he thought was an untouchable business. Those were two big things he wasn't willing to lose by causing a bigger scene than he already had.

I needed to confirm that the damn photos I snapped would be enough evidence for our family to take him down. I probably needed more, and letting my family down wasn't an option.

I thought about running after him, but I'd never run after anyone. I'd learned that very few people were worth my pride. There was always another way, and I was willing to get dicey enough to find that path.

I'd assess, adjust, and navigate my way into whatever we needed.

But first, I needed to get rid of the hot-as-hell fuckup who followed me to the bar.

CHAPTER 6

ROME

S HE WAS TRYING to kill me.

Or send me to jail.

Or have me lose one of my bars.

There was a motive to the shit she pulled.

There had to be.

When she sat down at the bar and ordered a shot for herself and the bartender, I tried my best not to tell my bartender to fuck off.

"Hey, Cole. Our customers can't knee a guy in the balls and then come drink here. We should be kicking her out." I eyed Cole for good measure.

He held up his hands. "You got her, boss? I'll let you take over making her drink or throwing her out."

I nodded, and he winked at Katie before stalking off to go help the few others that were out here on a weeknight.

I shook my head at the little tornado sitting in front of me. "Why are you at my bar stirring up shit?"

"I'm not. Little Georgie was supposed to be out of town."

When she didn't offer any further explanation, I went around the bar to pour her shot. She wanted a rum, some of the strongest I had on the shelves. If she wanted to get drunk, I didn't care about her enough to stop her.

I slid her the shot, and she curled her glossed lips at me. "You're not going to have one with me?"

I shook my head.

"Come on. I make it a rule to never drink alone."

I shrugged. "Not worth it to me."

She sighed and shoved some of her unruly curls away from her high cheekbones. "I'm buying. One shot's not going to set you back."

I laughed. "You're not buying either of them."

She glanced Cole's way. "He always makes me pay."

"Good. He should." I lifted a shoulder and spun one of the dark rings on my finger. "We don't hand out free drinks at Heathen's Bar."

She blew a raspberry and stood up on the footrest of her stool to lean over my bar. She grabbed a shot glass and the bottle from me. "Lay off him and the other bartenders. Girls flock to a bar where they get free drinks, not one where the owner has a stick up his ass and makes everyone pay."

My temper immediately flared. She knew just the button to press. "I'm not worried about people flocking to my bar."

"Right, because you don't make your money off Heathen's Bar anyway," she mumbled and wrinkled her nose as if the way I really made money disgusted her.

"And you don't make your money whipping up coffee drinks either." Every now and then, Katie made her way back to a little coffee shop that she'd taken a job at during her time in college. She was barely a barista and yet every guy waited in line to get a coffee from her on the rare occasion I stopped by. I wasn't proud to admit I knew because, over the years, I'd kept tabs on her. In my defense, the woman had purposely crossed my path over and over again.

She narrowed her eyes at me. "Mario needs me. You basically have us starting at ground zero because you had to confront Georgie for no reason other than to show him who was the bigger man."

"I was showing him he shouldn't physically harm you."

"You and I both know I can handle myself." She poured another shot and slammed the bottle down on the bar so hard the liquor sloshed over the rim.

"Can you now?"

Her grip on the bar was tight, her olive knuckles turning a paler hue. Katie was fumbling with the idea that she may not have been able to handle her latest victim. "Don't question my place in the family, Rome. I know what I'm doing and have handled myself since the day Mario brought me in."

"Do Bastian and Mario know you're actually seeing Georgie?" I asked the question because Bastian had finally stepped into Mario's shoes and was heading up the Chicago Family.

She had a death wish, and just looking at her in her next-to-nothing black dress, I wondered if my dick had one too. I constantly had to remind myself how she was bad news, how she'd been tied to my dead ex-fiancée, how I didn't need distractions, especially ones I might end up caring about. Yet she sat there unmoved, constantly trying to irritate the man who chose murder as his job within the family.

My little Cleopatra was just as fucked in the head as I was.

"Bastian has nothing to do with this. We needed intel, and I told Mario I would get it."

"By fucking someone who's going to throw you around?"

"It was barely throwing around," she snapped at me. Then she slammed her shot back and winced as she swallowed it. I watched her neck bob as the liquid burned her throat. "Look, I gave my word I would get the information. Just remember your place, Rome. It's not worrying about me."

"Mario may have brought you in, but I killed Jimmy. We watched him bleed out together. The man you'd tied yourself to had been lying to the family for years. You think I need to remember my place, but you stepped into the family with your judgment—"

"Exactly on point. I knew he was trash the moment he slid between my legs, but I pinned him there long enough to find a way to step over him and be a part of this family, didn't I?"

My jaw tightened, and I sighed. "Katalina, you looked at Jimmy like he was your savior and lover when no one else was watching. So I'm not ever going to say your judgment was on point. That man should never have slept with you when you were that young."

Her slate eyes shimmered like wet metal for just a moment before she glanced away from me. "Foster care was much worse. Everyone's got a story, Rome. Honestly, mine is one of the better ones." She picked at a crack in the bar like she was annoyed with it, like it was a chink in her armor she couldn't always cover up. Armor that was marred with experience and bruised by wear and tear.

"We both know that's not true." The way her stare went far away, I almost reached for her hand. I fisted my own instead and thought of all the ways a man that took advantage of children deserved to die. "I should have waterboarded Jimmy *and* Marvin for at least an hour."

A laugh full of sadness and maybe a little shock burst from her. Katie would never tell her story to me. We weren't close enough, but I knew that the men she'd been with had sex-trafficked women for years, that they knew how to torture a woman or a little gray-eyed girl.

"Well, I'll be honest," she said. "Georgie ain't got nothing on Jimmy. That's for sure. And I'm furious because I've barely got anything on him thanks to you. Next time you want to wave your manhood around and be pissy about nothing, do it somewhere else. Everything I do, I do with awareness, Rome."

I blew out a breath at her quick redirection of the conversation. She was small, pint-size, vulnerable. But I had to remember she'd danced with some of the most sadistic gang members out there. Her size was a jarring contrast to what she was capable of. Maybe it was her vulnerability that pulled men in, and maybe I was a sucker for it too.

I hated that she'd slithered into the family, hated that she'd intertwined herself in my life and I couldn't disentangle her.

Yet I knew she'd just been a kid trying to survive, a girl taken complete advantage of.

I knew but couldn't get her to know it too. She liked to remind me that her actions were consensual always and that she made conscious decisions.

She narrowed her gray eyes at me, as if trying to find the reason for my poor mood.

I came around the bar to sit next to her. "Do you know I could have spared Jimmy? I consider it a lot. Maybe my ex had decided to sleep with him. Maybe he deserved one more chance." I stopped for a second, not sure I wanted to say the next words. "You know what I kept picturing, though? *You* with him. The way you looked at him like he was your damn world and really he'd just created a world for you so fucked up you thought it was where you belonged, by his side. Did you know that he was sleeping with three other girls who were underage?"

Her eyes didn't widen; her muscles didn't tense. She wasn't at all surprised as I confessed all I knew about that dead boyfriend of hers. Mario would always give me a rundown of the victim, always make sure I knew I was doing justice rather than murder. Most of them I didn't care about. I would have followed through with it even if I didn't have the background. It was a way for Mario to try to save my soul, but I'd lost it long ago.

"Jimmy was the first *man* I slept with, Rome. Sure, I'd fooled around with kids, but he was different." She sighed. "He gave me money to make my father comfortable. No one else offered that. He loved me in his own way, I think. I was naïve and loved him a little too. I can admit that. It doesn't make me stupid, and it's ridiculous to think I haven't learned, that I wasn't learning when I was with him."

"Is it, though? They're all just as bad. You know Georgie's rap sheet. You're still getting yourself into shit situations."

"I'm aware. Mario doesn't send me in blindly."

"And still you slept with him?"

She laughed and then grabbed the bottle to pour more liquid into her shot glass. "We really doing this whole exchange? I don't want to know who you sleep with in your free time."

"Because who I sleep with isn't a part of my job."

She banged down the bottle to cut me off. "I don't sleep with men for money, Rome."

I tsked at her lie. "You've been Mario's bait for years now. You think they don't share some of your escapades with me? I have to know in order to do my job right."

She winced, like me knowing her secrets physically wounded her. Her voice was small but strong when she glared up at me and replied, "What you think you know about me isn't truth just because Mario says it is. I sleep with who I want, when I want, because I want. If it gets me off to control Georgie and his dick, then I do it. If I did that with the last guy, so what? I'm the best at this. I bring in the evidence and the information so that you can bring them to justice. You think I was a little innocent doll when I walked into that room with Jimmy years ago? You think he really was my world?"

I didn't answer her. I watched her body tense, her short breaths, the way she ran a hand through that mess of curls. She hid most of her vulnerability from everyone, but I searched

64

out those little movements that gave it away. She'd struggled with something saying those words, I just didn't know what.

Her gray eyes were hard as stone when she glanced back up at me, all vulnerability gone. "Jimmy was going to die by your hand or mine. Mario let you have him first, but remember he slept soundly next to me. Every. Single. Night."

I fisted my hand on the bar.

She glanced at it, knowing she'd hit a nerve. "I knew the exact time he would wake up to call his *four*, not three, other women. I knew where they all lived. I knew *everything*. When he held a gun to my forehead the night before his death, I quivered under the barrel, but on the inside, I was laughing, Rome." Her smile was as bright as a wolf's on a dark night. "I'd emptied the bullets out of it earlier that day."

I recalled how she'd laughed when she pulled the trigger in front of all of us the night she took her blood oath years ago. She was Cleopatra in sheep's clothing.

She downed her shot and stood from the bar with dignity. I almost withered under her stare. She was a whole head and a half shorter than me, tiny in every place. She made a man want to protect her, but then she morphed into a vicious siren, ready to devour those who did.

She didn't need protecting, and it made me want to protect her even more.

Or strangle her, depending on the day.

"One day, you're going to encounter someone you can't handle, Kate-Bait."

"And what? You'll swoop in to eliminate him?" she asked condescendingly.

"Don't be so sure I or anyone else will be able to rescue you, doll."

She scoffed and shoved back her hair. "Worry about saving yourself, Rome. I've never needed a knight to come rescue me.

I ride in on my own damn horse, and if it happens to buck me off and disappear, I can walk out—guns blazing—on my own."

She turned to leave. I should have let her go. I should have held my damn breath when she passed so I didn't smell the scent of her that I was addicted to.

My hand shot out and gripped her elbow, yanking her close enough for me to whisper in her ear. "You're not with anyone anymore tonight."

She licked her full lips and glanced down at mine. "So?"

"So stay for a few." I didn't know why I was inviting her, didn't know why I wanted her to stay.

"Probably not a good idea for anyone to see us hanging together as if we enjoy each other's company or something," she offered up as a reason.

"Who?" I shot back. "Our friends? You introduced me to all of them."

"Oh my God," she grumbled and pushed away from the bar. "I don't have time to bicker with you."

She glanced around as if racking her brain for the most ridiculous option she could come up with. "I'm going to go down the street to Crowned Ink."

"No the fuck you aren't," I blurted. "How much have you had to drink?"

It wasn't my business what she did on late nights by herself, but her walking ten blocks in the damn dark to a tattoo parlor seemed to be asking for more trouble than even I could ignore.

"I've had enough to know that the tattoo I'm about to get won't hurt that bad." She winked at me and sauntered toward the front door. Without looking over her shoulder, she asked, "You coming, Rome?"

I let out a string of curses as I went after her. The woman was more trouble than I ever wanted to be associated with—and I killed people for the mob.

Why the fuck was I following her in the dead of the night?

"You're asking for a problem tonight, Katalina." I growled her full name. It rolled off my tongue like an intoxicating drug, one I was scared I would never want to quit.

Her long nails, painted some dark color, waved at me as I caught up to her. "Don't follow me, then. I don't mind walking alone."

"I don't mind you walking alone either. In daylight," I spat back.

"I'm carrying and have a few tricks up my sleeve." She shrugged as we rounded the corner. One street light flickered in the night.

I had a chain and a trick up my sleeve too, but I was sure none of it would save me from the one thing I was in danger of.

Her.

CHAPTER 7

KATIE

"UNLESS IT'S A damn taser and a bodyguard, you've got nothing," he argued, like he truly believed there was no way I could be prepared if someone jumped me.

"I take self-defense classes. Dante's been training me for years. I've been in enough dicey situations to get out of most of the ones I encounter now. If not"—I shrugged and reassured him—"I'll live. Because if I don't, I'll die, right?"

He grunted at the words he'd said to me so long ago.

They'd echoed through me. They'd ricocheted around in my head for years, even in the darkest nights when Marvin and the men who paid him stood over me, when Jimmy held me down, when I was sure death would be a better option than life.

The tube lighting of Crowned Ink glowed a bright red as we neared the shop. Their logo was a red crown with bold colored skulls in a pile below it. I pushed open the heavy glass door but didn't hold it for Rome.

He grunted, but I ignored it. I took in the wall of magazines and, next to it, a large display of tattoos. All of them were intricate, popping with color or navigating the darkest shadows.

The leather seating didn't look too inviting, but I wasn't here to sit. It was late enough that no one else was in there getting work done. When I tapped the bell on the lacquered counter, I heard someone from the back immediately start shuffling toward us.

"This is a bad idea," Rome warned from behind me. He stood so close I smelled the mint on his breath.

"Then, leave. I don't need you here if you don't want to be." When the tattoo guy rounded the corner, I glanced back at Rome. "Okay, now I really don't need you here."

He growled at my wink, but my attention was back on the tattoo artist. His greenish eyes popped against the bright green of the walls. Black designs on his neck contrasted with the white collared shirt he wore.

He opened the laptop on the counter. "What can I do for you two tonight?"

"I just want a little writing on my ribs. Adding something to what I've already got."

"I've seen a little of it." He said, staring at my ribcage. I lifted an eyebrow but let him continue. "Exactly what is it that you already have?" Rome asked.

The tattoo artist nodded. "Can I see what you already have?"

I smirked at them both and stepped to the side. The black tiling on the floor shined with cleanliness—a much better establishment than the knock-off shop Jimmy's son had taken me to. They'd done my flowers with the jewels strung around them, even though I was underage. I'd told them I wanted it to look like the flowers were tangled in them, like the beauty was almost suffocating.

Every time I looked at it, the art made me want to cry and rage all at once. The piece was stunning, a testament to the fact that you could even find an artist in someone's basement.

I lifted my shirt to show them both. The art wrapped from my back diagonally forward down to my hip.

The green-eyed man stepped forward to examine the work and hummed low. "That's some good ink."

"I know." I bit my lip and shrugged when he raised an eyebrow at me.

He chuckled and stuck his hand out. "Name's Zane."

I dropped my shirt and took his hand. "I'm Katie. Obviously, I want the writing in the empty spot. I need a font that fits, and I'll write out what I want if you've got time to do me."

"Sure thing." He turned to Rome. "You want him in there with you?"

"That's why I'm here, Zane," Rome answered for me.

"You can leave the shit attitude on that side of the counter." I pointed behind us. "I need you being supportive, not an asshole."

Rome stalked by me as Zane handed me a form to sign and another piece of paper to write my words on. He explained his cleaning techniques, how I should sit, and when I should tell him to stop if it was too much.

"I can take a lot of pain," I announced as I lifted my shirt over my head.

When I glanced at them both, Zane was prepping his tattoo gun, smiling at my bravado, while Rome glared at me. "Is no shirt necessary?"

"I'm sure it's easier, right, Zane?"

The man didn't even lift his head, too engrossed in his process. "Whatever makes you feel most comfortable."

"I'm comfortable in less clothing." I wiggled down into the chair, settling in.

"Do you always have to do that?" Rome pulled a stool up so his massive upper body was close enough for me to see all of his abs, all of his chest under the tight T-shirt he wore, and all of his broody, strong-jawed face.

I hated how much I loved seeing that jaw pop when I pissed him off. He was ready to unleash tonight, and I wondered if it would be on me. I knew he was dangerous, that his temper flared and let loose something wild. The kiss we shared so long ago was a memory of that. I wanted it again even when I knew Mario would never let his right-hand man casually sleep with me, even when I knew we were two hurricanes blowing through the world and there was no way we could cross paths without leaving destruction behind.

Still, I stared at his lips for moments too long before I replied, "Do I always have to do what?"

"Fuck, woman. You know you're toying with me and every man you encounter."

"Zane doesn't care one way or the other. Do you, Zane?"

He inserted a new needle, tested his tattoo gun on a wet sheet, and spun around in his chair to start. "I only care that you get through these next fifteen minutes."

Leave it to a tattoo artist to get straight to the point.

"You ready?" he asked.

My heart picked up speed, and the adrenaline kicked in. The need to feel anything other than what I was feeling became overwhelming. Not because of his question but all because Rome's hand snaked up and grabbed mine.

Like he cared.

Like he gave just a bit of a damn.

I needed to feel anything but that. So I nodded. "Give me the pain."

Zane's gun pierced my skin, tiny needles wrecking it to produce something beautiful in the end.

Rome squeezed my hand, and I breathed out slowly as I looked his way. His other hand came up to tap my necklace. "Strong, like Cleo," he murmured.

If I asked him to kiss me right then, I wondered if he would. His eyes tracked every part of me in those fifteen minutes, and when they journeyed all the way down to my toes, I wiggled them. He smiled like he knew he'd been caught and didn't care.

"Thanks for coming," I blurted out and almost covered my mouth in surprise at my word vomit.

Rome didn't look at me but rubbed his thumb over my knuckles and watched Zane work. "Someone needed to come with you."

"I've gotten tattoos alone before," I announced and stared up at the fluorescent lighting just as Zane started marking over my rib bone.

"Doesn't mean you need to do it that way every time. Now, breathe out and squeeze my hand, woman," Rome coached me. "It helps."

"I know how to get a tattoo." I balked and tried to pull my hand away. He gripped it harder and leaned forward over me so that his lips were a hair away from mine. "Stop fighting me. Let out a breath on me, Katalina. I want to taste your air."

I knew he was just trying to get me past the pain. I knew this didn't mean a damn thing, but my nipples tightened, my body quaked, and my stomach dropped. Had I been standing, I may have fallen over.

I let out a slow breath. I wasn't trying to forget the pain. It'd already been forgotten. I was trying to quell the new feelings stirring in me, the ones that had always been there but grew rapidly as I stared into the depths of Rome.

From far off, I heard Zane mumble that he was done.

Rome's hand traveled along my collarbone as his voice rumbled through me. "Give us a minute, Zane."

Zane rolled away on his stool because I guess every person in the world listened to Rome when he commanded them.

Rome's fingers wrapped around my neck, but he didn't squeeze. "You got my words on you."

I licked my lips. "They're just words."

"They aren't. Come back to the bar with me."

"For what?" I whispered.

But I knew.

He tilted my head by pushing a thumb into my jaw, and then he lowered that dark head of hair to my neck where he took what he wanted. He devoured me without even kissing my lips, and his hand slid down to my cleavage where he dipped a finger in to graze my nipple. It puckered as I moaned.

His hand disappeared along with his mouth.

Suddenly, he was standing over me and throwing my shirt at my chest. "Put your top on. Let's go."

"I have to pay Zane." I jumped out of the chair and glanced at my tattoo. He'd already taped cellophane around it while I was being hypnotized by my damn kryptonite.

"He's been paid."

I spun toward the dark hallway Zane had disappeared down. "What do you mean? How? Do you two know each other?" That was a dumb question. Zane was right down the street from Rome's bar. Everyone knew him in one way or another, and Rome had a million and ten tattoos.

I pressed a bandage to the new ink and threw my shirt over my head. "I'm paying you back."

"Just move your ass."

I stalked out of the shop, irritated and completely unsatisfied. "I can pay for myself, and just so we're clear, I'm not for sale." I knew the comment would rub him the wrong way.

He grabbed my back belt loop and yanked me against him. His hand turned my chin his way. "Even if you do sell yourself as bait, I'm never paying for you, got it?"

I wore stilettos for a reason. I stomped into his foot, I hoped hard enough to hit the bone of his toe. He swore fluidly, and I left him stumbling after me on the sidewalk. "I never sell myself, and even if I did, you wouldn't be able to afford me, jackass."

CHAPTER 8

ROME

KATALINA HAD PERMANENTLY marked herself with the words I'd said to her the first night we met: *You'll live because if you don't, you'll die.*

Around it all were skulls and roses and dying flowers of all sorts, wrapped in jewels and strings of pearls in the most intricate detail I'd seen in a long time.

I'd never gotten that good a look at it all until tonight. It was art that represented her more than I think she would ever know. I saw her in the world of the family, trapped as a prized possession, trapped by the beauty she flaunted for us. She let herself be used over and over again as bait, and even if she didn't know it, it would kill her. The family would kill her just like they did everyone.

It was a beautiful lifestyle, but one that tangled you up and suffocated you until you were lying there bleeding out.

She'd made that bed. I couldn't change it for her, and I didn't need to get wrapped up with her.

Except she'd marked herself with my words.

Like she'd wanted to be mine.

My cock couldn't forget it, and I couldn't forget the way her neck tasted when I'd lost control. I needed to have her once, needed a reminder that I didn't have time for the shit she pulled, especially when there was no way her body would be as good as her bait.

When we walked back into Heathen's, she grabbed a few of her things she'd left near the bar. "I think I'll go call Bastian."

She purred his name, and the sound of it sliced through me like a knife sliced skin. "You're a fucking instigator, I swear."

The dim lighting of the bar allowed for some privacy to the untrained eye. A few customers idled around, drinking, minding their own business. The regulars were there, some leaning on the lip of the polished mahogany bar. The family and I had designed a space where people went to feel at home and lose themselves. It felt familiar with its wood floors and soft rock hits playing in the background on weeknights. The weekends, when college was in session, got rowdier.

The bar wasn't grimy, but it was lived in, worked over into a comfortable space. The college kids loved it, the ones out of college frequented it, and it held an almost iconic place within the city.

To me, it was my first successful venture as a businessman, and it had blossomed into other profitable bars throughout a couple of cities. They made for perfect gathering places for the family or a place to unwind when I needed it.

A place no one questioned anything I did, even if it was shoving Katie.

I grabbed her by the elbow and yanked her toward the back door of the bar.

She stumbled as I shoved her forward and smacked the swinging door open so she could fall through. "Are you kidding me?" I heard her say.

I moved after her into the back storage room. Bottles lined the shelves as the motion light overhead flickered on.

She turned to face me, her wavy bob flaring out as she did. "Don't ever freaking push me, Rome!"

"You're fine." I rolled my eyes. "You basically walked back here yourself."

She scoffed. "What happened to screaming at Georgie for manhandling me, huh? What happened to 'no man should put his hands on me'?"

"Except me." I eyed her up and down, taunting her with the something we'd always known was between us. "Definitely not Bastian."

"Well, Bastian and every other man on the face of this earth seems to at least flirt with the idea of being with me, Rome. You're hot as hell one minute and cold as ice the next." She crossed her arms over her chest, and it exaggerated her cleavage, exaggerated everything I shouldn't have.

"I'm not interested. My dick might be, though."

Her gray eyes narrowed. "Right. You saying that's all I'm capable of?"

"A better man will show you that's not true. I'm just not him."

"Whatever." She waved a hand like the conversation didn't concern her, like it was a fly buzzing around her head. "Are you going to tell Mario and Bastian you blew my relationship with Georgie tonight? Because that's really all we should be discussing."

I crowded her into the wooden table that was up against the back wall. "Fine. It needs to be discussed, anyway. First, Bastian knows you were baiting Georgie?"

"Of course." She put her hands on my chest to stop my approach.

"That fucker is pissing me off more and more. Second, I'm not telling them shit. You ruined it the minute you walked in here and he put his hands on you."

"I thought he was out of town. If I'd known he'd show up, I wouldn't have—"

"You wouldn't have come here?" I smiled. "Why, Kate-Bait? You scared to bring your boys here? We heathens aren't that bad."

She rolled her eyes. "The Heathen's bar boys are fine. No one gets involved except you."

"If he hadn't put his hands on you, I would have let it slide."

"I can handle a man's hands on me."

I gripped her hips in response, and she hissed when I squeezed and then lifted her up onto the table. "A man like that on a body like yours is a waste."

She looked toward the ceiling like she was trying to avoid the inevitable. When her eyes locked with mine again, her legs wound around my hips and locked on to me too. We'd only done this dance a few times before. We weren't meant to react to one another, and yet when we got close enough, we ignited and exploded.

"This doesn't mean a thing," she whispered and then bit her bottom lip as she looked at mine. "I do what needs to be done for the family, always. This attraction between you and me is just an indulgence, a dumb one at that."

I hummed low as I slid one hand up her smooth thigh. We were pushing each other, and I felt us getting close to something we usually didn't.

Tonight, we'd pushed our history too far. She'd brought a man in who'd reminded me of her vulnerability. She'd baited me like she did so well, even when she didn't know she was doing it.

I was taking the bait this time, even though I knew she was too frustrating, too volatile, and too chaotic to combine with my own wreckage. Us together, we were mayhem and ruination and mass destruction.

We both knew it, and still my hand slid higher and higher.

"You want to do this?" I rolled the question out like a boulder, knowing it would crush our sexual desires. This was Katalina, the girl I'd stared at the night she'd been inducted into the family, the girl who'd stared blankly ahead and didn't bat an eyelash as I'd taken the supposed love of her life in front of her.

We were both dead inside.

"Why wouldn't I?" Her voice shook as she said it.

"Because you aren't in control of this."

She smiled, but her lips quivered. "Of course I am."

"No, Katalina. We keep hooking up, we're bound to go off, and you can't control a nuclear bomb."

"Just watch me." She grabbed my shirt, and I admit she controlled the kiss. She dove into my mouth like it was hers to ravage. Leveraging her ass on the table, she dug her heels hard into my back, and her hands were on my pants zipper so fast, I barely kept up.

When I slid my hand to her panty line, I found nothing there. "Damn, not much of a barrier from the world. I should have known."

"I like to feel it, Rome. Every place I'm in, every situation I put myself in, I have the little knowledge that I could slide this skirt up and be taken by someone. Every bomb that goes off, I get to feel the explosion, and being that close to the edge makes me feel alive."

"There's something wrong with you," I grumbled, but my fingers slid into her, and she was so wet and tight, I knew I wouldn't back away, even if the whole world was wrong with her. Then she fisted my cock, and I bit down on my cheek to distract myself from coming before we even got started.

"Don't act like I'm the only one with problems. You've been eyeing me up since the first night you saw me."

I slammed a hand down on the table to shift some control back to me. "Don't talk about that night."

She rocked into my other hand and dropped her head back to expose her neck as she rode my fingers. She closed her eyes, trying to find her high. "Then, fuck me silent, Rome. I need someone to take me."

I heard the plea under her command, the hitch in her voice. Katalina was broken, shattered, left in jagged little pieces all over the floor. She wanted someone to make her feel something, to make life worth living, but I wasn't that person. I wasn't sure there was a person out there who could make her feel a thing. I was damn near positive they didn't exist, because I knew they didn't exist for me.

"You're not going to feel anything, Katalina."

Her slate eyes shot open, the storm in them dim and painful and raw. "No. I won't. You won't either. That's the beauty of what we're about to do."

She spread her legs wider, and I slammed into her. She wrapped her arms and legs around me as I pumped into her faster and faster. Clawing at my back and biting my neck, she didn't fuck nicely. She left her mark all over me, probably like she did to all her victims. And we were her victims. Katalina was poised as bait but never ended up just that.

I left my mark on her by sucking too hard on her neck, devouring her mouth when I should have pulled back, and gripping her hard enough to bruise.

Our touches were painful.

Just the way we liked them.

CHAPTER 9

KATIE

I SHOULDN'T HAVE SLEPT with him. I should have walked away and never indulged the pull I had toward him.

Rome said I wouldn't feel anything, and I normally never did.

Except with him.

With him, I felt every stupid thing I never wanted to feel again.

Pleasure and pain.

Hope and dread.

Longing and fulfillment.

Hate and love.

I told him I was going to the bathroom and slipped out the back door into a dark alley behind Heathen's Bar. Cole was out there smoking a cig and offered one to me. I let him light it and pulled in a hard drag before turning from him and walking away.

"Katie, sort of wanted to talk while you enjoyed the cig."

I waved over my shoulder. "Another time, Cole."

His laugh carried down the alley as I turned the corner quickly. I didn't need to stay any longer and face Rome. His dark stare would grate my raw nerves, and I would have to admit to enjoying him screwing me in the back of the bar more than I enjoyed sleeping with most men.

I sighed and took another drag of the cigarette before I dropped it and put it out with my stiletto. Then I bent over to pick it up and toss it in the trash. Just as I looked up, I saw the two figures rush me.

They were fast, and I was caught off guard, thinking about a man I shouldn't be.

The blow over the head was so precise, I didn't feel it.

———

When I came to, the white bed sheets and feather bedding under me signaled I wasn't in my own home. The night flooded back to my memory as I vaulted from the bed.

Mario and Rome rushed in from the doorway. "You're fine," Mario instantly reassured me.

I took a deep breath and shut my eyes for a second, putting my palm to the massive egg on my head. "I need some ice, I think."

Rome looked toward the ceiling as if irritated. "At your bedside."

"My bedside?" I looked over my shoulder and took in the mahogany nightstand where Advil and an ice pack lay. "Where are we?"

"The pent suite at the Hilton," Mario answered. "I need to get your doctor back up here. Rome can fill you in if you're okay."

I waved away his concern. "You know I'm fine."

"You take too many bruises to the head, little one, and you won't be. This job isn't safe for you anymore." He shook his head as if ashamed of himself. "It never was."

Mario Armanelli had a constant hang-up with the fact that I was better at my job than he could ever make a man. He didn't want me going in and doing the dirty work. It was the protector in him, the one who always wanted a daughter but got two boys instead before his wife passed away.

He always said I made him think of what could have been if they'd had a daughter, but he would never have let his daughter do what I did. I reminded him that if a mob boss had a daughter, she would never have let her daddy tell her what to do. Round and round we went, but he gave in either way because he knew I was right or because I was the best. Or both.

As he disappeared from the room, I downed the two little blue pills and took a gulp of water. I tilted my head to look at the man I'd left in the bar. "So, what's the damage?"

"Your head, for one." He pointed.

"And the two men?"

"Dead and gone. Bloodier than normal because I didn't have time to do clean kills with you lying in the middle of the damn sidewalk."

I winced at his tone. Rome never hid the monster in him well. I had a soft spot for the beast because he usually came out to play when protecting the family or me. "Sergio wiping the scene? Do we know who they were?"

Rome shrugged. Truth was, if Sergio didn't wipe the scene, it wouldn't matter. Our family had almost complete control of the police department at this point. Someone would cover it up. "Georgie isn't as small-time as we thought."

"I could have told you that. You blew my cover. I have some information on him."

"He's bigger than that. He's government big."

"How big in government? Is he pulling strings?"

"We're looking into it. They're going to be a juggernaut to deal with, and they seem to have their sights set on you."

Good. No part of me ever wanted to cower in the corner. My dad didn't raise me to be that way. I couldn't save my father, but I could make him proud. I'd stayed in the hot seat to make a difference for the helpless women who'd become prey for people like Jimmy. Mario took him down after I'd brought the right information to the family. Mario wanted trafficking out of the business for good. I would help them do that.

If Georgie was who Rome was saying he was, I could help so many more and solidify my spot in the family.

"I should have choked him out, then?" I joked and nudged Rome in the shoulder.

He glared at me. "No. You shouldn't have ditched out of the back of my bar into a dark alley. You should have stayed, Katalina."

The dark depths of his eyes, the way he ground out the words, the way he hovered in my space made me feel wanted, cared for, special.

I leaned away from him, not needing to get lost in the feeling. My purpose was bigger than finding out what love could offer.

I cleared my throat and picked at one of my fingers. "Don't do that."

"What?"

"Act like I have a place with or near you. I needed to go. What we did was over and—"

"That's bullshit. You don't walk out of my bar into the dark of the night."

"I do whatever I want." I raised my voice.

"Not after I sleep with you, you don't." He leaned into my face, and his eyes flicked to my lips. "Don't make me hate you even more, Kate-Bait. Don't make me regret it."

I sighed. Rome was the push to my pull and the enforcer to my plan. I baited and trapped the men, and he killed them all for the family. Still, our team dynamic was sandpaper to a wound as we brushed against one another. He couldn't forget who I was and that I was too close to the family for our relationship not to be messy. I couldn't forget how fast and effective he'd been at making me want him as he took the life of the man who threatened mine day in and day out.

I couldn't get any other words out to make him regret what we'd just done. My heart sped up thinking about his kiss, about the way he touched me. I needed Rome, even if I didn't want to admit it. Because I wanted to be more in the mob than just an untouchable—I wanted to be seen as a part of the family by standing on my own.

Above all else, Rome would never know he had my heart because I knew I could never own the monster that controlled his.

CHAPTER 10

KATIE

WHEN MARIO WALTZED back in with his sons by his side, I was sitting up in the bed. Bastian scanned the scene immediately, like a sponge soaking everything in. He'd grown up to be the tall, dark, and handsome Italian the whole city loved. Most everyone knew of him and his charisma, and he'd become the infamous heir to the mafia throne. He'd also kept a bit of his charm with me, was there when I needed him. Cade idled behind, like a feline never really concerned with what anyone else was doing. Maybe that was the benefit of being younger with less responsibility.

"Bastian has news," said Mario.

Mario's oldest son stared at me. "You're too valuable to be doing what you're doing."

His words pummeled me, made me feel like something more than I was. More than just someone who did a job for them.

"I'm fine. Nothing happened." I shrugged and tried to shake off the feeling of belonging. "I wasn't paying attention when I should have been."

"Even if you had been, it still could have happened because you're close to us, to me. We didn't consider the repercussions. You're a threat to many, and now you're extremely exposed."

I shrugged. "I can handle it. If you need me to call Georgie to—"

Bastian cut me off. "Move in with me."

Rome whipped his head around. "What?" he bellowed as my stomach bottomed out.

It was something I couldn't fathom, an invitation to move to the top of the mob family just like that. I hesitated.

"Katie"—he emphasized my name—"move in with me."

My stare jumped from him to Rome to Mario and back to Bastian.

"Why?" The question fell from my lips in confusion.

"Maybe I don't think you belong on the arm of our enemies," said Bastian. "Maybe you belong on my arm instead. We've staged you dating me before to lure targets. Moving in will piss them off more."

Rome huffed and his shoulders tensed, but he didn't object. I rolled my eyes. "We've only done that once or twice."

"You'll be protected under my roof and it'll be best for all of us."

"I get to decide that," I grumbled.

Mario scoffed. "No, I get to decide that." He cleared his throat. "Along with Bastian, of course. He's handling things here and he's right. Take some time at his place, huh? Let's regroup at the next meeting."

"I don't want that. Rome told me Georgie's government, Mario. I knew that; I had that information primed for you. He thinks he can bring you down and sideswipe Stonewood Enterprises in the process." I pushed when I knew I shouldn't.

We'd partnered with the biggest investment firm in the city a long time ago. If Georgie's people were going for that company, they meant business. "The government has been working on tapping phones, tailing you, finding ways to get you behind bars quickly."

"Georgie's only making that play so those damn Russians can get an upper hand," Bastian said, head tilted as if the only thing he didn't know were my thoughts.

"You think the Russian mob is involved?" I whispered. Another mob family working with the government and Georgie's gang meant navigating a lot more than I first imagined.

"I know they are. We've been working tirelessly to tighten up loose ends. We stumbled upon the information through those channels."

"Then we'll need everyone," I said. Bastian opened his mouth to respond, but I cut him off. "Including me. I'll play to Georgie's weaknesses. We've got to get as much information as—"

"Georgie's weakness is his manhood, Katie," Bastian said softly. "You on my arm will be bait enough to send him spiraling out of control. Men in love slip and falter, even when they know their love is misplaced."

"That's not a good idea," Rome said, and his hand went to my thigh under the thin white sheet. His touch was hot, searing, and reminded me of how his hands had felt on me just hours before. My pussy clenched like now was a perfect time to lust after him.

It wasn't.

Bastian stared down Rome with a sort of death glare I'd only seen him shoot at his enemies. "Get off her bed," he growled.

Rome's eyes narrowed, but he didn't move. "What?"

"You heard me."

Mario shook his head and tsked. "Bastian, we talked about this on the way over."

"We may have talked about it, but we didn't discuss it with Rome."

"Discuss what?" asked Rome.

"Your complete lack of foresight when it comes to our targets. You put her and this family in unnecessary danger," said Bastian.

"He had his hands on her." Rome's voice was low, and his eyes scanned the room. "Mario, you think that's okay?"

"It's not my father's choice anymore," said Bastian. "It's mine. Dad's got business in New York, which means I'm handling it here. And you don't get to fly off the cuff just because you think one of the family members can't handle themselves. It was unnecessary and reckless."

Rome narrowed his eyes and stood up slowly, on his own time. He straightened, and I felt them all shrink back, even if it was just a slight recoil. Bastian was the firstborn son of the Italian mob boss. He'd seen and experienced a gruesome, bloody life. But most of that blood had been spilled by Rome.

Rome enforced, he killed, he bled out victims who had wronged the family, and he'd never, ever misjudged a man's weakness. Even to the most powerful man, he was a menacing, brutal creature. If you weren't afraid of him, you were stupid. Bastian was anything but that.

Rome brushed imaginary lint from his shirt before he gently asked Bastian, "You know who you're talking to?"

Bastian ran a hand through his hair. "Don't do that, Rome. Don't warn me. I'm your brother."

"No. Cade's your brother. I'm your muscle, your protection, and also your weapon. I'm this family's monster. And if your protection finds something necessary, you better find it necessary too. Your life depends on it."

"Is that a threat?" Bastian took a step forward, and I found myself jumping off the bed. Bastian couldn't get in a fight. Especially not one he would lose, because then Cade would be in charge.

"Are we really arguing about a little rough-up from Georgie, you two?" I smiled at them both and eyed Rome with a look that said back the fuck up. He was dealing with the city's mob boss.

He canted his head quickly, and his neck popped. Cade and Mario—who'd taken a seat on the sofa across the room, as if to watch the two duke it out—stayed silent.

"It's not little, Katie. And everyone needs to know their place," Bastian stated, but I kept my eyes on Rome. His anger was palpable, vibrating off him in waves maybe only I could feel.

The thing about Rome and I was, we didn't really have a place. Our true families had died, and we had died with them. Now, we wandered around without souls attached to us, trying to be a part of something. We weren't actually blood family, although the oath made it sound that way, and we never actually abided by Mario's rules. They were loose instructions to us at best, and we navigated just well enough that they let us hole up with them until we met our maker.

Neither of us needed to meet that maker just yet.

Calm the fuck down.

"Bastian's right. If on your arm is where you need me, I'll be there." I shrugged like it wasn't a big deal. It shouldn't have been, but Rome's shoulders bunched like all of a sudden we had something new between us.

I'd only had him between my legs. And he didn't belong between my ribs and in my heart, I reminded myself. What we'd done in that bar would be forgotten just like he forgot other women.

"It's where I need and want you," Bastian emphasized. I snapped my gaze to him, trying to read his soft, definitive tone. "We'll get you set up at my place tomorrow. You can't stay at a hotel, and you've obviously worn out your welcome at Georgie's. Your apartment isn't safe anymore. So you come live with me."

"I'm fine with staying at—"

"My place. This week. Until then, lay low." With that, Bastian spun in his Italian leather loafers and walked out.

Cade and Mario got up and hugged me, whispering goodbyes, telling me to get rest. Mario grumbled to Rome that he would discuss everything further with him the next day.

Only one man remained. His massive back rose and fell to the rhythm of his rapid breathing.

"Rome," I whispered, knowing that saying his name was like poking an angry dragon with a mouth full of fire right then.

"You're agreeing to jump right into another lion's den after almost having your head bashed in?" he said under his breath without turning around. "You're agreeing to more danger when I just saved your ass?"

"Bastian isn't dangerous." I crossed my arms. "We both know for a fact that Bastian would never physically harm me. And I'm sure those men would have held me hostage. Although, I would have found a way out."

Rome whipped around. "Do you hear yourself? The head of our Chicago Family isn't dangerous? You'd be fine held hostage? Have you lost your fucking mind?"

"Me?" I shot back. "You put yourself in harm's way every day."

"I'm trained to do that. I knew how to kill a man before I was a teenager. This is my family, my life."

One part of me wanted to go to him and hold the boy that he was, to soothe the scared child who must have seen way too much, because I knew exactly how a child felt. Foster care for me hadn't been pretty. I'd been beaten, assaulted, and consistently taken advantage of. I knew what it was like to lose innocence too quickly. But the other part of me wanted to slide out the knife from under my clothing to hold at his throat.

"This is my family and life too. How dare you insinuate that it isn't? I've done just as much—"

"As me?" He laughed, but it was so cold it sent chills down my spine. "You didn't lose a baby or your father for the family.

My mother died because of mob ties too. It kills us all. My blood is their blood. They bleed, I bleed."

"They but not me?" I whispered because feeling excluded from what I constantly tried to be part of stabbed closer to my heart than I wanted it to.

"They don't care about you, Katie. Get out now."

"How can you say that? Bastian just asked me to move in with him." I threw it in his face, close to tears I didn't even know I had in me.

"Bastian would kill you. By escorting you around, that's basically what he's doing. The government and Georgie know you have intel. They fucking know you do."

"I barely got anything on them."

"But you heard conversations, you knew the whispers. You're a witness now, and you're a catastrophic danger that is on the arm of the enemy. The family is flaunting you in plain sight as bait. Antagonizing a monster will get you killed. You got out tonight because Georgie wasn't finished with you. He wanted to figure out a way to shut you up and keep you as his before the government found out that you knew everything. Now, with you on Bastian's arm...well, they'll torture you for that."

His words scraped at my soul. They gutted me and crushed all my hopes.

I closed my eyes and stood tall, took that deep breath I needed and let it go along with the other shit he was spewing my way. If what he said was true, it didn't matter. I'd climb to the top, prove I was a worthy partner, and be better than them all.

"I'll be fine." I shrugged him off in the way I knew he hated.

Rome's eyes bulged, and then before I could take another breath, he grabbed me by my neck and shoved me hard into the window. The glass and his hand on my neck were the only things keeping me from falling fifty stories to my death. "You're never fine, Katie. You're in danger here, right now, even with me."

"Am I?" I whispered.

93

He loomed over me and squeezed my neck so tight and so long, my vision blurred.

"You're a menace to yourself," he murmured before he let me catch my breath, but when I gasped, he kissed me like I was his to do with as he pleased.

I gripped his hair and jumped up to wrap my legs around him. He tasted like he was mine to do with as I pleased, too.

Our problem—we weren't anyone's. We were dead inside.

CHAPTER 11
KATIE

THEY LEFT A bodyguard outside my room the whole night. Which was overkill, considering I got the surprise of my life when I peeked out my door to find Rome staring at it from a chair he'd slid over.

I opened it wide to glare at him. "What are you doing? You should face the other way in case someone tries to kidnap me."

"That's what our bodyguard here is for. I'm here to watch for the real danger: you sneaking off and doing something stupid."

I slammed the door as loudly as I could. Then I opened it wide and slammed it again for good measure.

Still, I slept like a baby wrapped in a very safe cocoon. Was this what it felt like when my father was still living? Was this the family dynamic I missed so much?

The next morning, he was gone. I was left with just the security. "Dante, can you stop staring out into the abyss and make yourself useful this morning?"

"Katie girl, you're going to wreck this family, you know that?" he said as he turned to me with a sparkle in his greenish-blue eyes and a smile I knew he only had for me.

His sun-kissed skin made me wonder where he'd been the past couple of weeks. "You have some mission in the Caribbean and decide not to call me?"

Dante had done contract work since getting out of the military, and I knew he was flown places to do things in the middle of the night that only he and very few others knew how to do. I was lucky that he'd been an ally since the first day I'd met him.

"I'd have called you," he said, "but I heard you've been chumming it up with all the other men in the city. Georgie and now Bastian, huh?"

"Ha. Ha. You got a car here?" I leaned against the doorframe of my room and stuck my bottom lip out.

"Where you want to go, toots? I'll take you."

I needed to burn off the energy from the night before. I needed to get a handle on my thoughts. Decompression and centering of the mind worked for most. I got there by beating it out of myself. "You got time to train? I need to let off steam."

"Sure thing. But if Bastian asks...Ah, fuck it. They got eyes on us. They'll know."

"Sorry. If it's going to be that much—"

"Don't sacrifice your health, mental or physical, for someone else's comfort, toots. They might be important, but you're the most important thing to yourself. Got it?"

I didn't argue with Dante. The man's aura or spirituality or something just flowed through me, made me believe his words, and empowered me to push on with what I wanted without asking anyone else.

We jumped into a black SUV and made it to a gym we frequented.

Mats were reserved, but Dante walked up to one of the signs and pushed it aside. Reservations weren't something he ever had to worry about here.

The owner walked by shirtless and waved to us both. "You guys here for a few rounds? I'll jump in to spar in thirty if you got time."

"Nah." Dante shook his head. "Katie and I got to get dressed and train before we head out pretty quick. I'll hit you up later."

He winked at us and kept moving, eyeing up other members. The sweat in the air and the music pumping through the gym had me beelining to the lockers to get changed. My body yearned for workouts now. I craved getting knocked around and finding a way to get back up again.

Dante had begun training me when we'd first met. It'd started as self-defense. He'd called me tiny at a meeting, and I'd responded with some barb about how I'd find a way to take him down. He'd laughed and then offered to teach me. If he was in town, he called religiously to make sure I was meeting him at the gym.

I pulled my hair up into a ponytail and eyed the bandage on my ribs from the tattoo. Pain wasn't too bad there today, but if I wanted it to heal correctly, we'd have to be careful.

"Got a tattoo last night," I announced as I walked onto the mat in my tennis shoes and compression leggings.

My tight white tank didn't hide the bandaging too well, and Dante pointed at it. "What'd you get?"

"Just a quote to add to some ink I already had." I stretched my arms by pulling one close to my chest and then shaking it out before I did the same with the other.

"Hope it's inspiring." Dante went through the same motions.

"It's either that or depressing."

He chuckled and got on the ground with me to do a butterfly stretch. "Aren't they all?"

I nodded, and we continued to loosen our muscles for about five minutes.

"You probably need some more self-defense lessons."

I whipped my head up from looking down at my legs. "They told you?"

"Girl, everyone knows. You're our bait. No one gets to mess with you without repercussions."

I fell back on the mat with a growl. "Where's the damn confidence in me or at least the confidentiality for some of the stuff I do? Mario embarrasses me by sharing every single incident in my life with the family."

He poked me in the stomach. "Embarrassed by what, huh? We're here to protect you. How's that head of yours after getting knocked out?"

"Fine," I grumbled.

Dante had mastered a lot over the years, and one of those things was attacking when his victim least expected. His hand struck down onto my throat where he crushed my windpipe. Before I had time to react, he grabbed my hair and my head flew to the ground, but his hand was there to catch my skull before delivering any damage. It jarred me, rocked me, made me remember how quickly I could be caught off guard.

Would they miss me? Would they really always be there to protect me?

Or would I have to protect myself?

I knew the answer. Deep down, everyone knew the answer about the family.

I hooked my hand onto his wrists, making sure my thumb stayed aligned with my forefinger instead of wrapping around his arm like I had always wanted to do in the past. Dante had shown me that it was never good to have my thumb lingering on the other side of his arm. If for some reason the attacker yanked away fast, it could dislocate and leave me even more at their mercy. Instead, I had a stronger grip by keeping my whole hand together. I brought down as much weight as I could with my elbows onto his forearms. He didn't budge, so I lifted my hips and then brought them down with my elbows that time. I got just enough oxygen to keep moving by dislodging his hands somewhat.

I was small, agile, and flexible. I brought my legs up onto his hips and shoved him back hard. Normally, the next move would have been to grab his forearms as he slid away from my shove and try to hold him somewhat in place to kick his face, but I let him go, scrambled to my feet and motioned for him to come at me. "See how quick you can be now."

He smiled at me like I'd invited his devil out to play. Then he lunged. I blocked his first two punches and dodged a kick. I took the momentum from it and rounded to kick his knees.

He always had me beat, though, and today was no different. The man was trained to fight, to kill, to never be caught in a compromising position. He grabbed the leg I'd brought him down with while it was still in motion and shoved it up so high, I landed on my back, wind whooshing out of me, leaving me gasping.

I closed my eyes and let Dante laugh at me wincing at the pain. "Damn, Dante. That hurt the tattoo," I moaned.

I opened my eyes to see him standing over me. "You're a liar. The pain is only in your pride."

"Go away or help me up."

He took two steps back. "Little one, you only learn by getting up yourself and making sure you face your opponent again. The one who falls down over and over is the strongest of all in the end."

"Blah, blah, blah. I know," I grumbled as I got up. I wondered if he truly believed that, if he'd struggled over and over again in his life and finally found the place where he was strongest.

Dante stumbled into the family with his expertise, but he'd been an outsider for so long before then, I didn't know if he'd ever quite be comfortable fitting in with Bastian, Cade, Rome, and the others. The man was strikingly beautiful and also completely different from the other Italians. His roots were a mixture like mine, his eyes that emerald that shone bright like a panther's. He'd never fit in with the others with his appearance, but he didn't try to, either. I envied that about him, wondered how I could forget that I'd been left out too.

"Come at me again," I said, beckoning. "This time, go easy. I'm working with a banged-up head already."

Dante never went easy on anyone, but he worked me hard for the next hour, and I was thankful that I had to concentrate on only that in order to not get my ass beat.

"Give me a minute," I panted from the ground again. I'd never once had him on his back throughout the workout. "Then come at me again."

"Jesus Christ. We're done for the day, woman. Your forearms are bruising." I'd used them to block and break holds for the past hour, and they were sore enough to be damaged.

"So what?" I retorted as I scrambled up.

"You're wired from last night. Your body's tired, though. You need rest."

"I don't want rest," I said, hands on hips.

"Fine. Go shower and get your spare clothes on. I'll take you to work or something. I'm not sparring with you any-more today."

I blew a raspberry and stomped to the locker rooms. My legs screamed for me to sit down, but I didn't. My arms burned like they wouldn't be able to wash my hair, but I did.

By the time we left, I knew Dante had been right. I was fight-ing away the reality of the situation, and I didn't want to face the fact that things were changing quickly.

I made it my mission to reset the chain of events the rest of the day by doing exactly what I always did. If this day started the same as any other day, it meant it'd end the same too.

The sting of the new tattoo, the throbbing pain through my muscles after working out—and mostly the burning memory of Rome sliding in and out of me while he ravaged my mouth—were memories that needed to be forgotten.

Especially when he'd left me this morning without a word. Especially since we were probably back to where we'd started, and that was nowhere at all.

Especially since I wanted more, and I didn't exactly know why.

I argued with Dante the whole way back to my apartment. "This isn't anyone else's life, Dante. I'm doing what I want and I have commitments, a job. I'm not going straight to Bastian's."

"He's going to be pissed."

"He's going to be pissed I went to work out too. So, what's a couple more places? I have a week or two to get things in order. They got eyes on me. Go do your thing. We'll all be back together later anyway."

He sighed and I knew I had won the fight. He dropped me off at my apartment, and I got to avoid the drastic change to my life a little longer.

One week passed of Bastian and I being spotted here and there. We had dinner. We frequented a bar. We appeared as though we were dating. It was nothing over the top, but the few times Rome came with us to watch our backs, his eyes would meet mine, and my stomach would plummet.

Rome never said a word. He didn't even blink twice when Bastian would grab my hand or lean close to appear as though he had something intimate to share with me.

I stared at myself in the mirror a few days later and changed the bandaging over my tattoo before I pulled on a black crop top that barely covered it. After fluffing up my hair with a bit of cream, I added a dash of lip gloss. I didn't look bad. My curves were always on display, my skin was always clear of blemishes, and I liked to think men found me attractive. Still, Rome didn't say a word to me after that night.

He clearly had amnesia, and I was about to get it too. I didn't need to worry about a guy who never worried about me.

I hopped on the bus and went to my job at the coffee shop where I'd worked all through college. I'd graduated, good grades and all, and moved into the city with Georgie, but it didn't stop me from doing what I always had. Graduating was supposed to be this monumental time where I went off and got the job of my dreams, where I became a real adult, and where I was finally out on my own. College was supposed to be a stepping stone into adulthood. After graduation, though, nothing monumental happened. No mountain moved, and no river parted.

I'd been navigating on my own for so long, a diploma wasn't going to change anything.

I got to the shop and threw on the royal-purple apron. I turned on the machines Jackie hadn't started yet and let the low hum of music rock me into my usual routine. It was my little slice of normal. Jackie ran the shop and concocted me a perfect caffeine fix whenever I walked in.

"New drink for you!" she announced, bouncing with excitement when I returned from the store room. "Also, look who stopped in."

I glanced over and saw the only girlfriends I kept in touch with, Brey and Vick, munching on some granola.

"Bastian called Jett this week," Vick, a bubbly dose of blonde fairy, announced. Jett was the owner of Stonewood Enterprises and Vick's husband. She threw an oat cluster into her mouth and crunched on it way harder than necessary.

"Great. Everyone knows," I grumbled and pulled a metal stool over to sit.

"Are you okay to discuss this now?" Brey murmured softly, pushing a piece of her dark hair behind her ear before she continued. Aubrey Whitfield had attended the same high school as me, and we'd shared too much back then to ever sever ties. She'd become a friend I couldn't let go of even though I knew having ties to no one was smarter.

She ended up marrying Jett's brother, Jax, becoming a Stonewood just like Vick.

And I knew the Stonewoods did business with the family. Their name, along with the Armanelli name, ran the whole city.

I just wasn't sure how much they knew, how much I could tell them, how much I wanted to. We didn't mention business when we hung out. "I'm tired and have to work, guys."

"Not true," Jackie sing-songed as she wiped down one of her espresso machines. She motioned around the shop. "No one here to work for, and they've been frothing at the mouth more than my frother to talk to you about God knows what."

I rolled my eyes at her. "You're no help."

She shrugged in her green sweater. "Just being honest. I have a million things to do in back, including calling the owner of this place to figure out my lease. Watch the door and talk to them." She glanced their way. "They look too worried to be in here enjoying coffee. Bad for the aesthetic of the place and all."

With that, my excuse to avoid the conversation walked through the back door. I sighed and took another long drink.

"Brey's too sweet to start, so I'll go. We're all aware of who Bastian is. At one point in time, back when I was just dating Jett, you gave us all a scare by dating Bastian. We thought it fizzled out. Come to find out, maybe not."

I sighed. It was a long time ago when we'd staged Bastian dating me. We'd done it for a few moments to be seen by a target and that was it. Vick and Brey had only witnessed it because the target had worked at Stonewood Enterprises.

Vick continued, "Jett told me you two are seeing each other again." Her tone was grave, and coming from Vick Blakely, that was epic. She was never anything but optimistic.

I glanced at Brey, who'd pursed her lips and widened her green eyes a bit as if to say that I should at least indulge her.

Vick seemed so innocent, so naïve to the fact that life could be about making sacrifices and taking risks rather than just fairy tales and butterflies. It's what I think both Brey and I loved about her.

She was light while we were not.

Brey sighed. "I actually really like Bastian."

"As you should. The man would die for you," I said. "And Jax would be the one killing him."

I smiled, remembering a time Bastian had danced with her in a club, remembering the way he and Cade had acted as if they didn't know me. Back then, we weren't so high up, just kids of the mafia boss and a girl trying to fit into the family. So many nights I'd acted like I'd known Bastian, Rome, and Cade only as well as Brey and Vick did.

Now, Vick and Brey had married some of the most influential men in the city. Stonewood Enterprises had to have ties with the mob. So their women did too.

How long would they know my past wasn't exactly my past? How long would they believe I hadn't been a part of the mob until now?

The mob family kept their ties low-key. We weren't supposed to react when we saw each other. It was a new way, a way to keep our ties hidden, making it harder for enemies to figure out structures, dynamics, and mostly our weaknesses.

I was one of the biggest secrets of all.

Brey nodded like there was no denying my statement, her soft dark waves bouncing over her white top. "Jax and Bastian have nothing to fight over, though. At least, not right now because you want to be dating him, right? He's not forcing your hand?"

My best friend looked at me with concern. She wanted to know that I was okay, that there was no danger.

I'd lied to them time and time again about the men I was with. But they were both involved with Stonewood men now. "You both know you're hypocrites, right?"

"Excuse me?" Vick almost shouted, her straight blonde ponytail whipping around as she turned to glare at me.

"Vick, your husband owns one of the biggest corporations in the city—you think he isn't involved? You think he isn't working closely with Mario and Bastian?"

She stuttered and put her manicured hand to her mouth. "He's not...well, we aren't...the business is as clean as it needs to be."

I shrugged and pointed to Brey. "You know she's lying, right? All of Chicago couldn't be clean if they scrubbed their asses all day long. The Armanellis are everywhere. My family is—"

"Your family?" Brey asked, her eyebrows raised.

I groaned and pulled a hand through my brown-and-blonde-highlighted curls. "I should get to work, you two."

"You need to be dragged to an intervention," Vick grumbled. "You're hiding things from your best friends. That's absolutely not okay."

"This isn't black and white, Vick," I shot back.

"Nothing is more black and white than friendship. Specifically, our friendship." The conviction in her voice made it loud enough for everyone down the damn road to hear. "You say you don't care, and that means you very much do. So now I'm completely invested in bothering the shit out of you until I learn every detail and make sure everything works out perfectly. I think we need to call Rome." Vick started digging in her fancy purse.

I almost snatched it and threw it across the room. "You're so damn dramatic. I swear to God, I wish I never met you."

"I'm dramatic and yet you're saying you wish you never met me." She scoffed like my words weren't at all disrespectful.

That was the thing about Vick, she would gloss over everything negative I said. I could tell her that I was bleeding out on the floor, and she'd probably look at the blood, tell me it was a pretty color that accented my face, and then navigate the situation flawlessly.

She located her phone and scrolled through her contacts. "Was Rome there the whole night with you after the incident?"

I froze at her words. They both must have got intel about my night in the alley which meant they knew more than they should. "Rome has nothing to do with this."

"We want what's best for you, Katie." Brey put her hand on my arm, and when I stiffened, she slid it down to grab my hand and laid her head on my shoulder. "You're not going to hide it all. You might not care, but I'll care twice as much for the both of us. Vick won't leave any stone unturned either. We want to be there for you. And Jax and Jett do too."

"And Rome does too. Probably more than anybody," Vick chimed in, but she'd set her phone down like she was giving me a second to digest the information.

I stared ahead, knowing I'd lost my one family member at seventeen even though I fought hard as hell the best way I knew how to keep him alive. It made me a little colder to the world, a little more hesitant to have friends, and a lot more lethal within the family I had now. I was willing to do what it took and not look back, because I didn't have anyone that I really cared about to look back for.

Except Brey and Vick.

"You two are like little roaches that just won't go away, you know that?" Brey accepted me in high school when no one else would accept the foster child who'd hopped around men's beds. And Vick had attached to us in college, then stuck on like superglue. I sighed. "They've been my family since before you met me, Brey."

She squeezed my hand, and I felt her head nod. "Okay? Can you explain?"

"There's not much to explain. Dad was sick; I got in where I needed to so I could get him meds."

"So they're family?" she whispered as if trying to take it all in.

"As close as you and Vick."

Vick gasped and then grabbed her phone. "Jett's going to figure this out with us."

I snatched it away. "Jett works closely enough with Bastian to know not to dabble in this, Vick."

"My husband is going to dabble in whatever I want him to." She glared at me but didn't press the button to unlock her phone.

"Your husband and Bastian are dealing with government issues already."

"So what he said to Jett the other day is true?" She jumped up to pace back and forth in front of us. "Some guy hit you over the head, and he's concerned. Like how concerned? Like sleeping with you concerned? Like your boyfriend concerned? Jett said you're moving in with him."

I sat silently, not denying her statement at all.

"You can't just move in with him!" Vick slammed her hand down on the counter.

"You sound like a helicopter parent right now, Vick." I sighed and met her through-the-roof angry tone with a monotone one. "Calm down."

"Brey!" Vick whined and motioned to the one person everyone thought could talk sense into me. Brey was the rock and only foundation I would have listened to had it been negotiable.

It wasn't, though.

She studied me a second longer and then nodded. "She's moving, Vick." Then to me, "Do you need help?"

"I got it. Some of the guys will come by—"

Vick's honey eyes bulged. "Some of the guys? Oh my God, Brey!" She stomped her foot. "How can you think this is a good idea?"

"I think you calming down would be a good idea," I grumbled, but I had a small smile on my face that I couldn't hide. Normally, Vick would have shoved me into any man's home and told me to find my happily ever after. The fact that she wasn't doing that now proved she cared enough, and a little piece of my parentless heart warmed.

"I got the move under control. Promise."

CHAPTER 12

ROME

"**D**O YOU HAVE anything about this damn move under control?" I bellowed at Katie. She was shoving clothes into a cardboard box that Cade, Bastian, Dante, and I had brought over.

"Oh, shut the hell up!" she screamed, holding up a shirt against herself in the mirror as if this was the time to determine what she wanted to pack.

"Why the fuck are we doing this today?" I growled at Bastian. We should have given Katie a year to pack up her stuff because a week wasn't long enough.

Ever the know-it-all, he stood stoically and replied with his arms crossed, "Because it has to be done today."

I didn't hide my anger as I ripped the shirt from Katie and threw it in the box. "Try shit on later. Throw it in a box, and we'll carry it down to the moving truck. I got stuff to do tonight, and at this rate, we'll never be done by then."

She curled her glossed lip at me and peered around my shoulder to see Cade moving a vase from her table. "Be like Cade. Do something constructive like pack up stuff I don't need to sort through."

Cade's tattoos read *Cade* on one hand and *Chaos* on the other. It was a funny contrast, one everyone gave him hell for. Cade avoided most of the chaos and lurked in the shadows. His only job was to swipe data, tinker with apps, and pull intel for the family from security systems. He did it well.

"You're sorting through everything!" I swear to Christ my mind didn't work this way. I had precise times and schedules in my life for a reason. You didn't do what I did for the family without them. I needed some sort of structure, and she wasn't providing any of it.

On top of that, nothing was organized, which frustrated me even more. She'd known we were coming this afternoon, and her place was still a sty.

"What did you do all day?" I asked, hovering over her.

"Um, are you serious? I went to work, where I discovered that Bastian had announced I was moving..."

She paused, and I raised my hands to motion her on. I wanted to hear this story. It had to be a good one if not one thing was packed when we arrived.

"Wait. Why should I tell you? What are you, my daddy?" She raised an eyebrow at me. Then she leaned forward and purred out like a sex kitten, "Just remember, I like my daddies big, sort of like Bastian, and I'm not sure you fit the bill."

I knew I was going to hell because my dick jumped at her goading me. Cade snickered behind me. I would pummel his ass later, I swear to God. The guy inhabited his own head and got lost in his thoughts ninety-nine percent of the time but chose this moment to listen to our bickering. "Shut the fuck up, Cade."

He blew a raspberry, and I turned back to Katie to interrogate her some more. I wanted an answer. "Seriously, what did you do the whole day? You knew we were coming this afternoon. Why didn't you pack?"

Bastian stepped between us, his arms folded over his chest and his head tilted at me in question. "Rome, she worked and had coffee with Brey and Vick. Why are you up her ass? Let her be."

She bent at the waist to pop her mess of curls out from behind Bastian. "Yeah, Rome. Let me be."

I wouldn't have been surprised if steam poured out my ears as I glared at both of them. Katie took her taunting one step further and pushed up against Bastian's back. She wrapped one of her small hands around his waist and whispered up at him while holding my gaze. "Thank you for telling him to lay off, Daddy."

Bastian chuckled at her and then patted her arm. "You're fanning the flame, Katie. You want an explosion today?"

His choice of words, the way I told her that we were a nuclear bomb, it had me backing up as she looked at me with humor in her eyes and replied, "Maybe I do."

I threw out a retort I knew she would hate. "Maybe you need to stop toying with men that aren't interested in exploding, Kate-Bait."

Bastian had the last word, and that word rubbed me the wrong way. "He's actually right, babe. You appear to be mine now and shouldn't be goading him unnecessarily."

I growled, "You know, you're both a part of the problem. Katie's in danger, and we're letting her go to work? She gets to flit around town like she didn't get knocked over the head a week ago?"

Bastian sighed. "We got people watching Katie, Rome. You know this. We've been in contact with..." He shook his head as if he knew it wasn't something he needed to explain. He was the head of the family now, and he didn't directly answer to me even if I wanted to choke the answer out of him. "She's covered."

"She's being reckless. And her blood in the river isn't something you want to clean up, Bastian." I warned him because I was the only one who probably could.

He waited as he stared at me for a couple seconds and then said softly, "Katie, you'll need to put the coffee job on hiatus."

She narrowed her gaze at me as if I was the enemy, but she didn't argue. She nodded and licked her lips like she finally wanted to give me a second to breathe.

The woman was fucking with my head, and I didn't have time to play games. She was in a lot of danger, and so was my family.

I needed to stay on my game, not get irritated with a woman who wasn't mine.

I worked with Dante to pack up most of her dishes. I instructed him on the exact way I wanted them organized into the box.

He smiled at me slowly as I did. "You realize I pack shit up for a living, right, man?" He waggled his eyebrows and cracked his knuckles. Dante sometimes got rid of the bodies for us.

Bastian, on the other hand, commanded the damn attention. It never bothered me before. Yet.

Katie's eyes wandered over to him more than I liked. Her smile lingered when he gave her the attention she craved. And she licked her lips when she thought no one was watching. Was she hungry for his touch? Just enjoying the view?

She glanced my way and winked, making me stalk over to her. "You tell the coffee shop you quit yet?"

She huffed. "I text the manager, alright?" She waited a second. "Also, Brey and Vick know too much."

"That my fault?" I reared back at her accusation.

"Well, it's not mine. I didn't tell them anything. Bastian called one of the Stonewoods."

"You keep pushing boundaries, Kate-Bait." I shook my head because I loved and hated it about her all at the same time. "You should have never introduced those girls to me."

"We're all friends now." She shrugged and brushed at nothing on her shoulder, but she bit her lip. It was a sign she knew things were getting too tangled.

"Start taking this seriously." I told her, my voice low.

Her grey eyes narrowed at me before she licked her plump lips. "I always take what Bastian says seriously."

I couldn't stop the growl at hearing his name come from her mouth. She smiled at the rise she'd gotten out of me. She was just playing more games.

It wouldn't be a game if I ripped her away from him, from this whole family.

She needed to be punished for the way she baited men, especially men like me. Yet the punishment I wanted to inflict on her ended with me between her legs because she looked good enough to eat today.

CHAPTER 13

KATIE

"YOU'RE PUSHING YOUR limits with him," Bastian said from the window of his living room.

I was lying on his couch, swinging my legs back and forth in the air as he unfolded the top of another box. "Am I going to have to wear these knee-high socks here all the time, or do you turn up the heat ever?"

Bastian sighed and stalked toward me. "You don't want to talk about him?"

"What's there to talk about?" I asked, still swishing my legs, giving Bastian a sly smile.

He grabbed one calf and squeezed, stopping my rhythmic motion. His hand stayed where it was as he sat down next to my ass. Then he dropped my leg onto his lap. I let the other one fall down next to it. "I'm wondering about this arrangement."

"Well, I can tell you it's not the best plan you've ever come up with."

"Why not?" he grumbled, but he asked like he already knew.

"We're not nearly explosive enough to grab Georgie's attention, and I can hook him if I just go back there."

"Not happening." Bastian's commands were usually followed. Mob boss and all.

I put a pin in my idea for the time being. I figured I owed it to him to listen.

His hands rubbed up and down my thigh like it was a subconscious motion. It probably was, too. Bastian always had women around—hanging on him, tending to his every need—and he was a natural womanizer who charmed most of them with either the power he exuded or the natural way he took care of them. Hence the rubbing.

I didn't pull my legs away. I let his hand roam and wondered if it felt as good as Rome's on me, if I liked comfort as much as I liked Rome's heat.

The difference between them was that I felt safe near Bastian, like he would wrap me up in pillows and treat me like a treasure.

"The plan extends beyond you staying here, Katie. We have to work him hard enough that he approaches us alone, that he wants answers from you so bad, he's willing to step up to me with you on my arm."

"Georgie's a coward," I stated, as if that explained why he would never approach Bastian. They had to know that, right?

"For the next week, I'll take you out once or twice, but otherwise, you stay here. It'll drive him crazy. Come time for the gala, he'll have enough unanswered questions that either the men he's working for will be wondering or he'll be bursting at the seams to talk. We'll get him then."

"So, you want to keep me cooped up here twenty-four seven?" My voice came out as a squeak. I wasn't good at staying put, wasn't good at feeling locked in.

It's only a few weeks.

That sounded like years and years in my head.

I propped myself up on my elbows to look at him. "You going to be okay with me here all the time?"

He smiled like a Cheshire cat and dipped a finger in a tiny hole that had formed at the top of my sock, against my calf. These were my favorite socks, and I hadn't replaced them even when they'd worn through in certain parts. "I think I can handle you and your ratty socks. Don't worry about me."

"Oh, really?" I laughed and wiggled my calf away from him. "Our arrangement is going to make it pretty hard for you. In every sense of the word."

He lifted an eyebrow. "How so?"

I feigned offense by holding my hand to my heart. "Excuse you, asshole. I'm hot as hell." I curled my legs off him and stood up to do a twirl in my short shorts and cut-off top. With my hands on my hips, I popped my tits out in front of him. "I'll be walking around here however I want, in whatever I want."

"Even those socks?" he said as he feigned being scared.

"Oh, shut up. These socks just add to my appeal. You ready to remain celibate and have this right in front of you?"

Bastian bit his bottom lip and eyed me up and down as he leaned back in the chair, spreading his legs in his sweats like he owned the room and wasn't at all worried about me in front of him.

A fire sparked small in my stomach, a challenge almost. The man controlled a city and thought he could control me. Something about bringing him to his knees appealed to me. The way he looked at me with such arrogance and heat appealed to me too.

"Who says I'm remaining celibate, Katalina?"

"You think you're bringing women back here when I live here?" I shook my head. "Not happening. I'm not listening to that."

"I don't need to fuck in my own home. You think I can't take a woman wherever I want in the city I own? If I want to fuck in the alley, I will. If I want to fuck in a club, I will. If I want to fuck in the middle of Chicago traffic in broad daylight, I will."

My nipples tightened at his bold words, and he stared at them, watching them pebble. Something was happening between us, and I wasn't sure I should continue to indulge in it.

I turned my back on him and walked to his kitchen. "Whatever you say, Bastian." I waved him and the feeling off. This was supposed to be just an arrangement. Just for show.

"What do you have to eat?" I asked.

He got up and came over. "Why don't you finish unpacking, and I'll whip up dinner. You like pasta, yeah?"

"Doesn't every girl like pasta?" I said through a smile. "You cook?"

"Sure." He shrugged and rounded the counters to the refrigerator. He pulled sauce and a bowl of pasta dough from the refrigerator.

"Are those hand rolled?" My voice was higher than I wanted it to be. Pasta was actually a freaking weakness of mine, and this might have been the only time in my life I was trying handmade.

He side-eyed me. "Yes," he said slowly. "Why do you look like you want to fuck me on the counter right now, woman?"

"Did you make that?"

He chuckled as he pulled out expensive pots and pans. "Katie, my momma taught me to cook when I was young, before she passed. I promise she never disappointed and made sure I never disappointed either. We only eat handmade in this house."

"Oh my God," I whispered. Every other man was forgotten for a moment. This man held handmade pasta and sauce. "Please tell me you aren't joking. I don't think I've ever been with a man who can cook like a boss."

He laughed. "You really haven't ever been with a man."

I squinted at him and crossed my arms over my chest. "What's that supposed to mean?"

118

"It means I know most every man you've had a relationship with because you do that shit for the family. You're with me right now for the family. I appreciate it. I see your loyalty. I get your blood is my blood, but those guys weren't men."

"And you are?" I challenged him because my hackles rose the moment he talked about my role.

"I'm the man of most men, babe. You'll see."

"Hmmm, yes, I guess we will."

———

Unpacking my clothes while Bastian cooked was a little more challenging than I expected. "Where the hell do you expect me to go with my dresses?"

"The closet!" Bastian yelled from the kitchen.

The closet was miniscule. I could barely fit my ass in there, and my ass wasn't even that big. "Bastian, you're joking right?" I stalked back down the hallway to glare at him. "That closet is for Harry Potter and belongs under a staircase."

"Harry Potter?" he asked like he truly didn't know, and just like that, all my hope for him died. "Never mind. Don't even tell me. That's your closet," he stated like it wasn't a problem.

"I'll move your shit to that closet," I spat back and started for his room.

I heard a pan clatter, and then Bastian was in front of me, faster than a cheetah on speed. "You touch nothing in my closet."

"What's in your closet?" I eyed him with newfound interest, my head drawn back a bit in question.

"Nothing of your concern." His tone was hard and final, a stark reminder that I was a guest at the head of the mafia's home. He pointed toward my room, and I stomped back there.

"Georgie had a full walk-in closet for me, you know?" I taunted.

"Georgie just about killed you the other night," he replied, and I smiled at his retort.

Bastian and I were going to get along just fine.

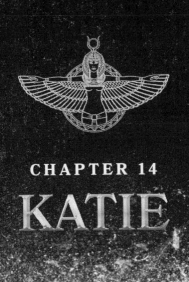

CHAPTER 14

KATIE

WE GOT ALONG more than fine.

Bastian moved mountains for me when he needed to. He wasn't home much, but food was brought in most of the time for me. The days he was home, he cooked. Like, gourmet-meal cooked. He made pesto chicken with arugula and prosciutto one night, and I seriously almost took him to bed.

We'd lived together two weeks, and the man was pretty much a saint every time he walked in. He removed his shoes, was quiet if he returned at night, cleaned up after me and himself. He even let me watch the shows I wanted to. Georgie always had on the news and wanted to talk politics, and Jimmy wanted to watch porn and do things a teenage girl shouldn't be doing.

Bastian was incomparable to the others. He was like a Stepford boyfriend.

"Want me to change the channel?" I asked one night while he scrolled his phone, sprawled out on the oversize chair near the couch. I realized that a historical romance with a duke telling the main character he wanted to marry her might not be his idea of entertainment.

"This is fine," he mumbled, scrubbing a hand over his face and sighing as he slid the phone into his gray sweatpants. He'd changed for the night finally, signaling to me that he wouldn't be going back out.

"Honestly, I can watch something other than a historical romance."

"The cinematography's spectacular, and the cast is talented. Plus, I'm intrigued with when they'll figure out the identity of the writer."

"You know already?" I asked.

He tapped his leg and smirked. "Google."

I stuttered and sat up indignantly on the white sofa, pulling my cropped black tank down in a huff. "You were looking that up? I thought you were working! What the fuck, Bastian?"

One side of his mouth pulled up in a casual smile. "I like knowing outcomes, Katie."

"That's not fun at all." I threw a pillow at him. "Don't you think it would have been nice to guess with me?"

"Not interested." He caught the pillow with ease and set it on his lap. His manly hand waved toward the television. "I don't want to waste all that time watching something if I won't like the outcome."

"That defeats the whole purpose of the narrative, of the viewing experience."

"Why waste time on trivial entertainment if you'll be frustrated when the ending isn't what you wanted?"

My jaw dropped in disbelief. I wanted to tell him that some things were best left as a surprise, that Google couldn't write out an experience, especially not a personal one. Yet his reasoning, which I'd never considered, made a lot of sense.

"You're bizarre," I conceded as I crossed my arms over my chest and fell back into the soft cushions of the couch.

"I like to think I'm efficient and prepared." Bastian unfolded from his leather recliner, chuckling. I shamelessly looked him over as he stretched and then walked toward me. He was a tall Italian drink of water, a perfect specimen of a man. His body moved languidly, like he was completely comfortable in his own skin. His broad shoulders framed his lean body, and I could make out the outline of a six pack underneath the T-shirt he wore. His bare forearms didn't need to be flexed for me to see the strong muscles where his veins popped.

We were getting along brilliantly, obviously.

Except that we didn't have sex.

He looked at me sometimes like he might try. I probably looked at him that way too.

Correction: I know I did.

I considered how our arrangement would change if it happened and didn't quite care about that. The only thing that stopped me was the memory of Rome's hands on me that night in the bar.

He'd burned something into me, imprinted on me, and left a mark I couldn't erase. I was stained with the idea of him, and no matter how hard I tried to wash away the memory, it stayed.

"Katie, do I need to throw those damn things on your feet away?" Bastian grumbled as he stood over where I was lying on the couch, feet up over the back because sitting properly on his overly expensive couch felt way too cushy for me. I wasn't that person.

"Only if you want a knife at your neck," I said.

He knelt down to get level with me. "You will never hold a knife to my neck. You know this."

"Maybe." I swung my feet around and jumped up. I pulled at my black shorts, but they didn't cover much of my ass, and my shirt didn't hide much of my stomach either. "Maybe not. I'm willing to bet I'll have an opportunity, though."

He glared at me for a second and then laughed his ass off. "You're something else, you know that?"

"If you say so." A knock sounded at the door. I lifted an eyebrow. "Takeout?"

"You know it." He nodded and went to get the food someone left on his doorstep. Perks of the mob.

I peered around him at the bag he set on the table. "What's in it?"
"Food."

"I'm starved. You leave me here to rot all the time."

"I leave you here to go to work."

"Your work is my work, right? My blood, your blood."

"Not right now. You're holing up for bait, and the intense bait dates start next week, actually. Do you know what you want to wear to the gala? We're supposedly raising money for a charity."

"Sounds fancy."

"Sounds like everyone who's someone will be there, including Georgie and the men he's working with."

The skin at the base of my neck tightened like I was an animal getting ready to pounce. I wanted out of this place and back to work. I clapped my hands together and unleashed a smile for Bastian. "When do I have to be ready?"

Searching my face, he didn't answer. He stepped close to me and moved one of my messy curls from the side of my face. "You're damn pretty when you smile, woman."

My eyes rolled hard. "Be serious, Bast."

"I am serious. You look like one of those big feral cats, ready to move in for the kill. To someone like me, it's beautiful."

If my skin was a tad lighter, he'd have seen my blush. "Are you being nice because I'm in booty shorts?"

"I'm being nice because I want to. If you want me to be nice for that, I'll be happy to just carry you to my bed now. Show you how much you don't really want nice."

Someone could have cut the sexual tension in that room with a damn knife. He glanced at my bare stomach, and goose bumps popped up right where he looked. I eyed the plump lips he would bite every now and then, like he was doing right at that moment.

"Tell me what's in the damn carry-out bag before we make this arrangement way more complicated." I shut my eyes to try to shake off my urge to jump his bones and pointed behind him.

He grunted and grabbed it. "Ramen from the restaurant down the road. Made special just for us."

"Someone forget to pay this month?"

"Nah. Their family's finances are tight, and I'm not in the business of collecting on every territory every month. Not the small ones at least."

He pulled out a white linen upholstered chair from the massive oak table and motioned for me to sit down. I ambled over and nodded as I slid in. He scooted it under me like I was fragile or something.

"You aren't supposed to pity the small guy," I said. "You take what's yours, or someone else will."

"Who taught you that?" Bastian inquired as he pulled out our bowls of steaming ramen.

"Your father did." Mario Armanelli ruthlessly collected, and every part of Chicago knew that.

"A good leader is feared, Katie. A great leader is loved. And an exceptional one is one you never thought you needed. This city will one day operate like that because I'll make sure they can say, 'Look, we did it all on our own.'" He didn't sit but rounded the counter to grab two glasses for us and filled them with ice water.

Bastian and I never drank at home. I didn't know if he ever drank at this point. He worked, and with his coming and going so much even in the middle of the night, I don't think he wanted to risk inhibiting his mental state.

"Without their acknowledgement, you lose their respect," I said.

"Or I gain their allegiance and they become stronger because they believe in themselves."

I shrugged. Our leadership views never coincided. He was philosophical while I was animalistic. The strongest survived, and cutting out the weak or pushing them until they were strong seemed to be the only way. "Or you wasted time on the weak when it's survival of the fittest."

"It used to baffle me how enamored my father was with you at such a young age. He even told me you sat in on some of the calls, that you gave advice." He rubbed his five-o'clock shadow. "Can you imagine, a seventeen-year-old giving the family advice?"

I let the silence seep in around us. Most of the family didn't know why I was wise beyond my years, but I'd lived with my daddy. He'd taught me love and pride. Then I'd been put into foster care where there was none of that.

I wasn't sure any of these men ever had love ripped from them, if they were ever loved like a daughter could be by her own father.

"Did you, Cade, and Rome grow up together? None of you were ever on the calls."

"My father wanted me to see the business, to know the duties of a boss. The calls were social, more of a diversion for those tapping our lines."

I nodded. "They weren't that important, but they were to me. I knew it was a way in for me. Jimmy coached me to never say anything too outrageous. He'd tell me someone could be listening, ready to take me away from him."

Bastian scoffed. "Not likely coming for you. But he gave you the right idea. My father strictly taught his heir to this mess of a family the bloody side of it."

"Cade too?"

Bastian shook his head. "Cade got lost in the world of the internet. He's free of responsibility. Rome and I saw everything while he saw next to nothing." His voice was laced with pain.

"At least you had each other." I tried to offer solace where I knew there was none.

"I didn't have Rome. I'll be honest with you because you look at him like you may be able to connect with him. Rome never connected with anyone. His mom was gone in a flash when he was born, and his father was our right-hand man for a reason. Our uncle was a sick, vicious thing that I wouldn't call human. He turned in the end. Rome doesn't say it, but he is the way he is because his father was who he was. And after all that time, we all thought we had him figured out. Rome may have hated him, but he thought he understood him too."

"But he didn't?" I was on the edge of my seat, my heart beating fast like a hungry animal scrambling for scraps. I wanted to know Rome's story more than I'd wanted anything in that moment.

"He shot his father when he tried to take my dad's life, Katie. My uncle wanted the power and was willing to kill his own brother for it."

"What?" I whispered.

He nodded solemnly. "Rome doesn't trust anyone because he almost missed it. We all did. He saved my dad's life by taking his own father's. It's a mind-fuck. And the damn power of this city did it to all of us."

I shook my head in disbelief. My mouth opened and shut as I tried to form words and wrap my mind around what he'd said. Rome was seen as the monster, but he was the monster that saved them all. "Maybe I understand him because he knew what his life could be, only to have it ripped away just like me. I had the love of my father and lived a life full of joy and being cared for until he died. It was all stripped from me then, and I had to adapt. Adapting and changing is sometimes the hardest thing to do. I knew what love was and was used to it."

He studied me. "True. I've always known this life, known what was coming for me. You both seem to have had a twist along the way."

"And I can't speak for Rome, but after my twist, I had to live a lot of different lives, none of which were good ones," I said quietly.

He stared at me, and I knew he was waiting for me to admit more. He commanded a lot from just one look, and I knew he could break most into admitting anything with it. But he wasn't looking at me that way. There was softness in his normally hardened features.

"Did you ever meet my daddy?" I asked after I took a bite of the ramen. "Aside from the time you all came to my house."

"Only once that I remember. He was trimming bushes in pants and a long-sleeve shirt. His shiny bald head sweat bullets in the humid summer air, but he kept moving quickly. I remember thinking his need to finish was astounding."

"He was always a hard worker."

"And proud of his work too. I walked over his freshly cut grass that day, and he yelled at me for not taking the sidewalk. He was the help, but he told me not to walk over his freshly cut grass." Bastian leaned back and chuckled at the memory. "I think he even scolded my dad for not teaching me better manners."

I smiled, soaking up any information about my father I didn't already have. "That would have been him. Proud as hell of his work always."

"His work was just that and raising you. He must have been proud of you too, then."

"I like to think he was proud of what I could have become, but not of what I was. He knew I got involved with Jimmy."

"Mm." He mulled that over as he stared at me. We were different in that sense. Bastian had always known where his life would take him. There was nothing else. "That's a hard pill for a father to swallow. Maybe for any parent."

"I'm sure your father worries about you too." I wasn't sure at all. Mario didn't seem to worry about his sons much. I liked to think it was because of the respect he carried for them, knowing he'd raised them for their roles the right way.

"My father doesn't care or worry much about anyone, Katie. My mother turned toward something else to numb her anxieties before she passed."

"I see." It wasn't my place to dwell, and when he glanced away, I let him know he wasn't alone. "My mother's been gone a long time too. It's probably better that way."

"Yes, maybe."

"Anyway"—I slurped up the last of my ramen—"I'm happy and full. Ramen hit the spot."

I started to clean up the table, but his hand went to my wrist. "I got it. Why don't you go relax, huh? I need to make a call anyway. Cade has been calling me."

"Your phone's not ringing." I pointed to it lying face down on the table.

"I silenced it. We were eating together," he said as if disgusted that I would think he wouldn't.

"You realize this is an arrangement, right? I don't care if you take a call while we eat. I don't care if you—"

"You're my guest."

"I'm your bait, Bast."

He rubbed a thumb over my wrist before he let it go and stood to collect the wrappers and bowls left from our food. "You're never just bait, Katalina. I enjoy having you here. If nothing else, you make good conversation and are pretty to look at."

I couldn't even bring myself to roll my eyes. Bastian's constant politeness was starting to rub me in all the right places. I was losing sight of everyone else in the world that wasn't inside of this penthouse, and I was forgetting exactly why Rome meant anything to me when I hadn't heard or seen him since I'd moved.

"Tell me something." I stared him down. "Is this how you treat all the women you bring here?"

He let out a breath and went to throw away the trash. Then he was back in front of me, dragging one finger down my arm and up again to my neck where my curls hung loosely. He let them fall between his fingers as if memorizing the way they did. "I'm starting to think I don't treat any woman like you, because there is no woman like you. You don't bitch about anything, you don't care to prepare for me to be back. You've worn ratty socks since you've been here, and you still look good enough to fuck on this counter right here. And to add to it all, you make for damn good company."

"Most women can do all those things, Bastian."

"I don't think so. I think that's why you're coveted bait and why I have to make sure you're never bait again."

With that, he wrapped his arm around my waist and kissed me. I met him halfway, sure I could erase every memory of any man before him with the way he treated me.

His touch was softer than I expected. He let me control the kiss, and I wondered if this was how he would rule Chicago, letting those around him think they were controlling, that they were a partner, that they could work with him to be the best.

I wrapped my arms and legs around him, trying to pull more from him, absorb more for myself. I was chasing a feeling that only one man could give me and it wasn't Bastian. He lifted me right onto his length, and I rubbed against it as he walked me down the hall to his room.

"We're moving quick, Katie."

"We're moving with purpose. You have calls to make."

I felt his chest rumble with laughter right before he threw me onto the white down comforter on his bed.

I glanced around his room. The whites flowed into warm wood tones and matched muted pictures on the walls. "Your room is welcoming."

He didn't take his dark eyes off me. "My room is here all the time. You in it, on my bed, willing to spread your legs, is not. So might be time to strip and look at my room later."

I scrambled to my knees and looked at him through my eyelashes, sure the power had shifted my way in this moment. "If we do this, it's probably going to change things."

He nodded but started unbuttoning his shirt like he didn't care at all. I lifted my top over my head to reveal an unlined lace bra. The stark white against my skin felt like a lie every time I put it on. It was one of the reasons I always wore it, like I could fool my body into thinking it was innocent again.

Bastian groaned as I dragged a hand over the lace and let my fingers linger on my nipples. He yanked his unbuttoned shirt off and unbuckled his pants at a rapid speed. Bastian was defined in all the right places, his skin tanned and taunt over his muscles. I wanted my mouth to water for him, for my desire to amplify, but there was nothing.

Nothing except for the need to feel in control of myself, to steer my longing for Rome to someone else.

"I'm not sure if I want you to strip the rest off or leave it on. Fuck, Katie." He breathed it out like he could barely contain himself.

I wished I felt the same. My eyes scanned up and down him, hoping for a spark.

None came, not even when I studied the lips that were just on mine. His kiss had been nice, but I didn't want nice.

I wanted ravenous, vicious, something close to monstrous.

Bastian smirked at me, his eyes dark and full of need. He moved toward me, his hand went to my thigh and slid up to my shorts where his thumb dipped into the leg opening. "No panties? Were you planning this?" he whispered near my ear.

The question had me jolting back. Rome had asked me the same thing, and it was at that moment, I knew this couldn't go further.

I leaned back, my heart thundering too loudly in my rib cage to ignore.

"Fuck, woman." His eyebrows slammed down, confused by my sudden recoil. "Do you want to do this?"

I smiled at him, but I knew it didn't reach my eyes. "I want to but I don't know if I can." I'd used sex as a tool and weapon before. Whatever I had to do for the family, I did. It was my choice, but for the first time in a long time there was a hurdle I wasn't sure I could jump over. I'd had Rome's hands on me, wished they were there again, and only thought of him. My body didn't want to cooperate, and I didn't know how far I would be able to go while thinking of someone else.

He scratched his head like he didn't understand. Then he tilted it. "If you can? You don't have to sleep with me, Katie."

I didn't know why tears sprung to my eyes or why he grabbed my shirt to push it back over my head before pulling me close for a hug.

We sat there for a long time as I silently let the tears run over my face.

He finally whispered in my ear, "Tell me what you want."

Those words would have had me drunk on the idea that I had the power over a man just a few weeks back. Yet, Rome had mixed me all up, made me think it wasn't just about the power and the control. And Bastian hugged me like I was something more than just the bait, more than just the tool the family utilized.

I was starting to want more, feel more, be more. Of what? I didn't know.

"I'm not sure I know what I want, Bast. But I have to figure it out before we go any further."

He nodded and backed away, holding me at arm's length. "We'll be okay, huh? Let's just get through the next few weeks."

He'd respected me, made it so easy and safe that I wondered if I should regret my decision.

To have lost so much of my innocence that I questioned protecting my mental health made me wonder what life would have been like had I attached myself to men like Bastian early on.

He left me that night feeling weighed down by a new burden of hope, hope for the future and fear that we wouldn't be able to achieve it.

CHAPTER 15

KATIE

WE WALKED AROUND each other on eggshells for a few days after that. He didn't try anything again. When he left me a couple of days later, he told me to take an SUV out if I needed to, to be careful about where I went.

He was trusting me and giving me space when he shouldn't have.

I tried to steer my mind to the fact that Bastian was here for me, wanted me, and that he trusted me to take control where I wanted to.

Still, my mind veered off course and found its way to the man who didn't want anything to do with me. Rome hadn't called, hadn't texted, hadn't come to visit Bastian in an effort to see me. He'd avoided everything we were, and now I wondered if it was because he was as broken as me. He'd lost his father by his own hands. The one person he should have been able to rely on made Rome exercise the monster in him in the most brutal way. He protected the family by taking his dad's life.

When I got to Heathen's Bar, the host greeted me with a smile and waved me in. Every heathen that worked there had a mouthwatering look, and the host didn't disappoint. His top bun was thick and his smile bright and white. Then there was Cole, who stood behind the bar in a tight T-shirt that showed off his muscles and his dimples were overkill.

"Is it too early for a drink?" I sat down on a stool and put my chin in my hand as I winked at him.

"Never too early for you, Katie. You're one girl I'm sure needs all the drinks she can get."

A patron who had been there much too long burped and swung his head my way. "What's that supposed to mean? You doing something I want to get into?" He waggled his eyebrows at me.

I rolled my eyes and didn't answer him. "Just get me a Sprite, Cole."

Cole stared down the guy who decided to get up from his stool and walk over to me. He wobbled on his way, and when he got within three feet, I could smell the whiskey.

"Cole, get me my Sprite," I told him pointedly. I could take care of a drunk and didn't need Cole getting into any type of trouble before the night even began. Bars were magnets for enough drama that I felt obligated to help out the bar manager every once in a while, especially since Cole was a papa bear on steroids for most everyone. He managed Rome's bar with precision and heart, making sure his employees and patrons always felt safe, while weeding out customers that caused the opposite quickly.

Cole filled up a glass just as the guy whispered something to me about going back to his place.

"I think you need to go home and sleep off the alcohol, buddy. You don't want a Heathen to kick you out of here for bothering me, do you?"

"I'm not bothering you, sweet thing."

I sighed and spun on my stool to glare at him. As I did, I lifted my loose dark shirt that covered the waist band of my jean shorts. My knife sat there, wedged in a case. When he looked, his eyes widened. I said quietly, "Leave before we have a problem. For the sake of the bar, huh?"

He stumbled back with his hands raised and then ran out.

Cole was laughing when I turned back around in my seat to face him and grab my Sprite.

"Do I want to know what just happened?" he said, his voice full of mirth.

"Nope. I need to go to the bathroom." I slid off the chair and headed to the employee hallway.

"I'm not sure that's a good idea. I think—"

I pushed through the swinging door, my heart pumping from Cole's words. If it wasn't a good idea, I might find something I shouldn't. Or someone.

The bathroom door next to Rome's office was cracked, but I heard rustling and the water running. I pushed it farther open.

The blood on his hands turned the water red as he washed them. The white porcelain sink blurred with the pink and red ribbons of someone else's life.

"Rome," I whispered.

He jumped, the muscles in his back rippling as he tensed. His dark head of hair was dripping wet, and as it shot up, droplets of water sprayed everywhere. Those black eyes solidified to a stone-cold stare when he looked at me through the mirror. "Why are you back here?"

"I had to pee. It's not like I don't come back—"

"Get out!" He delivered the command as swiftly as a sword slicing its enemy down.

I stood my ground. We still weren't friends. We were barely acquaintances at this point. He'd ignored me too many times for that and had acted as though I didn't exist for the past couple of weeks. And in those weeks, I'd almost slept with another man, one I knew could keep me content. Yet I still wanted only Rome.

"Katalina, you need to leave." His voice rumbled out low in warning.

I should have left like he asked me to. If he didn't care about me, didn't want me here, I shouldn't have cared either.

But I knew him. I knew his touch, the way his breath shook when he was with me, the way his mouth felt against mine. I knew the man under the monster.

More than anything, I knew the emptiness in his eyes. It was the same look that had marred my face over the years, time and time again.

I crossed my arms. "That's not just someone else's blood on your hands. Your face is bleeding."

He sighed and ducked his face down to splash some more water over it. "Get the fuck out of here, Katalina."

I leaned against the doorframe of the bathroom for support as my full name rolled from his pillowy lips. I missed hearing his voice, missed hearing him command me. "Does the other guy look just as bad?"

I got no answer from him. The silence ping-ponged around us, ricocheting off our tension and unanswered questions. Rome wanted me to leave.

Instead, I lightened my tone. "To be honest, I might act out and fuck up one of your customers tonight. They're out of control. I just had to threaten a guy. So I'm thinking I need a good fight story." I smiled at my own joke, trying to lighten the mood. "Please tell me you killed the other guy."

He whipped around to face me. His black eyes pulled me in and tried to swallow me in their hollowness. "I did."

Those two words—he said them so seriously, goose bumps popped up over my skin. "What?"

"Don't ask a question if you aren't prepared for the answer."

"Rome, seriously? You can't...Bastian didn't say anything about kills in the past few days. If you're not following the rules...Bastian doesn't want anyone acting outside of his control."

"You still staying with him, then?" The first real emotion from him was the pain as his voice cracked with the question. It hurt me just as much as him.

"What does Bastian really have to do with any of this? You know it's all for—" I stopped. If it were all for show, I wouldn't have kissed Bastian. But Rome hadn't called; he hadn't even asked about me. He'd left me to the mob without a backward glance, even knowing I'd had my head bashed in, even knowing people were out there looking for me.

"It has everything to do with it, Katalina. You know what the family is out there doing?"

"Rome." I glanced toward the ceiling, my heart wanting to break. "They don't tell me everything. So I don't get to ask those types of questions."

"You better start. And you better be prepared for the answer."

I combed a hand through my waves as I took in his words, the way his body vibrated with a rage that was barely contained. "Are you okay?"

He crowded me against the door, looked me up and down. "Bastian's world isn't the one you want—"

"And it's the one you do? You're in just as deep as me." I grabbed the gray shirt that had splatters of blood staining it. "How are you ever going to explain this? How are you going to come back from taking lives when Bastian isn't giving you permission? He's the head of the family now, Rome. Him! Not you."

He looked away, and the breath he took in was labored, like a wounded animal struggling for life. I felt him crumbling, felt the world taking him down, felt his pain.

My hand shot out, gripping his bicep where blood lay wet over his tattoos. "Hey," I whispered and squeezed. The blood rolled down over my fingers. Warm. Still full of life. It was that vibrant red, like roses on the sunniest day after a summer rain. "If you're hurting, if you're about to break, break me instead. I can handle it."

"Are you offering what I think you are?" His gaze ran up and down my body, searing it and branding it as his with just a look.

I swallowed and then licked my lips, knowing deep down that I was his at the end of the day, that Bastian—that no man—could tie himself to me like Rome could. He'd been there for me since the beginning, and so I would be there for him until the end. "Yes."

His hand shot out so fast to wrap around my neck that I jumped and fell back into the brick wall behind me. Little fragments of the aged cement crumbled onto my shoulders as I leaned farther away from him. My body was accustomed to pain and suffering. Still, this once, I was sure this was the most danger I'd ever been in.

He squeezed, and I felt my windpipe start to close. "Kate-Bait, I will break you. And I won't put you back together."

"I'm already broken," I murmured, but it sounded far away. "And I don't expect a handout from anyone."

"At least you've learned what it's like to be in the family." He grabbed my hand and slid it under his shirt. I felt the warm liquid before it registered that he was bleeding, that he was running my hand over his wound. "My blood is your blood. I bleed, you bleed."

I whispered the oath back. "I bleed, you bleed..." He squeezed harder so that I couldn't finish it.

Then he yanked my neck toward him so he could devour my mouth. He moved like he was ravenous, sucking on my lips and then making his way down to my neck as his hands roved over me to the jean shorts I wore. He unbuttoned them, his big hands taking control and not fumbling at all. He didn't wait for me to nod as he shoved them down over my ass to the ground. "You still clean?" he panted into my ear before he went further.

My heart pounded as anger sliced through me. "I should be able to say I've slept with someone else since you." I pounded his shoulder. "I don't want to wait for you to have me in the back of a bar. And yet, I'm fucking clean because all I think about is you. All I remember when another man touches me is you."

His dark eyes pulled me into their depths and held me hostage there. His voice rumbled out soft and low. "No man but me should ever be touching you. You're driving me insane just living with him, Katalina. It's driving me fucking insane."

He plunged his cock into me so hard, I got shoved into the wall. I moaned at the feeling of him filling me up, at feeling like I was connected to the one person I felt separated from for weeks now.

I'd been chasing the high, chasing the feeling of him with Bastian, but couldn't find it.

I squeezed his hips between my thighs and writhed as he kissed me. "Why does it take us weeks to get to this point?"

He shifted and pulled out before he answered, leaving me empty. I stared at his cock, glistening with my arousal and throbbing in front of me. His arm muscles flexed on either side of me and his jaw ticked when he answered, "I'm never supposed to get to this point. I'm supposed to protect you, that's it. I can't protect you when I'm fucking you, Katalina."

"I should decide who protects me and who gets to be between my legs, Rome."

His cock flexed, and my pussy clenched in reciprocation. "You want to choose this? Choose the man who can kill you in a heartbeat? I'm the family's monster, Katalina. I don't have a heart to give you except a fucked up one."

"It's the only one I want." We held each other's gaze, speaking a language I wasn't sure either of us really understood. Maybe there was love there. Maybe we were sharing that sentiment but we couldn't have known. The world had jumbled all our emotions and made us forget that love could be shared by anyone, even the darkest of souls.

I rolled my hips in front of him, drew his attention back to my core, right where he wanted to be. He stepped up and slid his length into me centimeter by centimeter. When I glanced up at him, he said, "Watch my dick slide into where it belongs. If nothing else, this works and works very"—he thrust so hard into me I arched—"fucking"—he pulled out and then pounded into me again—"well."

I saw his pupils dilate as I clawed at his back and screamed his name.

Maybe this was where our end began.

CHAPTER 16

ROME

I PULLED HER DOWN into the black hole. It swallowed us up and ate us whole.

Our light was gone.

She orgasmed in my bar's bathroom with one lone tear streaming down her face as I took her heart and soul.

I pumped my cock into her almost violently two more times before I buried my seed in her. Our breaths were labored, struggling for life after reaching something way beyond it. I hadn't come like that with another woman ever.

I backed away from her and took in her bruised lips, her wrinkled clothing, her mussed hair, and knew if I couldn't keep away from her, we were doomed. With her, I only had tunnel vision. I couldn't see past her blinding light to real threats to the family, couldn't keep a clear head, and definitely couldn't put the family first.

I'd marked her neck, and the beast in me wanted to do it again and again, to lay by her side and snarl at anyone who looked at her. It didn't care about anything else.

And that was the problem.

I was the monster. I had to keep it together. I had to let her go and get her out of this mess of a family instead of pulling her further in.

I told her to leave. I yelled at her to stop fucking with me, and then I punched the wall numerous times when she did just that.

A few days later, I got the call that Katalina wanted to go dress shopping for the and swore fluently at Bastian over the phone.

What the fuck were they thinking?

I drove there enraged that we were taking no precautions, that we were pandering to the whim of a pretty little girl who thought she needed to try on dresses while rival mobs who worked with the government wanted her dead.

I got there and kicked a chair over to sit in.

"Seems like you're in a great mood," Cade grumbled, not looking up from his phone.

"Shut the fuck up." I snatched his phone and threw it on the floor just to piss him off.

He glared at me. "Pick it up."

I laughed at his command. He knew I wouldn't do that shit if he held a gun to me.

Bastian walked over and picked it up for him. "Stop being children," he mumbled as he handed the phone to his brother.

I huffed and crossed my arms over my chest.

Then the damn woman who haunted my every thought came out of the dressing room, and all my muscles tensed. "That dress is unacceptable." The throbbing pain at the base of my skull intensified. She had the uncanny ability to give me migraines, to make me hurt in places I'd never hurt before.

I needed to keep my distance, and yet today, I couldn't risk her safety even to save my sanity.

"I'm sorry." Her frosty gray eyes narrowed. "What are you even doing here?"

Bastian chuckled from one of the black leather chairs near me as the saleswoman fluttered about. "He's here because he's family."

Katalina stood before me in a black couture gown with delicate beading strung in swirls over a mesh fabric. Everyone would wonder if they could catch a glimpse of her tits in that gown. I wondered too as she swished back and forth and her eyes jumped to Bastian, then Cade, then Mario.

"Mario, you're family," she said. "Cade's family too. Maybe soon to be my brother-in-law." She smirked at her dumbass joke. I didn't find that shit funny in the least. "But Rome's your cousin and the muscle. Dressing the girlfriend for a party where we introduce ourselves as a couple doesn't need muscle."

"When the girlfriend is just the bait, it does," I shot out, even though she wasn't looking at me. "You need eyes on your asses because this is tempting fate. It's being idiotic when you could have just been sent a dress."

She glared at me. This was probably all her idea. The woman was obsessed with finding some sort of perfect outfit for every occasion. I wasn't sure if she was trying to look deadly and completely fuckable all the time or— Then again, that was probably exactly what she was doing.

The messing with my head had to stop.

I growled and surveyed the store. The windows at the front of the building were wide open to onlookers, but we had two watchmen who would alert me via a ping to our watches if something was off.

Everything was fine. We just needed to get this over with.

"Not that dress, Katalina." I turned to the saleswoman. "Find her another one."

"Actually…" She bent her arm behind her and pulled the zipper down. I took a step in her direction just as she let the dress drop to her feet.

Fuck, that woman.

All-black lingerie and heels contrasted with her smooth skin.

Bastian jumped out of his chair and strode to her side, beat me to her. "Katie, not okay."

The smirk she donned pissed me off and made my dick twitch at the same time.

"You're playing with fire, Kate-Bait," I said over Bastian's back.

She had the audacity to flip me off and then put her hands to Bastian's lapels. "It's fine, Bast. It's not like you haven't all seen a woman before. In particular, you've both seen me."

Bastian whipped around to glare at me just as I cut my glare to him. "What the fuck is that supposed to mean, Bastian?" I spat at him.

Bastian's nostrils flared, and I knew he was pissed at Katie or himself. Maybe at the both of them for indulging.

None of it mattered.

Not one single thing carried any weight other than what she'd just revealed. For the first time, real jealousy throttled through me.

Katie was always this wild thing I couldn't tame, this sort of chemical I knew was too unstable to handle. And I knew that every man that had her wasn't really going to keep her. No one could stabilize that. No one could control the uncontrollable.

Staring at Sebastian Armanelli, I suddenly wondered if he'd be stupid enough to try.

The idea heated my blood, tightened the muscles in me that I used to kill, and my hand itched to grab a weapon. He may have been family, but Katie was, or had just become, *my* untouchable.

"Your crazy is showing." Bastian nodded toward my hand like he knew I was about to grab my gun.

And while we stood there measuring one another up, the host of all our problems practically skipped back into her dressing room.

"Fuck, man." Bastian sighed and closed his eyes as if trying to rid himself of the frustration she caused. "She's intoxicating. It was one time and it didn't go further than kissing. It probably shouldn't have—"

I lost it. My fist connected with his jaw so fast I swore in surprise.

Cade grumbled that he wasn't dealing with us, not that he ever did. He'd been on his phone since we got here. Still, he stalked off to the other end of the boutique.

Mario groaned and pulled at the collar of his shirt while Bastian rubbed his jaw. "Rome—" Mario started.

Bastian cut his gaze to his father. His jaw worked more than it had a moment before. "It's not your place to handle the situation here anymore."

"It's always my place."

"You're not the boss anymore. You gave that up, right?" His question was laced with acid because Bastian had never really wanted to be the heir to the throne. He took his place out of obligation, not desire.

Mario nodded solemnly. "Doesn't mean I ever gave up being your father, though, son. And that goes for both of you. You're brothers. Remember that." He stalked off, his loafers clicking on the white tile.

"You're here to protect and control our surroundings, not inflict harm on me." Bastian stuck his hands in his pockets, surrendering to any fight.

I shook my head at him. "I answered to your father."

"And now you answer to me."

I restrained my immediate refusal. I didn't belong to a family where Mario wasn't boss, and Bastian had just crossed a line

I knew Mario would never have crossed. "I work with you. I don't answer to you. Never have. Never will."

"The family doesn't work that way."

"The family doesn't work any way without Mario at the head of it. You're going to have to build it from the ground up."

Bastian nodded. "So I've told my father."

I curbed my retort and turned away from him to school my expression as I realized he agreed with me. "Then, as you build, you should know I take lives. No one ever takes mine, physically or metaphorically. I don't answer to you. You're only as strong as your right-hand man, and if I'm going to be that for you, well, you don't fuck with what's mine."

"Meaning Katie is yours?"

I sucked on my teeth. "I'm not sure yet."

"Be sure, Rome. She sleeps under the same roof as me. She's either untouchable or not."

"She's untouchable in one way or another."

"Now, that I can agree with. Just not sure if I'll be able to follow through on the damn request you aren't even making. Draw a line, Rome. And make it as clean as you slitting a throat. A request for an untouchable should always be that way."

He made sense. Bastian always made sense. He was the immaculate, controlled head of the new mob. New in that they wielded their power with reason, built allies instead of enemies, and ran a flawless business. It was a new reign, and for the first time I saw the appeal. A smart man cloaked his request with a compliment and befriended the man he knew could leave him open to be murdered.

I wanted to gut him for it. I wanted to hug the fucker too.

"She does all this shit on purpose, I swear," I grumbled and ran a hand through my hair. "If I didn't know better, I'd say she was pulling all our strings. What the hell are we doing here picking out a damn dress?"

Cade chose that moment to amble back over. He didn't glance away from the phone in his hand as he typed, but he did manage to add, "I sent her a list of designers she could choose from. She said she had to try everything on and refused to have it all delivered because it was a waste of money."

Mario and the saleslady had also returned, both laughing at something Mario had told the woman. His Italian accent, his gray hair and bright smile, and his strong posture always charmed women, even if they were half his age. "What are you talking about, Cade? Waste of money? Don't be ridiculous."

"Katie said it. Not me," Cade replied almost robotically.

"Said what?" The woman of the hour popped her head out from behind the dressing room's sleek black door. "I need help with my dress."

Bastian searched her face, like he was reading whether or not she wanted him to be the one to offer.

"Oh, yes! It has a very intricate back." The saleswoman jumped at the chance to play mother hen. I tried not to smirk.

Katie looked like a deer caught in the headlights. "Well, actually..." She cleared her throat and then wide-eyed all of us.

Bastian folded, bastard that he was. He cracked his neck and waved the lady off before he grumbled to me, "Draw the line, Rome, or you'll end up lying in a pool of your own regret."

I stared at that door like I stared at victims I was about to put a bullet through. I contemplated the repercussions of banging it down and telling them both to stop fucking around with my emotions.

But Bastian was right. I hadn't claimed her as an untouchable, and that was something that never changed within the family. We didn't have many ties to the outside world. Our men were supposed to be loners. Family was family, and that was it. Except for the women we loved. Except for the kids we had.

Untouchables.

It was a list that wasn't taken lightly. Mario had swiftly ended men's lives when they harmed or got into bed with another man's untouchable. It made for trust between us, and it made for a hard line too.

But Katie was something different, a part of all of us already.

As if to solidify my thoughts, our watchman texted and said the area was still clear, that he was stopping in. Two seconds later, the boutique's bell jingled to signal Dante walking in. My eyes had stayed on that door long enough to know we weren't in any danger, but the bell still put me on high alert.

"Where's our Cinderella? I haven't seen that girl in a minute." Dante's white smile popped as his bright greenish eyes searched the store. He regularly made trips in and out of town and had only been gone about a week this last time. I knew they worked out together, though.

I didn't ask a lot of questions, because I was sure the answers were a lot like the ones I gave when I was interrogated.

"Dressing room," Cade grumbled with a wave over his shoulder.

"Bastian?" Dante asked, eyes going wide.

"Dressing room," Cade answered in the same monotone voice. Dante's gaze cut to me.

"What the fuck are you looking at like that?" I shot at him.

"You." He smiled, and I considered punching him.

"What for?" I crossed my arms over my chest. I didn't know why I was asking. It seemed everyone was privy to the fact that Katie and I had issues.

He just shook his head. "She an untouchable yet?"

"Fuck off," I grumbled.

"Jesus." Cade sighed. "You need a drink, man. I need a drink just being near you."

"Would you stop talking to me about shit happening in the room when your head is buried in that phone?"

"I'm working." He finally dropped it to his side and smirked at me. "You need my full attention?"

148

"Stop smiling. You look like a lunatic."

"He is one." Dante laughed and lifted his chin at Mario, who now seemed to be shopping for someone other than Katie.

"Why are you here instead of scoping the area?" I asked.

"We got it handled. The crews need training, and we already know the area is secure."

Dante was a mixed bag. His father was a distant cousin of Mario's, making him family, but I didn't know much about him. He'd lived a pretty normal life with his mother other than secret meetings with our family. Then, he went into the army at eighteen, coming back the same but also completely different.

"Plus, I knew I didn't want to miss this." He walked forward in his combat boots and rapped his knuckles on the dressing room door. "Katie, Bastian. Let's see the damn thing before Rome's patience wears out."

"Dante?" Katie squealed like she could exude actual happiness and excitement about something. The door swung open, and she flew at him. "My hero's home from war!"

"Oh, for fuck's sake," I grumbled. The woman hugged, slept with, or made some connection with every man she encoun-tered. Why any of them wanted to be around her more than a minute was beyond me.

Except I was the one contemplating her status within the mob. I was the one on the edge of claiming her as mine.

As Dante set her down, he placed his hands on her bare shoulders and mumbled, "Let me have a look at this dress."

She smirked and shrugged. "It's mostly for show. Gotta draw them in, right?"

He nodded, but his eyes devoured her like every man's in the damn store at the moment.

Sure, Katie was a sort of family to them, but she was also what we knew her to be.

Bait. And damn good bait too.

I stared at her as Dante spun her around in the boutique and wondered if they were all a little in love with her. This black dress sparkled with her movements, the beading a dark, shimmery reflection that drew the eye. It hugged her like a second skin and was sheer in the waist and near her thighs. Black feathers along the sweetheart neckline hugged her tits, made them look good enough to eat, serving them up on a fucking platter.

Although the dress reached the floor, the combination of the open back crisscrossed by a black ribbon, the bare shoulders, and her ample cleavage made this dress worse than the one before.

Dante whistled, and Mario clapped as he walked over.

Bastian leaned on the doorframe of the dressing room and nodded slowly. "It'll bring any man to his knees."

Katie smiled at him. "Thanks, babe." She was in rare form. I felt it the moment I'd walked in and when she finally made eye contact with me, she didn't disappoint. "And can you imagine me in it on my knees?"

Bait.

I was pretty sure I wasn't okay with her being that any longer.

CHAPTER 17
KATIE

I THOUGHT SEEING ROME with Bastian would be easier. He stood there in that boutique unscathed by my being there with another man. I was certain he had no true feelings except hate toward me after screaming at me to leave the bar.

Not that I cared.

Except that I did. Except that I couldn't stop thinking of him sliding in and out of me, of how his eyes pulled me in, of how my body gravitated toward him and was repelled by anyone else now.

He was supposed to care a little too. We were supposed to be bound by our inability to bind to anyone else.

So I pushed every one of his red do-not-touch buttons.

"Get the fuck back in the dressing room and change," Rome said in a low voice.

151

"What crawled up your ass?" I put a hand on my hip and waited for an answer.

"You're purposely trying to rub me the wrong way today, Katie."

"Maybe I'm rubbing you just the right way." I winked at him.

One of his massive hands went to the back of his neck, and he pulled on it hard as he sighed up to the ceiling. Then he said, "Yep, I'm doing it," to no one in particular and dragged me into the dressing room by my elbow.

I fought him. He fucking deserved it. "Don't manhandle me, you big asshole."

Mario shook his head as he walked away to confer with the saleswoman again. I swear, the boutique must have been used to our type because none of them batted an eye. I tried to stomp one of my heels into Rome's shoe, but he sidestepped and threw me over his shoulder.

"No help?" I yelled over his back. "Bastian? After everything we've been through?"

He looked a bit wounded, but Rome said over his shoulder, "You come near us right now, I'll step aside the next time a bullet comes your way."

Bastian's jaw ticked; I saw it. But he didn't step forward.

Rome dropped me down in the dressing room, and I stumbled back into the wall. "A little overly dramatic?" I raised an eyebrow as I readjusted my sweetheart bodice.

"You're out of control, woman." His eyes were wild, wide with fury when normally all I saw was emptiness.

Good.

I was finally getting a reaction.

I crossed my arms over my chest, and his gaze flickered down for a moment. "Oh my God. It's a dress, Rome. Can we get past it?"

"It's a hook, line, and sinker dress. It's a here-I-am-on-a-platter dress for a fucking event where you could die because of it. Pick something less in-your-face."

"I like in-your-face."

"Too bad!" I yelled. "I like you. They like you. The whole city likes you. Too damn much! We can't keep you safe when you're tempting everyone's rage, everyone's pride."

"I can keep myself safe, Rome." I smiled with extra smarminess. "But thanks."

He crowded me into the corner of the fitting room, and his hand went to my favorite place—wrapped around my neck—so he could lift my chin and glare into my eyes. "You know every time you say that, I think of how easy it would be for me to snap your neck."

"It'd be the hardest thing you've ever done, Rome, because you wouldn't be able to live with it like you do all the others. You'd have to find a way to get over the fact that you actually care about me. You may act like you don't, you may act like I'm just a nuisance, but you wouldn't be in this fitting room if that were the case."

"I have a job to do, and that's protecting this family. You're a part of it. I take my job seriously, even if it means dealing with your shit."

"That's what you're going with? I'm your job?"

A line formed between his eyebrows, like I was confusing him, like he was working through what I said but wasn't catching up quickly enough. I knew the struggle. I knew his fight not to care for me. I was fighting to shove him aside and move on to Bastian too.

In that fitting room, under the fluorescent lights that amplified all our imperfections, I found my most glaring one.

His calloused hand on my neck sent shivers across my body; goose bumps rose along with my nipples as if they would only ever peak for him. My hands had a mind of their own as they inched the mesh of my skirt up and then gripped his shirt while I wrapped one leg around him.

His hand gripped me tighter, and my mouth dropped as I sucked in air and felt his length against me. His other hand gripped my upper thigh, and I bit my lip as it slid higher.

He swore over and over again, strings of whispered obscenities mixed with insults about how reckless I was as I let his hand creep farther and farther.

Abruptly, his hand raked hard up the rest of my thigh. He pulled his hips away just enough for him to move my panties aside and plunge two fingers into me.

I would have screamed out, but my voice was gone. He was cutting off my oxygen, watching me ride his fingers, watching me lose my control and consciousness. I held onto his shirt, felt my nipples tightening against the fabric, felt his eyes watching me, my tits, and my body riding him.

I should have stopped.

But I couldn't.

I was on some roller coaster of Rome, some fucked up feeling of wanting him and then hating him and wanting him to want me too.

I saw spots as he pressed his thumb into my clit and rubbed back and forth, hard and slow. "Please, Rome. Please, please, please." I begged him like I begged no man. I climbed to a higher mountain with him than I had with anyone else. I was willing to give in, willing to give anything to reach the peak with him.

He moved his fingers faster. "You beg me and only me, Katalina. This part of you belongs to me."

I wanted to tell him to fuck me, to unzip his jeans and let us get a quickie in, but he took my orgasm too fast by sliding a third finger in and curling them to hit my G-spot while rolling his thumb roughly on my clit.

Just as my core tightened, he released my neck and covered my mouth to muffle my moan while I convulsed around his fingers.

When he knew I'd be quiet, his hand gripped my jaw, making me look right in his eyes. All I could see was hunger and rage as he said, "Buy the other dress."

I didn't confirm or deny that I would do anything. He slowly removed his hand from under my dress, and I tried not to mourn the loss immediately.

"If I buy the other dress, what do I get out of it?"

"A happy monster for the night? That not good enough for you?" he said without looking up. He was turning me around, trying to find a way to help me out of the bodice. "Where the fuck is the zipper?"

"I'm tied in."

He groaned. "I hate this thing."

"Sure?" I said as I glanced down at the swell in his jeans. My mouth watered, and I just about licked my lips. I knew how he handled that dick, and I knew it was some of the best handling I'd ever had the privilege of witnessing.

"My mind and dick rarely agree on things."

I turned quickly to hide my smile and pointed to the tie at the bottom of my back. "Untie me?"

His hands held my waist for a moment. He stood a whole head taller than me as I looked at us both in the mirror. Rome was this mammoth of a man, full of muscle, tattoos, and darkness. I knew firsthand that he used every one of those muscles, that every one of those tattoos meant something, and that his darkness was all-consuming.

"This dress is hypnotic, Katalina. *You're* hypnotic." He rested his chin on my forehead, and my curls rubbed against his five-o'clock shadow. "What am I going to do with you, huh?"

I stared at him in the mirror, wondering if we could ever just be normal, just together. "Why do you have to do anything different than what you've always done with me before?"

"Because before I was sure I didn't care. Now I'm not so sure. Caring makes me vulnerable when I can't be. Not for the family."

I prided myself on not getting emotional. My dad had been there, then he wasn't. I went into the system swiftly and knew emotions were taken advantage of. I didn't cry. I didn't complain. I took it all—the beatings, the abuse, the neglect—in stride.

Why was it that now, all of a sudden, with just the slightest bit of truth and attention from him, I wanted to let the unshed tears go?

"Probably should get me out of this dress," I whispered.

He nodded and then stepped back to start loosening the ribbon.

As he did, my waist spilled out. I breathed in deep as his fingers dug between the ribbons and my skin to slacken the fabric's grip.

"Jesus, are they folding you in half when this is tightened?"

"Beauty is pain." I chuckled at his disbelief.

"Katie, there're marks from the waistline," he said like it was ridiculous.

I glared at him. "Rome, you get to throw on a jacket and look nice. We do this to look nice."

"This is like bondage. Seems pretty uncomfortable for a night of show."

"But bondage for foreplay and show is what it's all about." I waggled my eyebrows at him.

He had the ribbons in his hand, and for a moment he cinched them tighter. "Don't play, woman. We're getting this shit off you, and you're getting the other dress."

"You still didn't tell me what I get."

"What do you want?" He sighed, like he'd finally tired of me and was admitting defeat.

Maybe that's what I needed. For him to step aside so I didn't truly become a victim of heartbreak in all this. Rome was my most dangerous downfall. I didn't care about my life being at risk, because I knew that losing myself would be much less painful than losing someone I loved.

"Should I ask you to step aside?" I said. "Bastian and I could be comfortable, Rome. I've enjoyed being there with him. Should I ask you to stop whatever the hell we keep doing?"

"You could."

My heart sank. He would let me go so easily. I knew it was an indicator for me to turn away, to leave him behind and ask him to do the same for me.

"You could, Katalina, but it wouldn't matter." His solemn tone signaled that he was in as much turmoil over what we had as I was. "I don't step away from what's mine, and you're quickly becoming that. Even if I don't want you to be."

I looked up at him and ran a hand over his jaw. "Then I guess what I want is for you to claim me, because the harder you both pull the more I'll relish the pain of splitting in either direction."

"Ever the masochist, huh?"

"Takes one to know one."

CHAPTER 18

KATIE

"I'M SORRY, YOU said you're coming over?" My friend's announcement over the phone didn't make sense.

"Yeah, we're all coming over for movie night," Vick repeated so loudly that I held the phone away from my face and curled my lip at Bastian in question.

He was lounging on the couch as he watched TV and scrolled through his cell. When I mouthed that it was Vick and she wanted to do a movie night here, his cheeks hollowed out and he widened his eyes, sucking on a chunk of pineapple from the bowl of fruit on his stomach. He looked absolutely ridiculous, and I could tell from the smirk that followed his loud eating that he was mocking me.

"You're in on this, aren't you?" I popped my hip out and raised the phone back to my ear. "You talked to Bastian already about this, didn't you?"

"Well, my husband was working with your boy toy this morning," she started as if she was going down the list like the girl in *Legally Blonde.* "I might have mentioned last night that I haven't seen you in a very long time. They discussed business quickly, and business is good, Katie. You know that. All of our businesses within Chicago are operating very well." She emphasized each word. God, she was way too bubbly.

"I don't understand how we ever became friends," I groaned and flipped off Bastian when he started chuckling. I should have chucked my phone at him. He'd been weirdly available all afternoon, and now I knew why. He'd planned a damn movie night behind my back.

"Well, I can remind you. Brey and I became college besties. You and Brey had been high school friends despite all the baggage you both have. Lo and behold, you found you loved me."

I sighed. "Vick, tonight probably isn't the best—"

"We all need a night to relax. What better way to do that than with movies and friends? We're coming over. I need to see you. Brey needs to get away from her little rascal. And I think Rome will—"

"He can't come!" I shouted and then spun around to stalk toward my bedroom. My heart pounded as I tried to come up with excuses for why this was a bad idea. "It's not the best time. Bastian and I have business to—"

"Business is good."

"Look, I'll see you all at the gala in a few days."

"The gala will be all stuffy, and we'll only be able to drink champagne when we should be able to drink vodka." I heard her husband say something in the background, and she replied with, "Well, babe, of course I'm still going to drink whatever I want."

"Vick, let's just cancel. I'm not feeling that good."

"Oh, get real, Katie. You've never been sick a day in your life. If you're going to act like a badass all the time, suck it up and be one. We'll be there at eight." She hung up like she wasn't at all scared of my badass vibe.

I knew why. It was because I wasn't at all frightening. Instead, I was the one panicked.

I needed to stay away from Rome; I needed to keep this relationship with Bastian separate from my friends. I didn't want to be in front of them with my feelings all mixed up.

I stormed down the hallway and grabbed a pillow to throw at Bastian.

"What the hell, Katie!" he yelled as his fruit went flying.

"You planned a freaking party without consulting me." I threw my hands up. "What happened to I'm your guest and you want to make me feel comfortable?"

"I thought having your friends over would make you feel comfortable."

"Why the fuck would that make me feel comfortable? I'm basically staying here to bait a goddamn government deal and bait my ex into slipping us information about it. Now, I'm going to have to pretend it's something more."

He sat up. "It's not? We kissed a few nights ago."

I stuttered at his assessment. "I'm sorry. Do you want it to be something more?"

Something shifted in the room. The fun we normally had slid over to allow questioning to roll in.

"I'm not sure, Katie." He narrowed his eyes and looked me up and down. "I enjoy you, that's for sure. I know another man does too. He's supposed to be the man who will give his life for me, though. Rome is supposed to be my brother, woman. We need to find a balance."

"So you're throwing us all together."

"What better way to figure out how we all work than to get us in the same room?"

"It's absolutely ridiculous," I replied and stepped back as Bastian unfolded from the couch and walked toward me.

"I've never seen you look so uncomfortable. Everyone who is coming over here is everyone who cares about you," he pointed out.

I took a deep breath, knowing that was exactly why I was freaking out. My dad had cared about me. I was okay with one-on-one care. I did that fine. Having a best friend from high school stick around as long as she had proved my point. Brey and I had gone through a lot together. She didn't know my whole story, but she didn't need to either.

No one did.

And I didn't need any more than one person who cared about me in the same room. The idea had me itching. I checked to make sure I didn't have hives.

"I don't think that's a good idea," I mumbled.

"If it makes you feel better, I won't bite that sensitive spot on your neck when Rome is looking," Bastian taunted with a smile, but there was question there too.

Were we toeing a line we shouldn't be? Playing too close to the sun?

"I don't care what you do in front of Rome." I scoffed at the idea.

"You do." Bastian picked at imaginary fuzz on my shoulder. My body didn't heat at his touch the way it did with Rome. The low sound that escaped my throat as I shifted away from him was frustration.

Bastian tilted his head. "You told me you needed to figure things out, and I'm trying to do that too. I'm trying to figure out what you want, Katie. I'm not sure I can, because I don't think you know either."

I pinched the bridge of my nose and closed my eyes. "Why can't we just move on, Bastian? If something else happens between us, then so be it."

"I think it's because I could really fall for you. I could really rule an empire with you too. We'd make a fascinating and devastating team."

His words were like warm caramel poured onto vanilla ice cream. Enticing, delicious, and not good for me at all. My mouth watered at the idea of what we could be, of what I could

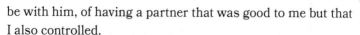
be with him, of having a partner that was good to me but that I also controlled.

We stared at each other's lips, and I wasn't sure who moved in first.

We kissed each other for a minute, taking in the feel. I moaned at the sensation. It felt good, great, so soft.

Safe.

But there weren't fireworks or explosions.

It wasn't me kissing Rome.

Wasn't love supposed to feel this way though? Safe. Wasn't a relationship supposed to be about give-and-take and feeling comfortable enough to do all those things?

At one point, I'd thought I'd loved Jimmy for that very reason. A young girl's mind gets murky around a man pushing her to be an adult.

Bastian's worshipping me was much more innocent. His fingers massaged my lower back as he tilted his head to pull away and whisper to me, "You're beautiful, Katie. So beautiful you could stop the world."

My heart clenched at his words. Beauty had gotten me this far. It'd made men trip over me, made them come to my door in the middle of the night while their wives slept. It'd also given me what I needed to survive.

The beauty was part of the broken side of me. Did he see the cracks? Did he see the shattered pieces, or was he just fixated on how my beauty could shine?

My mind wandered. Bastian's stare was bright on me, but Rome's had always been dark. That man only saw my jagged edges, the ones that were so broken he thought I was a lost cause inside. He saw the ugly under the beauty. Still, he wanted me.

Maybe that's why I wanted him too.

CHAPTER 19

KATIE

BASTIAN BACKED AWAY from me after he saw my face. He stared at me with this inquisitive look that seemed mixed with a little fear. I taunted him a bit, telling him to deliver the goods and the home run.

He shook his head no and told me to get ready for a night with my friends.

Our relationship was wobbling on a balance beam, and neither of us knew which side we wanted it to fall on. He'd started to become my friend, and I didn't have a lot of those—not men, at least. If we were going to continue down this road, the lines needed to be clearer, and I was sure he felt the same.

I let my curls fall loose in the shower and air dried them after. I pulled on a cut-off sweatshirt that hit just below my breasts and some matching pants. It wasn't a night for me to go all out. It was a night to chill, to try to relax with those that supposedly wanted to be around me.

Or it was a night I needed to feel comfortable in my clothes because everything else was going to be uncomfortable.

The first knock at the door had me jumping.

"There's wine cooling in the cellar, Katie. Go pour yourself a glass before you scare away your friends." Bastian waved me off before going to answer the door, and I walked through his kitchen to the oak barn door that led to a cooled cellar.

The air was crisp, the brick walls lined with expensive wines, and I was a fish out of water. Wine had never been my strong suit. Hard liquor, I knew. Not knowing what to pick, I grabbed a red one and shrugged. Then I threw two more under my arm because alcohol was going to be needed.

I reentered the kitchen to find my friend, Brey, standing there with her massive husband, Jax. His arm was draped around her as he glared at Bastian.

"All I said was that your wife looked nice tonight." Bastian leaned against the island counter and folded his arms across his chest.

"You know better than to look at her," Jax threw back at him.

Brey shimmied out from under his arm. "He never gets out," she said as she took a bottle from me and then hugged me before I could back away. "I never get out either, so just indulge me."

I rolled my eyes at her. "How's the little monster?" I asked. Brey had the baby a few months back, and after we all got to see and hold her, their family basically disappeared. They were overprotective and in love and completely content in their little bubble.

I didn't blame them. I didn't aim to pop it either. Brey and I were the type of friends who could go a year or ten years without seeing one another and still drop everything for the other if need be.

"Good. She's a little tyrant, that's for sure. She wants to go everywhere with me and never wants to leave my side. I tried to leave her to go to the center for a few hours, and Jax showed up thirty minutes later with her screaming and a look of terror on his face."

I laughed. "I guess that girl is just like her daddy. Neither of them can be away from you for too long. Anyway, I'm sure the kids were happy to have them there." Brey owned a center near a reservation that housed kids in need. We'd all visit once in a while, but Brey put her heart and soul into her work there.

Brey nodded as the doorbell rang again and Bastian let Vick, Jett, and Rome in.

"Look who my hubby and I found in the elevator!" Vick announced as she pointed to Rome.

He smiled at her antics because no one could hate the bubbly side of Vick if they tried. It exhausted and excited you all at the same time.

Rome's smile for once was genuine, like he actually enjoyed the company of the people around him. He and I had somehow formed friendships with the same damn people over the years, and it crippled me to see him looking so damn refreshed and carefree around the people I loved most.

Then his gaze fell on me, and his smile dropped off. We took one another in, and I licked my lips at his attire, the dark hoodie hiding the tattoos that I knew snaked around his muscles. The slim sweatpants that hugged his thighs in just the right way had my mouth watering too. When his jaw popped, I reminded myself that we needed to keep our distance, even if he'd kissed me in that fitting room.

We sat down for a movie that I couldn't watch at all. I couldn't name the characters if my life depended on it. I sat next to Bastian, and his arm draped around my shoulders while Brey and Vick sat near their husbands. Rome took the solo chair but burned holes in Bastian's arms with a fiery gaze most of the movie.

I couldn't stop wondering what he'd been thinking by coming tonight.

I gulped down my wine and reached to grab more when Rome murmured, "Get me some?"

His voice made me jump, and I knocked the open bottle onto the wood flooring. The swear word flew from my mouth before I could stop it. "Shit."

Brey beelined to the paper towels in the kitchen. "I got it, Katie."

"Thanks for saving my floors, Brey," Bastian said, completely unfazed by the mess. When Jax tensed, Bastian smirked. "She's one in a million."

"You better knock it the fuck off, Bastian," Jax growled.

He chuckled at Jax's jealousy. "You'd think he'd get over us dancing together in a club once, honestly."

Brey rolled her eyes as she cleaned the floor. "It's not like I slept with Bastian."

"Right." Vick laughed. "He barely gives Rome shit about the fact that he slept with Aubrey."

Rome coughed, and Jax growled at him. "Thanks a lot, Vick," Rome said, but he was smiling like he wanted to taunt Jax too. Then his eyes jumped to me. "I'm not ashamed, though. Brey and I had an agreement that worked. It worked very well."

It was like he'd stabbed my stomach with a dagger. Jealousy dug deep in the crevices of my body and festered. I hated the feeling, wanted to rid myself of it immediately.

"Oh, Jesus," Brey grumbled as Jax stood up, ready to leave.

I sighed and wiped my forehead, trying to shake my anger. "I'll go get another bottle," I said to no one in particular.

Rome nodded, but when I passed him on my way to the cellar, he got up and silently followed. If our friends questioned it, they didn't say a word.

When we got to the cellar and he closed the door behind him, I spun around and glared. "What are you doing following me in here?"

"I'm getting a moment alone with you because you're practically shaking out there."

"I'm fine." I waved off his assessment.

"You're nervous or uncomfortable. Or both? Is it me?"

I didn't know what it was. It was all of them and feeling like I had this unit even when I really didn't. It was him too, knowing I wanted him and knowing I shouldn't, feeling the jealousy of another woman when it'd been years since they'd hooked up. "I'm just on edge."

His hand went to my jaw, and instinctively I tilted my cheek into his palm. The anxiety subsided; the shakiness of the world steadied. "You're okay, huh?"

"I'm okay." I nodded.

"Good. Now"—he smiled before he threw out what he probably thought was a joke—"let's make both of us happy and not have you sit with Bastian's arm around you. It's only fair since my mouth was on you last."

Thinking of him with Brey, with any other woman, had me acting out. I wanted to witness his fury and inflict a jealousy in him stronger than mine.

"No, it wasn't." I dropped the words out one at a time as if dropping pebbles into a well and waiting for the splash.

"What did you say?" he whispered like he couldn't believe my admission. "We were just at the boutique. We just... You're telling me that since then, you let him have you?"

I looked down at my nails and contemplated whether I needed to paint them deep red. By the time we were done here, they probably already would be. Rome's stare grew darker and darker, like a predator who was out for blood. But I was a good fighter, and I'd claw him apart before he drew any of mine. "Bastian's a gentleman. We kissed. Nothing more, nothing less."

"'Nothing more,' she says. Fuck me." He spun away from me, and a guttural sound came from deep in his chest. When he twisted back, he was a man on a mission. He didn't say a word, just grabbed me by the hips and turned me to face a wine fridge with a mirrored door. I saw our reflection there, how his body stood so big behind mine.

I put my hands on the door and looked over my shoulder at him. "Want to kiss me again and see if this time you can make me yours?"

"I'm not here to fall for the bait anymore," he murmured as we both looked in the mirror. Suddenly, the hands that killed, that I knew were extremely deadly and had inflicted painful pleasure on me before, were light as a feather. His fingers danced over the sensitive parts of my collarbone, played with the chain of my necklace for a moment, and then swooped up to hold my chin high so that we were staring at one another, his chest against my back. "I'm only here for you now, woman. Not to be a pawn or play a game with Bastian."

"Wasn't that the game you played with me out there? You tossed your relationship with Brey right in my face."

"That was a few years ago, and we all know it wasn't a relationship."

"You fucked her just like you fucked me."

"I slept with her to fill a void. I have sex with you despite knowing you'll probably create a bigger one. Fuck, woman, I should never have looked twice at you."

"Why? Am I that toxic?" I whispered because I couldn't stop myself from asking.

"You're intoxicating, that's for sure. I'm supposed to protect the family, not lose myself in the mind-fuck that you are."

I didn't take lightly to the insult. "Fine. Don't, then. You shouldn't have come tonight, anyway. Bastian and Brey wanted friends here. We definitely aren't that."

"I'm their friend, though."

I crossed my arms. "Not mine."

He twirled me to face him. "Yes, yours. I'm your whatever the fuck you want me to be. I have been since the moment you walked in with Jimmy. Shit, probably since the moment I stood in your room staring at you wearing that necklace."

I clutched it to my chest. "I'm not asking you to be anything to me."

"And yet I'm yours and you're mine."

I bit my lip as he said the words. The room suddenly felt so small, and Rome felt bigger than life. He took up so much space with his massive muscles and broody-ass personality. I wanted to scream at him for claiming me and then rip his clothes off so he could show me just how much I belonged to him. I couldn't stop my breath from coming faster, couldn't stop myself from pulling him close and leaning my forehead against his.

"You're tangling Bastian in our web," he said. "You always think I'm trying to punish you for taking pleasure from him. You know you're mine and I'm yours. What the fuck are you thinking?"

"I don't want to be yours!" I yelled. "You can't put me before the family, and I can't sacrifice my place in the family for you. I don't belong on the outskirts. And if I'm with him—"

"You'll be what? What's it matter where you are?" He narrowed his eyes like he was trying to figure me out.

"A long time ago, I was a little girl with dreams, Rome. I can't remember a single dream now. When I lie awake at night, all I see is different men standing over me and showing me that my worth is between my legs."

Rome's face paled and he fisted his hand, but I held up mine to stop him from spewing something comforting I didn't care to hear.

"All those little girls are out there feeling how I feel. I still think about the one I met at Marvin's, how we stared at each other with not on flicker of emotion in either of our eyes. We'd been stripped of life and were dead inside and out. What if my dream gets to be stopping the men from standing over us?

Maybe I get to change something, and isn't it better to have a dream like that than nothing at all?"

"You should never have had to go through any of it." He sighed. "But that has nothing to do with Bastian and you."

"Sex trafficking is big business and at-risk youth are perfect targets. We've pulled our family's business away from it, but the Armanellis could do more."

He shook his head and shut his eyes in frustration. "You can't change the family. Even with Bastian. You'll be just another girl on his arm. Family is blood, Katalina."

"I deserve that family title just as much as any of you."

"Maybe." He sighed. "You're as close to them as any woman will ever get."

"And that should be good enough?"

"No, it should be motivation for you to leave this shit behind for somewhere you'd get equal respect."

I turned around and poked him in the shoulder. "And where would that be? Give me one good place where I got a shot at that."

His stare was desolate. We both knew the only place I could be comfortable now was with all of them. I found myself longing for him to make me feel at home for just a second, to make all the nightmares disappear.

He leaned away just as our lips were about to meet. "Not this time. You need to figure this out, Katie. We can't kiss in the dark and then you have motivations with him in the light."

"Oh, really? It's not like you're about to tell the family we're exclusive. So why not?"

"Because remember—the man who kissed you last isn't the man who can fuck you into oblivion, am I right?"

I licked my lips, thinking about our time in the bar. I didn't answer him one way or the other.

"We're two very different men," he said.

"You're kidding me, right?" I said in frustration. I wanted Rome's lips on mine. Didn't he want to taste me the way I wanted to taste him? Hadn't he missed my lips as much as I'd missed his?

"Did you know he told me to choose if I wanted you in that boutique, Katalina? Me. Not you." His hot breath moistened my mouth as he let go of the breath he was holding. He shut his eyes as if the pain of what he was about to say was too much. "Shouldn't Bastian know by now it's not my choice, but yours? Me or him, right?"

Then he gave me what I wanted. He took my mouth in his and seared his heart there. I wanted to melt into him, get lost in him forever as his tongue roamed my mouth like he owned it.

"Choose me, Katalina," he whispered. "Let me consume you. Pick our destruction, not his safe haven."

"Pick you, how? How, Rome? All you want is the family's safety. You won't change that. So what? We hide in the shadows forever?"

"Shadows are better than the light sometimes," he responded, but he was already backing away and nodding like he knew he couldn't have me. Like, all of a sudden, he didn't really want me.

"I don't want just little corners of darkness. I want it all. I want your darkness and your light if there's anything left. And if not, I want the monster in you because it's the only thing that saved me so long ago. If I can't have that, I'll take a dream with Bastian."

He winced before he spun and left me.

I stood there so long the light turned off in the cellar. The darkness swallowed me up as my heart thumped, pulsing rage through my veins at being left behind again by the only person I wanted.

CHAPTER 20

KATIE

"SO, YOU HAVE to go with Bastian alone?" Brey asked me again, like I was the worst friend in the world a couple days later on the night of the gala.

"It's best just this one time. We're running late, anyway."

"It's been more than just one time now, and Jax and I can wait. We have the babysitter all night."

I winced at the reminder that my high school best friend, the one I'd somehow managed to keep by my side all these years, had a child. She had a family. A good one. A solid one.

One I would not put in any type of danger.

"We're probably going to run really late, if you know what I mean." I paced around the counter in Bastian's penthouse with my beaded black dress all zipped up, heels clicking on the tile while Bastian chuckled softly as he read a newspaper.

"No, I don't know what you mean," she deadpanned, totally and completely knowing what I meant. She was pissed, but my friend had the manners of an etiquette coach. I knew pushing anyone's boundaries was hard for her. "Why don't you enlighten me, Katie? Because I have it on good authority that Bastian isn't really all you're saying he is. You forget I work for Stonewood Enterprises and that company runs the city along with Bastian."

"Can you hold, please?" When she started to say no, I cut her off. "You'll hold."

"Does she know, Bastian?" I fumed from across the room. The man had a dumb smile on his face, like he did every time he knew something I didn't. He'd come home numerous times with intel that he wanted me to drag out of him, like a kid hanging onto a secret with slippery fingers and a big mouth.

"Know what?" he said, his eyes crinkling with a silent laugh he was holding in.

The fucker.

I stalked over and snatched the newspaper from his hands. "Who reads newspapers anymore anyway?" I seethed, balling it up and throwing it on the floor. "Are you all talking about this dumb show we have to put on tonight without telling me about it?"

"Only her husband knows. Probably his brothers. Now that I think about it, most likely their wives. Yeah, I'm guessing Brey knows."

"What happened to no one talking about the family?"

"The Stonewoods are family by proxy. For business purposes. For all purposes, really, at this point."

"I have kept that part of my life separate for a very long time and for good reason." I enunciated each word and folded my arms across my chest. "Do you remember what happened to Vick a few years back?"

My friend had been sideswiped by a car. No one was found guilty. No one was found dead either. Which meant Jett Stonewood and Bastian had tracked them down and made them pay in more ways than one.

He stared at me, his eyes darkening with a malice I barely saw there. "Nothing like that will happen again."

"How can you be sure? You weren't sure then."

"I wasn't the boss for more than a minute when that happened. It won't happen again. Not to Brey, not to Vick, and never to you. You're all protected now. Untouchable."

"They are?" I squeaked out. "Do they know?"

"Of course they know."

I stalked away, leaving the piece about me being an untouchable for another day. I didn't want to be untouchable; I wanted to be a part of the family. Did he know that? Did he know I wasn't like the other women, the other children and friends of the mob? I was part of *them*.

"You're an untouchable, and you didn't tell me," I said softly into the phone. It wasn't a question.

"I was waiting for you to tell me about your life before I imposed on it. You've been a part of the family for a long time, you said. I didn't know how deep."

"Brey, that's not something I ever wanted to put on you."

"I put my life on you before. I put a lot on you. I expect the same from a best friend. Lean hard."

"Leaning could get you killed," I shot back, glaring at Bastian for good measure. He waved me off and mumbled he was going to get his shoes and suit jacket on.

I watched him walk away. I was in the apartment of the most dangerous man in the city, and I felt no fear except for my friend on the phone. Fear that her affiliation with us would cost her her life. "Jax and you are—"

"Very careful. And we're very much on the outskirts. You know his music app keeps us more isolated from the business than anything else. I've stopped working as much. We're protected, not really involved."

I sighed with relief. "And Vick?"

"Probably much more invested than me. Jett owns half the city, Katie. Mario and Bastian must have told you—"

"Not much. I'm…" For the first time I didn't want to say *bait*. I didn't want to tell the only person who'd been in my life as long as she had that I was a tool they used more than a family member they took care of. "I'm helpful to them in a lot of ways, but I'm a woman who's not married in. I'm just me."

"That's a pretty formidable thing to be, if you ask me." I heard a muffled, "And me," in the background.

"Hi, Jax."

"Always a pleasure, Katie," Jax said like he always did. The man never found pleasure in anyone taking his wife's time. I was a necessary nuisance to him. "So, we'll see you at the gala?"

"You'll see me. I'll find you both when I arrive."

And somehow Jax had navigated the situation between Brey and me perfectly.

Brey sighed. "I love you, Katie. Don't get so lost you can't find your way out. And if you do, find us."

"Of course," I replied quickly.

I never would, though.

Brey was blood much thicker than the family's. She was my home. And I'd barely ever had a home after my father died. Not one I felt safe in, not one I was loved in, not one I cared for at all.

When I was with Brey, though, I got a friendship that was immovable and love that was freely given. When you found a home that safe, you never ever tarnished it.

But for some reason, I couldn't admit within my safe place with her today that I was the mob's bait. It made me wonder for the first time in a long time if I'd let them all take advantage of me. I was a woman, but I was as formidable as Brey said.

I'd never backed down.

I'd never given them a reason to doubt me.

I'd delivered important information time and time again.

178

Was bait as good as blood, or was bait a couple of drops they were willing to waste?

I paced the kitchen, round and round that counter, until I'd talked myself into believing I was more. Then I strode back to my room down the long hallway and yelled to Bastian, "I have to check my dress. Be out soon."

I slammed my door and eyed the walk-in closet. The dress I had on was sleek and black. It was the first one I'd tried on, the one Rome conceded to having me wear. But I'd called the saleswoman and had the other delivered.

I still didn't know why. It was a hell of a dress. Like the devil himself conjured it up for me to do bad things in. The feathers felt like heavenly clouds brushing against the swell of my chest, but the cinched waist, the boning digging in, and the tied ribbon squeezing my lungs reminded me that most days could be heaven and hell mixed together. The feathers were woven into the lace and tapered off just at my hips where beads and mesh swirled over my ass and pooled down my legs. The material would swoosh with each step I took, and I knew every man would love it.

I'd straightened my hair and dyed it onyx black, and painted my eyes dark and smoky. With my hair in a high ponytail and red lipstick on, I knew I was asking for every man's eyes.

Tonight, I wanted them.

I wanted an audience, and I wanted to be the juiciest bait yet. I just wasn't sure if I would allow anyone else to save me tonight.

I was starting to think I needed to save myself. Save myself from everyone.

Even the family.

"You ready?"

I jumped, and my hand immediately went to where I'd just slid my knife under my armpit. The metal fitted there perfectly because the knife was small, crafted to wound but not necessarily kill. I'd have to twist and truly gut someone if I wanted to. I never used it, but my hand flew to it much more often than necessary.

"Carrying into the gala, Katie?"

"A little extra back-up is always nice."

"For what? I'll be by your side all night. We get Georgie alone and he'll admit everything to us. He won't be able to stand us together, and he'll confront us. He just needs to admit something about Russian ties. Cade and I discussed it with lawyers. We could potentially get him on arson or RICO laws if we get audio too. Supposedly a burned-down factory was a part of all this. That's it. If you feel unsafe at all tonight, though, you press the button on your bracelet."

I glanced down at the nifty device that appeared to be a diamond bracelet. It had a tiny black button on the clasp that signaled distress.

Distress? As if I hadn't been alone with Georgie hundreds of times on my own, as if now I was important enough to hold on to. But why?

"Is this necessary?" I lifted my wrist. "I've never needed this before."

"Before we didn't realize you were dealing with men capable of murdering you, Katie. We were fucking stupid."

I narrowed my eyes. "Anyone is capable of murder. Georgie's fine."

"If we get more intel on Georgie, our lawyers will take care of the rest."

"This isn't how your father would do things, Bastian," I said as I turned toward the mirror. "What's the plan? Have me on your arm and get him so worked up he comes over and confesses all his dirty deeds? It won't work." I moved a few feathers around and dragged my ponytail to my front to comb a couple of the curls into submission.

"It'll work," Bastian responded, but his shoulders were bunched, and I saw the question in his eyes.

These men didn't understand how other men worked. It took a woman, someone like me, who'd lain with them in their most vulnerable moments, to know what made them tick. Georgie was proud and slimy all at the same time. He wanted love for his manliness and did just about anything to obtain it.

"He'll never approach you, Bastian," I murmured, but I decided to concede for the time being. "Don't worry. This will work. I promise, you won't need backup. We got you." He huffed, and I knew he meant well, but I was on edge, in a place I'd never really been before.

I'd avoided telling my best friend that I was bait and Rome's words echoed in my head. The thought of being alone, of the family not really being mine, of not belonging had infiltrated my soul. It was uncomfortable and real, and it exposed me to the one thing I didn't want to remember—that I didn't really belong anywhere.

But I did deserve to be somewhere. I'd earned that right.

If they wouldn't give it to me, I'd take it.

CHAPTER 21
ROME

S HE WORE THE dress.

It was like the devil himself wanted a damn show and had wrapped her up, helped her get ready, and served her to all of us that night. He was laughing in hell right now. I could almost hear his cackle.

She strutted in on Bastian's arm. Regal, fuckable, mesmerizing. That dress was a waterfall over her legs, but every curve of them was visible. The beads shimmered under the crystal chandelier light, and her dark stiletto heels elongated her stride down the carpet.

I tensed as she looked up at Bastian and smiled adoringly. It may have been a show, it may not have been.

Either way, it didn't matter.

The back of her bound up by that black-as-ink ribbon and the way her ass flared out from her waist, I heard some of the men visibly moan.

Fucking breathtakingly beautiful.

Feathers and beads and black strings had been wrapped around the most dangerous woman here. The mob and the government were watching. Everyone wanted her for different reasons, but we'd all take her for one.

Georgie's suit strained over his gut as he leaned back farther to keep his eye on her while she strode down the steps of the ballroom with Bastian. Her nails dug into his arm, the only sign they were together. Other than that, Katie stood tall in her red-bottomed six-inch stilettos and stared off into the crowd as if she wasn't too concerned with any one individual. Her eyes didn't scan the area; she didn't turn her head to clock anyone's whereabouts.

She was above everyone, and no one could bother her for a glance.

Instead, every man's eyes scoured her and her body. The devil wanted a show, and I knew for a fact he was going to get one.

"Enthralling, nyet?" He let his Russian accent twist the English I knew he spoke perfectly.

"You here as a part of the bratva tonight?"

He lifted his eyebrows as if to say, So what if I am? "You think she's worth the fuss?"

That man had always been a rogue Russian, dabbling where he shouldn't. The string quartet started to play a low, lonesome melody, and one man glared at another as Katie walked by. I saw one shake his head at the other, and they lost their expressions just as quickly. Katie and Bastian walked right past me to meet Mario at a table.

I lurked in the shadows, watching others watch.

We'd had eyes on Georgie for the last hour. He'd mingled with every big name there. He'd disguised himself much better than we expected, and for some reason that bothered me most. I'd let Katie walk into a lion's den without being aware.

I was supposed to be aware of everything.

"You're going to shatter the tumbler you're holding." Jax nodded at me while we stared toward the doorway of the club.

The crystal in my hand was strong enough to withstand a tough grip. We were in the most elite club of Chicago. Still, I set it down much harder than necessary.

Brey glanced at the glass and then at me. "She's not committed to anyone right now, you know that, right?"

"I'm not interested in her commitments," I shot back and then pinched the bridge of my nose when I saw Jax pull Brey closer to his side. "Sorry, it's been a long day."

"It's going to be a long year if you plan to stick with the story of not being interested." Jax lifted an eyebrow at me.

He and I never really got along. I'd met him just as I'd stopped sleeping with his wife. We never saw eye-to-eye, and yet we saw everything the same. We had an understanding that the women in our lives were much more important than any disagreement we could have had. Brey had needed us back then, and now, it seemed Katie might need something from us.

"Give me a break. I'm protecting her and everyone else in this family tonight."

Brey smirked, and her green eyes seemed to mock me. "Protecting her? Katie's never needed protection from anyone. She needs someone to show her life is more than a series of events, that she doesn't have to keep moving forward every time something bad happens to her. She needs someone to take her in while she learns to feel again."

"Maybe Bastian will give that to her," I muttered.

She scoffed. "It's not my place, but I'll say it once anyway." She glanced at her husband. "Cover your ears."

"Oh Jesus." Jax kissed her cheek and walked away as if he knew what she was about to say had something to do with our past relations.

"I've lain next to you after sleeping with you, Rome. I stared into your eyes and tried to find something other than what I was feeling. We were both destroyed back then. You had your demons and I had mine."

185

We'd mixed our pain with pleasure, drowned out our misery with sex. It worked because we had each other for company, but it didn't erase the pain I felt at losing my unborn child, at missing something back then that I should have caught. Brey was a filler, just as I was for her.

"Okay?" I responded, waiting for her to continue.

"Katie pushed us together. I'm realizing that now. I'm not sure why, but she trusted you to be nothing but a comfort to me. And you were. But you never, ever looked at me like you did her."

A *ha* escaped from deep in my chest. "And how do I look at her, Brey?"

"Like she's your heaven and your hell. A dream and a nightmare all wrapped up in one tiny little warrior."

"Ain't that right?"

"I hope you both work it out." She patted my back and gave me a solemn look. "You've been circling one another for years."

She turned and left me for her husband, and I wondered if she and I ever would have worked. We shared our misery but not much more. It was an understanding within the bedroom at best, and she'd found someone who understood her beyond that. Quite frankly, she'd always had him. They just had to dig through the shit before making it to the sunshine.

I sighed and wondered if Katie and I would be able to do the same.

Except our shit was deadly, and her enemies stood there eyeing her and whispering. If Georgie made a move toward Katie, we'd be ready.

Tonight was about pulling him into a room with both her and Bastian. Katie was the arm candy that would pull Georgie in, and we would get him to crack.

When I refocused my attention on our targets for the night, they were nowhere to be found. I loosened my collar and strode to Bastian and Mario. "Where's Kate-Bait?"

"Bathroom." Mario waved me off. He'd already had too much to drink.

"Bastian? You let her go to the bathroom on her own?"

"She's capable, Rome," Bastian answered. "We've got eyes everywhere."

"Georgie's—" A ping went off on my watch, and both Bastian and I shot each other a look before I read the message. "Dante has a visual of them on the balcony."

"Fuck. She told me she was going to the bathroom." Bastian fisted his hand and then shoved it in his pocket. "Don't make a scene."

"I should kill you now," I growled as we both tried to move fast enough to get there in time without drawing anyone's attention. "With the way you're running things, we're in for a fucking bloodbath."

"If you weren't like a brother to me—"

I looked over my shoulder. "I'm more than a brother to you. I'm the man who makes sure you don't take a bullet to the head. Lose the power trip."

Bastian didn't say more. He was already looking past me to the two blond, blue-eyed men who'd stepped in front of us as we got to the double doors.

One ran his hand over his buzz cut and said, "Sorry. Boss is having a private meeting."

Bastian exchanged a look with me. We could spar, and I could cross a line with him every now and then. Russians didn't get the same privilege. "Move or I'll have you killed," he said.

Buzz cut bulked up and rested a hand under his suit jacket exactly where I knew he was carrying. I shifted my eyes between the two of them.

Bastian spoke softly behind me, "I don't want a war. I've told Dimitri that, but if you don't move now, you'll have one."

He said it so smoothly, I almost thought I'd misheard him. Bastian had been skirting around his power for so long, I was sure our family would crumble. He led with negotiation, rather than confrontation. Tonight, he'd finally grown some balls.

The smile that spread across my face must have looked menacing. I was ready to do damage. I wanted a fight. Everyone was pushing too many boundaries lately, and Bastian never had near enough jobs for me.

The monster in me stirred.

The man in front of me took the smallest step back. And Bastian repeated one last time, "Move."

Both men nodded and stepped aside, knowing their place. Armanelli blood was still king, and they were mere pawns not looking to rock the boat. We pushed past them, and Bastian let out a breath.

I glanced at him and saw him scan the balcony, eyebrows furrowed, lips pursed. Fear surfaced in the way he flexed his neck. I realized that Bastian was finally scared of losing something. Katie was more than just a game piece to him.

I wondered what he'd do if he lost her to me tonight instead of the bratva, if I claimed her tonight as an untouchable, as mine.

CHAPTER 22

KATIE

MEN, BY NATURE, had to be stupid. I was sure of it. Bastian had given me numerous lectures about not leaving his side, as if I were a sheep, only accustomed to being herded.

I played the role well enough and nodded at his requests. Then I promptly faked having to pee.

He didn't even question me.

Women should have been leading the world, not men.

It took one coy look Georgie's way and a lift of an eyebrow for him to excuse himself. He knew better than to draw a crowd. He wanted time alone; he wanted an explanation.

He wanted me.

I strode out onto the balcony. The wind chilled me, and the night air washed over me like a calm before a storm. The stars from this far out of the city shone brighter, louder, and more vividly.

The cool cement railing was just thick enough to allow me to lean on it and really peer up into the night, get lost in the darkness of it all. This was the place I felt most at home, surrounded by nothing but myself in a fine outfit, bathed in ink-black shadows.

"I could push you over the edge for the shit you've been pulling."

"Georgie." I spun around.

His face had already reddened with the anger he wanted to release. He was bursting at the seams to unload on me. He stepped right up to me, making me distinctly aware of his size advantage over me, and stared me down. "I should kill you, shouldn't I?"

I shrugged. "You could. It wouldn't do you much good, though. Things are bad enough already. You're sleeping with the enemy, Georgie. Dipping your toes where they shouldn't go."

"No!" he spat. "You're doing that! How could you jump from me to him? Bastian? An Armanelli?"

"So what?" I asked innocently. "He's a nice man."

"He's not. He's one of the most dangerous men in the city."

I jerked back, feigning shock. "Don't lie to me, Georgie."

"God damn. I told them you didn't know!" He threw his hands up. "I told them all."

"Told who?" This was the reason I was out here. I was the woman he trusted.

"God, you're beautiful, Katie. But you're naïve. That man you're with tonight, honey, he's got big ties everywhere. He's dangerous." His hand went to my cheek and rubbed it slowly.

I didn't cringe or shudder, even though my stomach clenched. The old feeling of my gut twisting when I was with a man I didn't want seemed amplified. After being with Rome, after having hands I wanted on me instead of ones I needed on me for the family had bile rising in my throat. "No one's that dangerous, Georgie."

His hand slid to my neck. The snarl that came from him was feral. "That what you think after the stunt you pulled in that bar? You're a tiny thing, and just because you got one over on me doesn't make you invincible."

He'd started to squeeze my neck, his sweaty hands trying with all their might to scare me. I knew I could hold my breath for at least thirty seconds. Choking someone out was much more work than people thought. Remaining calm was a tactic that would afford me energy, extra oxygen, and enough time to let him keep talking. I'd turned my recorder on. He'd been dumb enough to start this conversation without searching me.

His emotions, his love, his recklessness were getting the best of him.

It made me wonder how anyone who was in love could ever be useful. Is that why Rome had avoided our relationship? Had avoided every relationship?

I widened my eyes in mock fear and scratched at Georgie's hand half-heartedly.

"The bratva will rule this city. It's only a matter of time. I burned down that factory to send a message, Katie." He got bold, his other hand skirted up my thigh. "The Armanellis are floundering to figure it all out. We'll have the city by the time they do."

I shook my head. My vision was starting to blur, but I let him continue his perusal while I slid my hand into his pocket and grabbed his phone. Cade would be able to glean information from it.

I kneed him hard in the balls before I passed out, before he got close enough to take real advantage of me, and his grip loosened immediately.

"Georgie." I wheezed in a breath and rubbed my neck as I stared at him bent over in pain. "I should kill you. I could stab you in the back right now and enjoy seeing your shirt turn red."

He barreled toward me like a blubbering walrus, still doubled over, but not in any doubt about his own strength. The man seriously thought he could tackle me at that slow pace.

"George!" Bastian's voice cut through the night air and had us both freezing. My date for the night walked out onto the balcony where the moonlight shined over his dark hair and dark suit. His pace was slow, calm, measured.

Behind him, his right-hand man.

Rome always drew everyone's eyes. Or maybe just mine. But they immediately went to him like water pulled by gravity down a steep hill. I wondered if he knew that even lurking in the shadows, he was the center of most women's attention. He moved almost silently, as if he never wanted to be noticed.

Still, I couldn't look away.

Out on that balcony, there could have been hundreds of people and I would only have been drawn to him. He was the moon among the stars, brilliant in the dark and brighter than every other human around him. His suit was tailored to fit perfectly over his massive arms and chest. He'd opted for all black, as if to match the tattoos that peeked out when he turned or stretched just right.

Together, the new mob boss and his lone wolf advanced on us with malice in their eyes.

Georgie was already scrambling away, shaking with eyes wide. He'd turned from a walrus to a mouse, scared of the predators that had just invaded his space. "I didn't do anything," he announced. "She asked me to come out here. I'm done with her. I've been done."

Bastian walked to the edge of the balcony to look out at the gardens below. Then he checked his watch, completely unfazed by Georgie's explanation. "I don't want to turn this city into one that bleeds out day and night. The ruler of an empire should breathe life into it, right, Rome?"

Rome stared at me, eyes glistening as black as the sky. "I think a ruler does what has to be done so their empire can thrive. If blood must be shed, let it be the blood that tainted the empire in the first place."

"Spoken like a man that kills for a living." Bastian chuckled. "Still, George, I think the place we call home shouldn't be one where we all live in fear." He spun on his heel and bent down to Georgie's level to meet his eyes. "Should it?"

"No. Of course not. I'm here on business like everybody else. I don't know anything."

"Is that right?" Bastian glanced at Rome, who cracked his knuckles and then let the rusted chain fall from his sleeve. "I don't think my cousin is in the mood to get his suit dirty. You know what I mean, huh? Why don't you just—"

"Bastian!" Another man appeared from the entrance. Tall, blue-eyed, blond, and extremely well dressed. He moved so fluidly across the balcony to Georgie's side, the only way to describe him was as a snake slithering toward its nest. "Did Georgie introduce himself properly?"

Georgie's gaze ping-ponged around and settled on the tall man next to him. "Dimitri, I didn't know if that was official."

"It is. Georgie is a Vor for my family now."

I shook my head, floored that Georgie had gotten that far in any mob. It meant they respected him now, that they would miss him if he was gone.

Dimitri continued, "And I see you've poached one of our women. Katie, is it?" He stepped forward and held a hand out for me to shake.

He stared at me with eyes of such a pale blue, they were almost white. His skin was light as porcelain under the night sky. As he smiled down at me like he knew me, every part of me screamed to run the other way. Even so, I took his hand in mine and felt dread wash over me. It was like he saw a part of me that was all bad, and I knew at once how dangerous he could be.

I tried to pull back my hand, but he held fast, narrowing his eyes. "Nice to finally meet you."

I yanked my hand away and wiped it on my dress. "I can't say the feeling is mutual."

"But it was inevitable. I'm hoping you and Georgie resolved whatever matter was between you?"

"Other than him trying to cop a last feel? There's nothing between us now." I glared at him, and Georgie spat into the night air. "You got what you came here for, huh, Georgie? Why don't you two be on your way?"

The snake turned his head back and forth, taking in the scene. The cackle he let loose echoed through the silence of the night. "Don't you know who I am?"

A ball of anxiety grew in the pit of my stomach.

"The only people I need to know in this city are the ones who run it." I walked to Bastian and Rome's side. I stood tall between my men, where I belonged. "The Armanellis don't care who you are."

"Oh, they do," said the snake. "And you should too, Katalina. Your blood, their blood? You bleed, they bleed? They family?"

It was like he'd seen through all my layers, straight to our weakness. I glanced at Rome and he nodded slow as he searched my eyes. My heart squeezed because I wasn't sure if he was saying I belonged with the family or just him. I just knew he wanted me to understand I meant something in that moment.

He meant something to me too.

Maybe all it takes is a look, just a feeling exchanged between two people to know that their story isn't finished, that there's hope.

I whipped my gaze back to Dimitri, ready to tear down whoever threatened our future. I took a step toward him, but Rome grabbed my arm. "Yes, my family bleeds for me and I for them."

Dimitri's mouth stretched slowly across his face to reveal his teeth. They were white, straight, and the fangs pointed a bit farther than most. "Remember those words. When I see you next, I'm going to enjoy reminding you."

He motioned to Georgie, and they disappeared back into the party.

I waited for Rome or Bastian to give me the lowdown, to tell me what I already knew. When neither of them spoke, I glanced at them. "Russian bratva *Pakhan*? He the boss now?"

"Technically, his father still runs the bratva, but it will be passed down to him soon enough. He's the heir, the one everyone listens to out of fear," Bastian said.

"So?" I waited. "Why are we tiptoeing?"

Bastian sighed. "As you know, we think they're working with the government. We didn't get—"

"I got the information we needed." I held up my phone and let the two minutes of recording go. It had caught some of my muffled gasps. I saw Bastian's jaw tick and Rome's back stiffen, but I waved at them both. "I'm fine."

Bastian nodded, and as the recording ended, one side of his mouth kicked up. "You didn't listen to me about staying by my side at all, but you got what we came for."

"I'm fully capable of always getting what I came for," I murmured, handing the phone over. Then I pulled the other phone from beneath my dress. "Got his phone too."

He shook his head, pocketed it, and pulled me close to murmur into my neck, "You're brilliant, woman."

I let Bastian's mouth brush over the soft skin in the crevice of my neck as I glanced at Rome. My body yearned for him while my mind reminded me that we weren't on the same page.

Bastian pulled back and turned his head toward Rome and then me. "If either of you have something to say to one another, you should do it now before we go back inside."

Rome still held his chain in his hand. He fisted it. "You can't keep letting people run astray under your rule, Bastian. Katie didn't listen tonight."

"But the night was still a success."

"One night it won't be," Rome shot back. "Then what?"

"Give me a break," I let out under my breath. He was pushing us both because he wanted something to be pissed about, not because the original plan didn't pan out.

"Give you a break?" The menacing rumble in his voice sent shivers up my arms. "What about a break for me? I told you not to wear that dress. We told you to stay next to Bastian's side. You never, ever listen. Now, not only was George looking at you, Dimitri was too. The future bratva boss. You need his attention too?"

I stepped away from Bastian and Rome. I stepped into the moonlight, let the wind brush over my bare shoulders and flutter the feathers at my sweetheart neckline. "I did whatever I had to do. We needed that intel."

"And we were going to get it without throwing you in the line of fire!" Rome bellowed.

"I'm as involved as you, Rome. I'm not just the arm candy. This was easy because I helped make it that way. This is for the family. Isn't that what we do, everything for the family?"

He glared at me, eyes licking with fury. "I do that. Not you! My life is for their protection, not yours."

And maybe that's why, at the very end of the day, I did it. I wanted him to understand that if that's what he lived for, that's what I would live for too. "Without me and you, without the relationship between us, that's what I live for too. I don't have any other ties. I get that or I get my dream. At least with that, I'll have something to be proud of, huh?"

"Your dream?" he whispered and then he shut his eyes tight because he knew that dream was me with Bastian, trying to change the bad in the world, trying to be at the top of the family to pull strings for little girls all over, for better lives for everyone everywhere.

Rome stalked past Bastian, setting his chain down on a table, and then he was right next to me. His body shoved mine, and I stumbled backwards into the cement railing. "You don't need a dream; you don't need to be proud. You should be already… don't you see you've changed us all already?"

"Meaning what?"

"Meaning I'm sure he's as fucked in the head for you as I am. Meaning we'd die on a damn stake for you if we had to because you've jumbled up all our shit and stuffed it into a bag you control."

My jaw dropped. "I'm not some voodoo—"

"No, you're Cleopatra," he hissed as his hand skittered over my neck. "Where's your necklace?"

It was the smallest thing to notice, just a single raindrop of attention on his part. Yet it drowned me like no one else's thunderstorm ever could. I cleared away the ball of emotion forming in my throat. "I left it on my nightstand at Bastian's."

He scanned my face, his head close enough for me to breathe in his breath, taste the air that went through him and then straight into me. He sighed and squeezed my shoulder before the deep timbre of his voice rumbled out. "Okay, Kate-Bait. Okay. Games are over. We choose dreams or destruction tonight."

His hand dropped from my skin, and he pivoted to face Bastian who met his stare head-on.

Two of the most powerful men in the city stood on that balcony with me, looking like gods ready to attack each other. Bastian would have thrown lightning, and Rome would have met him with thunder. I wasn't sure who would have been the victor. A sick part of me wanted them to figure it out, a part that was broken and used, a part that was accustomed to being a pawn instead of the one they really wanted.

"You claiming her as an untouchable now?" Bastian asked, as if completely unfazed, as if he hadn't kissed me more than once in these past few weeks. He appeared resigned to the fact that this was bound to happen.

"You think I can claim Katalina?" Rome's voice seemed to shake the whole balcony, and I felt his question so deep in my bones, I wondered why I'd ever thought a man could claim me.

Bastian's stare cut to me, and his brow furrowed. He sucked in air like it was suddenly hard for him to breathe. "I'm sure she can't be claimed. I'm just not sure who she wants to claim for herself."

They both turned to me, two men in dark suits, gold rings on their fingers glinting in the moonlight, identifying them as part of the most powerful group in all the city.

My knees weakened, and I grabbed the railing to try to regain my composure. "You want me to choose?" I murmured as my gaze jumped between them. "I can't choose."

"And really there's no need. You live with me, you sleep under the same roof as me, you came here with me. You *chose* me," Bastian emphasized. "I told Rome to draw a line, and he didn't. Now, we have one. You and me, right?"

My mouth opened. I wanted to say yes. It was the smart thing to do. I had a place finally. I finally fit in a box, had finally climbed to the top where I would be respected.

No words fell from my lips, though.

Rome chuckled. He scratched at the scruff on his jaw and let whatever joke he'd thought of roll through him. His laugh turned maniacal as he glared at Bastian and then me. He rubbed his hand over his head and tilted his chin toward the sky. The tattoos on his neck stretched as his laugh died, and he breathed in a massive sigh. When he angled his face back toward me, my stomach tightened, the hair on the back of my neck stood up, and the instinct to run rushed through my veins.

Rome's eyes were cold, dead, empty as he said, "Let's see if it's you and Bastian, huh?"

I shook my head no as Bastian whispered, "Rome, come on."

He prowled toward me like a panther, slow and menacing. I swear he swayed like he was drunk on the knowledge that he would own me before the night was over. "Come on, Katalina.

Does he make you feel the way I do? You want his touch over mine? His tongue down your throat more than mine? You like the way he tastes that much more?"

My nipples tightened as I stole a glance at Bastian. He was watching me, studying the way I panted at Rome's words.

I couldn't control my quick breaths. My bodice suddenly felt too damn tight; the way the dress flowed out and into the wind between my thighs brushed all the right places.

Rome leaned back on the cement railing next to me, his shoulder butted right up against mine. He leaned in and whispered, "Do you want to show, Katalina, or do you want to tell?"

I licked my lips. Rome was giving me the option, letting me take the lead like he never did. My pussy clenched. With every man I'd chosen to be with, I'd been in charge. It was how I reached a high because I hadn't had control with the others, the ones who forced themselves on me.

Except with Rome. Rome took what he wanted from me; he dominated our sexual escapades and made the rules. And I loved that only with him, that he didn't need to treat me nicely or feel the need to give me control, like he knew my broken pieces and could navigate their jagged edges better than anyone.

Yet tonight he was asking me. Like I was his ruler, like I wore the crown, no matter how broken it may have been.

Bastian didn't say a word. His gaze jumped between us, and a small smile played at his lips, one of knowledge, of forfeiture.

I turned to Rome. "You ready to show the family that you're better for me? That we can be together, that you get me to my high better than Bastian ever would? Show me. Show him. Show us all."

He grabbed my neck and yanked me to his mouth so fast I yelped. The sound was muffled by him devouring me, feasting on me like I was his last meal. He sucked on my tongue, ravaged my lips, and then licked over them to soothe the pain.

I moaned as his free hand grabbed my ass to shove me straight into his hard cock. He was rock solid, longer, thicker than anyone I'd ever been with. I clung to his back, trying to get as close to him as possible, but he ripped his lips away as quickly as he'd dived in and shoved me around so that I was facing Bastian. His muscular tattooed forearm wrapped around my waist and pulled me back against his chest. I felt his dick at my ass, felt how he gyrated against me just to cause me to gasp, cause my mouth to water, cause me to arch back into him.

"Now, what first, Kate-Bait?" Rome purred. "Raise your skirt or lower your bodice? Should we show Bastian how you beg for it?"

Bastian's eyes burned into mine with question. What a perfect specimen he was, all smooth tanned skin over that strong jawline with a full head of hair to grab. His gaze trailed the length of me, and my skin seared under it. A blush wanted to rise, as hot as I was underneath my skin. My core clenched with need. Something was happening with these two men putting me in the middle of them, one dominating me and the other watching, waiting for instructions.

"Don't tell me that, after all this time, you've lost your voice, Katalina," Rome whispered for only me to hear.

I didn't turn to him to acknowledge his words, but my hands fell to my thighs where I gripped the skirt of the dress. Inch by inch, I bunched the fabric into my hands, raising it higher and higher until it was just below my pussy. "If someone comes out here"—I glanced behind Bastian—"you two are killing them."

I was offering Bastian a way out, a lifeline if he wanted to leave, because I knew he was about to see me in a whole other light. Instead of seeing the games Rome and I were playing, he could go check the doors, make sure no one would come out onto the balcony.

He crossed his arms over his chest, narrowing his eyes at me like he'd read my signal loud and clear. "We have two guys guarding entry." He stepped forward and breathed in so deep, the lapels of his jacket expanded. "If I'm to lose you, Katie, I want to see what for. If you choose out here on this balcony tonight, I intend to witness it." He licked his lips like he already knew I'd chosen, or maybe he knew he'd forfeit me that easily.

I set my jaw and leaned back into Rome, finally provoked enough to taunt them both. I yanked the material higher, and Bastian hissed when he realized I hadn't worn any lingerie.

The cool night air flew across my slit. It chilled and heated every part of me. One of my hands went straight to it, ready to push myself over the edge.

"Don't you dare touch yourself," Rome grumbled in my ear. "If you're going to be in the middle of both of us, take what we give you."

Were his eyes closed when his finger slid inside me and his thumb ran over my clit, or were they on Bastian? I couldn't be sure.

My men, my night and my day, my dark and my light, my comfort and my torment, were colliding. I only had myself to blame, or maybe I could blame Rome for the way he pushed my limits, made me submit to this scenario in the first place.

"You feel me, but you see him," he said. "What turns you on more? My touch or him in front of you?"

I didn't answer him. I closed my eyes to shield myself from the ever-changing looks on Bastian's face.

"Is this what you want? Him on your arm in public giving you power, or me in the dark taking it away?"

I whimpered, not sure how to answer, not sure I really wanted to. Bastian had become my path to a dream. I wasn't sure I was ready to let him go, but Rome owned me. He knew the dark parts of me that I hid from everyone else, what I'd been through, why I was the way I was. And still he was pulled to me like I was pulled to him. He owned my thoughts, my body, and my orgasms.

He owned my heart even though I'd tried so hard to keep it from him. I bent to his will time and time again. "Please just finish me off," I whispered, hoping that Bastian wouldn't hear my plea.

"Already begging." I felt the scruff on my neck disappear. Rome was looking straight at Bastian, and Bastian's gaze moved past me. "Do you want me in you? Or him?"

I craned my head over my shoulder to glare at him. "You'd hand me over that quickly? That all I am to you?"

"Kate-Bait, you've climbed over me time and time again for another man," he murmured, and his hollow, dark eyes shined with a black jealousy I wasn't used to.

I wanted him to say it out loud, wanted him to claim me as his. "If you'll step aside so easily"—I turned to Bastian even as I felt Rome's fingers moving in me slowly, languidly, almost punishingly—"Bastian has been happy to step in and be there for me all this time when I barely got a glance from you. You'd fuck me in a bathroom and leave me in silence the next day."

"You think it was easy?" he ground out. "I've tried to be without you, forget you, leave you behind. You've rooted yourself in my every thought though."

Bastian combed a hand through his hair, shaking his head once like he couldn't believe he was this far down the rabbit hole with us. "I'm sure this is a bad idea, Katie. I'm sure we belong together after this display."

I nodded, but even as I did, Rome's one hand still sat on my collarbone while his dick ground against the bunched fabric over my ass. I moaned, rolling my hips back like I wanted it. My body had a mind of its own, a magnetic sexual force that was only drawn to Rome's pull.

Bastian's eyes locked on my hips, on my dress still bunched there, and I started to let go of the fabric just as his hand shot out. It balled into a big fist, and the tulle of my dress tangled in his fingers, covering the mafia ring I stared at from time to time. Each of the men at the top of the mob had them, like class rings, but with skulls imprinted on them and a teardrop on the side that symbolized the family's blood.

Bastian yanked me forward, but my body didn't budge an inch. Rome still had a hold on me and wasn't letting me go. Bastian's eyes jumped to over my shoulder, and then his head shook in disappointment before he twisted my dress fabric so hard, I gasped at the fabric biting into my skin and at seeing the veins in his forearm pop. "Let him watch, Katie. It's my turn."

His dark stare met mine as he breathed in deep. "You're going to be my untouchable or his. Tonight, you're the boss. You get to choose." He pressed his mouth to mine.

Choosing whose untouchable I wanted to be was a slap in the face. Didn't they understand I'd worked for my place beside each and every one of them? I didn't want to be protected; I wanted to be *equal*. And I wanted a love big enough that the person beside me would fight for that equality with me.

I tried to focus on the way his hand gripped my hips, on how it moved up closer to sliding into me. His touch was soft, measured, and sweet. I didn't know why it didn't move me like Rome's did. He gently sucked on my tongue, and I just knew.

We all knew on that balcony that night. I'd only beg for one man, and it wasn't the one with his lips on mine.

Rome, the freaking monster everyone was afraid of, was behind me. I arched, and my back pushed into his length as he thrust forward, reminding me that no one really had my attention except him. His heart pumped fast, like some emotion was getting the best of him, and his scruff on my neck scraped harshly as he turned his face back and forth into my sensitive skin.

Then his lips were at my ear and he whispered, "Come on, Katalina. Who do you want?" His chuckle was evil, and then he bit down hard on my earlobe. His hands went everywhere at once. I felt him roughly shoving down my bodice to free my breasts. The wind cooled them as he heated them by pinching my nipples and then roughly rubbing over them with his calloused hands.

Our relationship was just the same, pain and pleasure always. He hit me where it hurt, asking me the questions I didn't want to answer, and yet it was the most alive I'd felt for days. Rome had dug a dagger somewhere deep inside my heart, and I couldn't dislodge it, no matter how hard I tried.

Bastian pulled back, his mouth glistening, but his eyes dull with defeat.

"What do you want, Katalina?" With the question, Rome's hand went to his suit pants' zipper, and I knew he was releasing exactly what I wanted. When he yanked the back edge of my dress up so that his cock rested between my ass cheeks, I practically screamed in frustration at not having him in me already. He pumped against my skin once and let out a string of swears.

"We have to stop," I whispered. "This is too much."

My eyes tracked Bastian's expression as Rome's thumb rolled over my clit, as my body welcomed the man that was supposed to be there. His middle finger slid right up into me where it belonged, and I couldn't hold back the moan, couldn't hold back how my nipples and body reacted.

Bastian's hand reached out, but Rome's low rumble at my neck told us both he was done sharing. His hand went to my throat and squeezed. "Get off this balcony, Bastian, and let Kate-Bait fuck her man." His command was swift and filled with more authority than I'd ever heard.

His words echoed through the night. Maybe I was the only one who heard them over and over in my head, the way he hadn't claimed me, but had submitted himself instead to my ownership. He might have owned my body, but he knew I owned his soul, that we owned one another.

Bastian's dark eyes hardened, and he nodded at us. "She's your untouchable, then."

The word caused my muscles to tense as I stood before Bastian, skirt up and bodice down, wrapped up in his right-hand man, on the brink of a climax to rock my world.

Rome's voice reverberated against my back as he answered the city's ruler. "She's something to us all. It isn't that."

Bastian's eyes searched us both for a second longer before he spun on his heels and stalked off.

Rome didn't give me any warning before he spun me to face the balustrade. He shoved me forward so my breasts spilled over for all to see and my ass and pussy were easily accessible.

He lifted the skirt of the dress higher, and his hands went to my hips, then my ass, as he rubbed the globes hard with his calloused hands. "I was getting nervous you would keep kissing him while I fucked you to prove a point."

I rolled my eyes into the wind. Of course he was mad at how far I let the charade go. "You could have stopped it, Rome," I shot back. I placed my hands on the stone of the railing without looking back at him and arched my spine a tad more just to piss him off.

His deep hum and the return of his dick to right back between my ass cheeks signaled I'd gotten the response I wanted. His fingers worked themselves into me again, and I moaned, wanting more, but so far gone I was willing to take whatever he gave me.

Then his thumb slid to my other hole, and I gasped as it puckered with the pressure he put on it.

"I don't stop you from anything, Katalina. I'm just here to keep pushing you farther and farther down whatever damn path you decide to take."

I bit down on my lower lip because my whole body was shaking, anticipating and adjusting to the idea that something foreign might slide into that virgin place. I'd never let anyone there, and yet having him rub a slick digit over it had me panting like I wanted him to.

"One day I'll take this from you too. This body is mine," he growled, and then both his hands were on the cement banister, anchoring him so he could pound into me so ferociously that my whole body pummeled the stone. I lurched forward, my tits bouncing in the night air as he hammered into me again and again.

I took each thrust in complete and total submission because I knew this was Rome unleashed, unhinged, and completely vicious in his mission to reach a high with me. He slammed into me so hard my hips scraped and bruised against the stone. It didn't matter, though, because my whole body had been waiting just for him.

Rome and the monster that stirred in him belonged inside me. I was his home, his vessel, the place he'd always come back to.

Or so I hoped.

And when he did, he would be the only man I'd submit to, the only one I'd let fuck me over the balustrade of a balcony.

"I should have left you with him," he grunted with each thrust.

"Just finish me off," I begged into the wind, not sure he could hear me.

An evil sound much more menacing than a chuckle came from him before he pulled himself fully out of me. He gripped my ponytail right at the base of my neck and jerked my head around to face him. "You don't tell me when, Katalina. You may own every part of me now, but I own these moments. Always."

The truth of his words stabbed at my heart. If we owned one another like this, how would we ever disentangle ourselves?

He thrust hard into me again to prove his point. I screamed into the night as my monster took me and brought me to climax before I fell apart in his arms.

CHAPTER 23

ROME

THE WARM CANDLELIGHT flickered on the face of every man watching Katie too closely as we walked back in. I wanted to leash her and drag her from the gala. Yet no wild animal like her was meant to be tamed. I only got that privilege when I was making her moan my name.

She glanced at my watch. "It's probably time for you and me to go our separate ways."

"As long as they intersect at some point later on," I mumbled as I nodded and started to back away from her.

Her dark cat-eye makeup had smudged around her misty gray eyes, and her hair wasn't bone straight anymore. The wave that broke through her ponytail was a sign of the heat that had passed between us before. That look of dishevelment only worked in her favor. As the music swayed the guests, her presence mesmerized them. For the next hour, I watched her bounce around while hungry eyes tracked her movements.

I should have been satisfied. We'd settled on the fact that her place wasn't with Bastian. He'd agreed to let her go, agreed that I owned some part of her that he never would.

Still, my body vibrated with anxiety.

Something was off.

The lighting flickered too much, and one violinist always seemed to play just a tad off from the other musicians. Even my drink tasted a degree too strong.

I twisted the watch on my wrist as someone carried on idle conversation with me. I didn't miss things. It was my job to feel the irregularities and shifts in the night in order to protect.

I filed through each moment of the evening and went back to the men glaring at Katie as she walked by. It had started with them. Their stares jumped from her back to each other like a plan had already been set in motion, like they were baiting us when we thought we were baiting them.

I straightened my suit jacket and nodded to the man talking to me. He waved me off, aware that I wasn't listening to a damn thing he said anyway.

My constant awareness of the surroundings and people allowed me to track down the culprits easily. I rounded a corner where only staff for the event were supposed to be. Yet two men stood there, whispering angrily.

One grabbed the other by the collar and threw him up against the wall. "If we're going to do this, it's going to be my way."

"If we bring her in, she's taking his place. It's the only reason he's seeking her out now."

"Or he's bringing her in to do that himself. I'm not stepping on his toes, you dumbass."

"We just say she did it herself. One bullet to the head is a reasonable story."

"That's his granddaughter. I'm not fucking with his granddaughter," the other one spat.

I stumbled back. His words echoed in my head as I tried to regain my footing.

They were wrong.

Katie was the daughter of a black man...

But we'd never looked into her mother.

I strode back to the gala, back to where I could make sense of things, and scanned the crowd for Katalina.

How could we not have known?

Mario held his gut as he laughed at something Katie was saying. His eyes sparkled, and his smile stretched wider than it ever did with me or his boys.

Mario Armanelli was hiding something, and I was going to figure out exactly what it was.

CHAPTER 24

KATIE

HE VANISHED LIKE a phantom in the night. We'd walked back in together, and he'd disappeared, claiming business was a priority.

Rome had gone in for the kill, ripped my heart from my chest to claim it as his, and then vanished just like he did after every one of his other kills.

He could call the family for a cleanup of those he left for dead. But not for me.

I stood there, heartbroken and waiting. I scanned the party for him, but he never showed.

Bastian must have taken pity on me because he came to stand beside me at the oak bar. "Stop looking, Katie. He'll show when you least expect it, huh?"

"You're the last person who should be coming to lick my wounds." I glanced at him before I looked back down at my drink.

"And why not? Because you chose him? You chose him long before tonight." He took a moment to sit down on one of the velvet-upholstered barstools. "I'd hoped you wouldn't, but then again, I knew you would. I only had to test which thirst was greater—love or power."

"Power?"

"I run this city. I know what it means for you to be on my arm. And you do too. You're one of the only women that truly does." He ran the back of his hand down my arm, and his touch still felt as warm and safe as ever. "It's why I would have let you stay there. It's why I would have trusted you to be there. Only if you wanted it, though." His hand fell away. "And you don't. You want love or hate. I'm still not sure which feeds the two of you."

I sighed. "Maybe we feed off our love and hate for each other. Or we feed off the void in us."

Or maybe it was the darkness. We'd come to terms with the fact that we lived in the night, and now, after all this time, I found I was most comfortable there with him, where we knew the demons lurked because we were demons ourselves.

"I'm not proud that I want power," I confessed. I wasn't proud that my motive for becoming a solidified member of the family was to control the city and never be under someone's thumb again, to find a way to rid the city of sex trafficking. But I knew I didn't want another Marvin standing at the bottom of my bed at night or another Jimmy who would hold a gun to my head to control me. They needed to shake with fear. They deserved to.

Not me.

And that thirst for power, that thirst to make others shrink away from me, wasn't something you let shine in the bright of the day. At night, our desires consumed us, and I knew it was where I belonged.

"It takes someone being powerless over and over again to make them crave power like I do, Bastian."

He nodded. "You know better than I do. The blood that runs through me awarded me my position. I'm navigating this with education, not experience."

212

"You'll learn," I told him because I saw fear in his eyes for the first time. Bastian was calculating and educated beyond his years. He had a wise look to him, like he knew the world or the world knew him and they somehow worked together in harmony. But Bastian was still a boy in the world of killers and criminals. His father had educated him but hadn't dragged him to the dirty parts of the job. If anything, I'd seen more than he had because of the men I'd been with. "And I'll help. If I can."

"You've helped enough by being bait for us this long. Take some time, huh? Figure it out with Rome." He nudged his shoulder into mine, and we looked down at our drinks.

I nodded and took a breath, not sure if I would take his advice. I knew I needed to do something about it all. "I'm going to find Brey."

"Dante will go with you," he said, and I realized Bastian's trust in me had shifted. He'd learned from my last little bathroom stint, and his quiet tone was firm.

Our mob boss would step into his role well.

I sighed. "That's annoying as fuck, Bastian."

"Not as annoying as you pulling what you do on me, Katie," he singsonged back.

Dante was by my side while Bastian gave him strict instructions not to let me out of his sight.

"Come on, big boy." I patted his massive arm, and he grunted. "I'm coming by the gym later this week to let off some steam."

"Good idea," his deep voice rumbled back. "You've got a hell of a lot of tension in those muscles of yours." After years of training with me, he could probably tell by the way I walked that I needed an outlet.

"I'm just frustrated with some stuff. I'm working through it."

"Coming to the gym will help."

I nodded as we walked the dimly lit hall that led to a back staircase. I was sure Jax and Brey had gone to the upper bar at

213

the back where there were less eyes on them. They both hated attention, and mingling wasn't their strong suit.

I glanced back at Dante lumbering slowly behind me. "You like the view from behind or just not in a hurry today?"

The smile that spread across his face made him look like a giant teddy bear. "I'm keeping an eye on the perimeter, woman. Give me a break."

I twirled back around but slowed my walk. "Sure, sure. Just taking your time on the—"

The grunt and thud happened so fast, I barely witnessed what occurred.

I spun quickly on my heel and caught just a glimpse of the ski-masked man who'd taken down Dante in an instant. He had a cloth over Dante's mouth as the big guy's eyes rolled back in his head.

I gasped when I should have screamed. I froze when I should have run.

He moved with precision, like a trained professional. I'd always thought I'd prepared myself for something like this. I'd fought Dante in self-defense classes and slept next to dangerous men. I'd put myself in pretty bad situations where I knew I'd get slapped around. But I always outmaneuvered those men. I knew their emotions, that their feelings for me would hold them back from taking my life.

But this man, whoever he was, dressed in all black...I couldn't even catch a glimpse of any markings before he'd pinned me to his muscular body with his arm around my waist and covered my mouth with the cloth.

I clawed instinctively at his hand, dug my nails in as I wildly searched the hall. No one was turning the corner. No one saw him drag me into the shadows.

"Be calm, Katalina," he whispered.

Just as I remembered the knife in my dress, I blacked out.

CHAPTER 25

KATIE

I CAME TO, AND the first thing that hit me was a migraine from the chloroform hangover.

I didn't move. Waking up as a captive and waking up next to an angry, violent lover were very much the same.

I relaxed my body and kept my breathing slow. I listened for any sound—voices, TVs, footsteps, traffic outside; any clue that could tell me where I was.

I lay across a cushioned surface that felt much like a leather couch, and some cloth was draped over my body. I felt the tulle of my dress still wrapped around me, but the knife that should have dug into my ribs was gone.

My kidnapper had wrapped me in a blanket and laid me on a couch? Left me dressed? It seemed they'd be playing nice once they knew I was awake.

With just the sound of cars in the distance, I knew we must still be in the city, but whoever was with me, they weren't giving much away. No one talked or walked around, and I couldn't smell anything except…a hint of metal mixed with aftershave, like he'd washed away the blood of his kills but couldn't completely shake the scent.

Rome.

My eyes shot open.

There he sat, leaning forward on a brown leather chair. The ski mask dangled from his large hands, and his head hung low as he looked at the ground. His brown hair fell over his forehead, damp like it'd just been scrubbed clean.

"What"—I cleared my throat at the pain of talking as his eyes sliced up to meet mine—"In. The. Actual. Fuck, Rome?" I winced as I pushed up on my elbow to sit and noticed that my wrists were zip-tied together. "Are you kidding me?" I lifted them in front of me and wide-eyed him.

"Take a minute to relax, woman. I'm going to explain."

"Relax?" I screamed and then gripped my throat. The burn was excruciating.

He jumped up and grabbed a glass of water from a slatted end table next to the couch. "Drink this. It's just the drug you inhaled."

"*Just the drug I inhaled*? Do you hear yourself?" The shock was wearing off, and the rage was setting in. I snatched the water with my two bound hands and chugged it down. I was going to need all the strength the water could give me in order to kill the man standing in front of me.

"I needed to get you out of there quietly and quickly, okay? If it hadn't been me, it would have been the Russians. I figured out their plan in just enough time to do what I had to do to get you out."

"You made me breathe chloroform!" I choked at the burn. "My throat is in hell right now, and I could have died. Did you know—"

"That chloroform isn't very stable within the body at high doses? Yes, I'm aware, Katie," he said with absolutely no remorse.

"So you were willing to risk my life. And Dante's?" My voice went up a notch at the thought of Dante smiling at me for one second and then—

"Dante needs to learn to take in the surroundings and not your ass."

"Oh, get real, Rome. We aren't even dating. Don't act like a man can't eye me up." I wondered if I could stomp a heel into one of his boots.

"We're past dating. You chose me up on that balcony, woman. And you sank your claws in so far, I'm convinced you can feel my bones."

"We aren't past anything. Not after you freaking kidnapped me!" I pointed my finger at him. "You could have killed us."

He scoffed and sat down next to me on the couch. I fell over into him, unable to keep my balance with my hands tied. Some of the water sloshed out of the cup.

I stared at it and then glanced up at him before I poured the cold liquid right on his junk.

"What the fuck, woman!" He jumped up, sputtering and wiping at his crotch.

I dropped the cup on the floor but kept my stare on him. "I don't take kindly to being dragged around unconscious, nor to being drugged."

Something danced within his eyes. He backed up and sat down in the leather chair, spreading his arms over the back of it, and smirked at me. The ski mask still swung from his hand, mocking me. "You know I'm the best at what I do, right? I wasn't going to hit you with chloroform knowing the dosage could be off and kill you. We have ties to pharmaceutical companies around the world. The drugs I use now are much more refined. You breathed in a chemical that purely knocked you out but wasn't at all harmful to your body. I wish I could say the same for what you do to me." He mumbled the last bit to himself as he looked toward the ceiling.

"I'm not harmful to you," I shot out. It was a defensive mechanism now because my mind was running through what he'd said. He'd utilized expensive drugs he probably shouldn't have to get me here. For what?

"You're the most toxic chemical known to man, Katalina. You're a beautiful woman who is smart and happens to know it. You know you're powerful, but I wonder if you really know how powerful. It makes you dangerous, unstable, and extremely volatile, especially since the whole damn city seems to be looking for you."

"I don't get the charade. I don't get any of this. I don't even have that much on Georgie. You're being dramatic and over the damn top." I wiggled my wrists. "Argh! Get me out of these."

"Things are happening, and I'm not exactly sure who's involved. So this gives me a little time to work it out."

"What do you mean 'who's involved'? You couldn't tell Bastian and Mario? They aren't involved with their sworn enemies, Rome. This"—I held up my hands and waved at my face—"is fucking ridiculous."

"It's not. I need a day or two to get everything straight. And I need you to sit patiently while I do that."

"When have I ever given you the idea that I'm patient, you idiot!" I yelled, wiggling around on the couch in fury. "I'm the last person to sit around and do nothing. What info do you have? Let's call Bastian and work through this."

"He could be involved. I'm not disclosing anything to him."

"He's going to figure out you took me."

"And by that time, I'll know if I can trust him."

"How do we figure that out?"

"*We* don't need to figure out anything."

"Argh!" I screeched and pounded both of my fists into my legs. "You're all idiots, you realize that, right? It was ridiculously easy to slip past you all tonight to get Georgie alone. I'm good at finding clues, I'm good at getting people to trust me, I'm good at figuring out the missing equations. You need me. You all do. And without me, you'll fail. You'll miss something. And I'll squeal. I'll find a way to run to Bastian. You know I will."

"Katalina, why can't you just cooperate?"

"Because I wasn't born to do that, and you and I both know it."

"This time, I need you to let me be the boss, Cleo."

"Not going to happen, Rome."

"So be it." He sighed and got up to set his ski mask on a black storage cabinet near the door. Above it was a weathered slab of wood with metal hooks. Each hook held a set of keys. "Which room do you want?"

"Which?" I hesitated and then blurted out, "I'm not staying here."

He hummed. "You'll stay with a man you barely want touching you, but refuse to stay with me."

"I was fine with Bastian's touch," I shot back, ready to argue with him about anything at this point.

"My room will be fine for you. I don't have all the bells and whistles of Bastian's, but I have a bed. You need to sleep." He took one keychain and spun it around his finger as he smiled at me. "Maybe to work out some of the anger too."

"I don't need to work out anything. I can control my anger. I need you to untie me"—I twisted my wrists, and the zip ties dug in, not budging at all—"so I can strangle you."

"Katalina." He tsked and walked toward me. "I just saved your life. Keep a low profile for me, huh? Just for a few days, maybe a week."

One thing I'd learned in all my years of being on my own was that I was forgettable and useless if I wasn't kept in the loop. If you were useless, you were dispensable, and that was never a good thing to be in the family. Rome needed to share what he knew.

Fuck him and his waiting. I made a beeline for the kitchen. It was just ten steps away.

One step, and Rome's eyes widened.

Two steps, and I figured I'd grab the closest knife in the block.

On the third step, Rome lunged and his hands shot out. He still wore all black and moved like a damn ninja.

I reached forward on the fourth step, sure I could outstretch and outmaneuver him.

He swung one big arm around my waist and hauled me up. "Why do you always want to fight me?"

I thrashed around like a maniac in a ball gown.

And wasn't I? I was fighting for freedom from my lover. If that didn't sound twisted enough, he'd bound my arms and was dragging me back to his room like I was his captive.

"You're not keeping me here," I said firmly when I lost the energy to wail into the air.

He hoisted me up onto his shoulder like a caveman taking his food back home. "It's happening, Katie, with your consent or without it. It'll be more comfortable with it, though."

We finally made it to the end of the hall, and Rome pushed open his bedroom door. For some reason, I expected there to be chains, weapons, knives, and all-black everything. I'd never ventured into the place he slept in all the years we'd known each other.

The shaded grays and black-and-white decor humanized him and made me wonder if he wanted the normality that some his age had. Did he decorate this space to escape the life of the family?

"Put me down," I mumbled as I looked around over his shoulder. He must have heard that my interest had shifted because he let me slide down his body and stepped back so I could take in the space.

"You decorate this place?" I asked, pointing to a picture of a woman and a man at a table, him lighting her cigarette.

"So what if I did?" he shot back, his voice gruff.

"I like it. Sort of Italian romance meets the '50s meets modern design. I wouldn't have expected that." I shrugged and ran my hand across the photograph that hung over his dresser. "You know them?"

"Nah. Just a photo I used to love," he murmured, staring at it. He shook his head, and a lock of his dark hair fell over his brow. He spun away and ground out, "It's not important. Forget about the pictures. You stay here if you're going to cooperate."

"And if I decide I'm not going to cooperate?" I lifted an eyebrow and sat down on the bed that sported a faux fur comforter. It warmed me immediately. I wondered how many times he'd actually slept in it, how many times he'd had someone else sleep in it too. Jealousy came swiftly. "I don't necessarily want to sleep where you've slept with others."

One side of his mouth kicked up, and a dimple I rarely saw dented his cheek. He pulled the keys from his pocket and inserted one into a barely visible slot between the wall and a photo. "If you'd like"—the wall popped forward, presenting us with a secret entryway—"you can sleep in there."

Curiosity killed the cat, but I figured I had one or two lives to spare. I gravitated toward the hidden door. As I curled my fingers around it, I looked up at him. "You're not going to kill me in here, are you?"

"I should, but I'm a masochist for the pain you're undoubtedly going to inflict on me in the future."

"Is it sad for me to admit I'm the same way with you?" I whispered.

Rome's finger dragged across my collarbone. "We're speeding toward a train wreck, you know? And I can't seem to stop. I want this with you. I'm fighting for this with you. It won't end well, though."

"Why?"

"I'll always put the family first, and I've been bred to trust no one."

My chest tightened. "You don't talk about your upbringing."

"Not much to say."

"Bastian said your father—"

"Was a liar. I took his life for it. I'd do it again." The darkness in his eyes deepened, and he glanced down like a memory weighted his gaze. "He gave me that chain. And now it reminds me that each part of the family is connected, but it only takes one link to break us all."

I nodded, knowing the strength of the mob but also how fragile it was. "It's not your responsibility to hold us all together."

"It is. I'm the monster. I protect us. I save the family before I save anyone else."

I sighed. "We're aiming toward the same goal."

"Yeah, but when I'm with you, the monster quiets. I'm starting to think his loyalties are different to mine."

She shook her head. "Worry about protecting the family, Rome."

His tongue ran over his teeth. "That includes you, Katalina."

"I'll never be one of the family. An untouchable, sure. But not part of the family."

He kissed me then, and this time it was soft. His lips were gentle as they rubbed over mine, and his hand on my jaw soothed away my worries. I melted into him because it was where I'd always belonged, the one place I felt most secure and most scared. No one wants to lose their safe haven, and Rome had the ability to rip mine away from me. My heart warred with itself. Would I be a part of the family he always protected or become a detriment to them all?

I wondered if one day the man who kept me standing would destroy me.

Until then, I took in the taste of him, absorbed the feel of him, and clung to the hope that maybe we could make it in the family together.

He pulled back and leaned his forehead on mine. "My blood is your blood, baby. I promise you that."

I nodded because I wouldn't argue with him now, not after a kiss so tender.

"I'll show you the room." He stepped back, breaking our connection, and motioned for me to step forward. "I need you in here for a few hours while I gather information."

I opened my mouth to argue with him.

He cut me off. "If I get the info I need, I'll share it with you first. No one else."

"You expect me to believe that you won't call Bastian?" I jutted a hip out, trying to look menacing even though my hands were still zip-tied and I was in a damn poofy, over-the-top dress.

"Our relationship should be built on trust," he tried with an eyebrow raised.

I blew a raspberry and started to walk down the dark hall of the secret entrance. "You don't trust anyone, Rome." That was the problem between him and every single person in his life. His father had broken him, and maybe his ex-fiancée had too.

I heard his footsteps behind me, and we came to a dark oak door. I turned the knob, not waiting for him to give me permission, and walked into a room lush with leather and rich, luxurious creams. A king-size bed sat on one side, while a large desk topped with four computer monitors stood on the other.

"Room for you and your lovers?" My stomach rolled with jealousy.

"No. A panic room of sorts. You're the only one who has been in here."

The muscles coiled in my neck relaxed. "So, what? You want me to stay here? Instead of a panic room, it's a prison cell."

"Don't be so damn dramatic. You have everything. There's a bathroom over there and—"

"There're no windows!" I turned toward him and glared at how ludicrous he was being. "You need to start talking, or I'm going to start freaking out. What do you think is going on?"

"I think you're too volatile right now for me to share that with you." He stalked toward his computers and started unplugging them.

"Are you kidding me?" I screeched and ran over to bang him on the back with my two fists. It felt like I was pummeling a brick wall. "Untie me now. Forget Bastian. I'm calling Mario."

He turned around with wires in his hand and a big-ass smile on his face. "You're in no state to argue, Katie."

I was in a hidden room with a killer who could dispose of a body very easily. The only people who would miss me were Brey, Vick, and maybe him.

He was right. I wasn't in any position to argue or tell him what to do. I should have been begging, strategizing, anything. Most people would have been scared at this point. But I wasn't ever scared that Rome would physically harm me, even though I'd seen him break my former boyfriend's bones. Instead of the fear I should have felt, I only felt frustration.

"I'll argue all I want. This is stupid!" When I stomped my foot to emphasize my point, he stared down at it. Before I knew it, he'd burst out laughing. Rome, my serious lone wolf, bent over and laughed his ass off at me. "Are you kidding me right now?" I pursed my lips so I didn't join him. I probably looked ridiculous standing there with my hands tied in a ball gown and heels.

The whole thing was preposterous.

A giggle slipped out, and he glanced up with tears streaming down his face. "I can't believe I got you commanding me even tied up and at my complete mercy."

Our laughter grew and grew. I tried to stop, but it would just explode from me again and again. "Oh, my God. I can't stop."

He shook his head and didn't turn toward me. "If I look at you, I'll never be able to quit."

That had me sliding to the beige carpeted floor and rolling with laughter.

He grabbed me by the waist and sat me up against the footboard. He studied me as if to make sure I was comfortable giggling there, then sat next to me, shoulder to shoulder.

We let the joy bounce around the walls. I took in how relaxed I was in the middle of his panic room, a room that would basically be my prison cell if I agreed.

I wanted control of everything. I felt it deep in my bones, yearned for it everywhere I went. The world had been cruel to me, and I, in turn, wanted to be cruel to it.

Yet, sitting on that floor next to him, I didn't really want anything more at all. I sighed. "How long do you expect me to stay cooped up here?"

"Just a day or two. I'll be back every few hours."

"What if you're not? Why here instead of out there?"

"I don't trust that someone won't come looking, and I need you hidden until I iron out the details." I opened my mouth to ask more questions, but he held up a hand. "Katalina, I'll tell you once I have the facts."

"I don't like being at anyone's mercy, Roman." I admitted to him the one thing he had to know by now.

"Because you're clawing your way around the world, Cleo. Sometimes, you need to let someone else rip it apart for you. It'll be a nice change, huh?"

"And this is for me, not to get rid of me?"

"Don't insult me, woman. I could have done that easily tonight more than once."

I nodded. Outmaneuvering Rome wasn't ever in the cards. He'd been trained by his own father, and I knew from the stories that he'd been the best.

"Maybe so." I said what I had been told so many times. "You're not your father, though, Rome. Would he have holed me up here?"

"I don't know what he has to do with this." He eyed me curiously.

"I'm trying to figure out if what you're doing is smart or stupid. Is it easier to kill me or go looking for whatever information you think is out there about whatever you won't tell me?" I shrugged my bare shoulders.

Rome glanced at them and got up to grab a throw off the bed so that he could wrap me up in it. Just as he was closing the front of it around me, he whispered, "My father would have killed you. Probably long before tonight."

"Why?" I breathed out.

"He didn't like complications. He hated them, actually. Instead of a woman potentially messing with my heart or his, she would be dead."

"Sounds ruthless."

He set the edges of the throw over my chest after I was tucked into it like a caterpillar in a cocoon. "Ruthless doesn't always get you to the top. He got cocky, cocky enough to step out of line with the family."

"I'm sorry you lost him, Rome."

"Why? His death is a good reminder that even those people who have been steady all your life can be the ones to completely change. He taught me a lot—nothing good, really, except to trust myself and no one else."

"Not everyone will change like him."

"Sasha lied too. Everyone does. If you're a survivor and life puts enough obstacles in front of you, you'll do what you have to."

"Or you'll sacrifice yourself for the one you want to survive more than you." I believed what I said deep in my bones. "I'm a testament to that."

"You're a warrior, Katalina. Your father would be proud of you."

I picked at my nail and let his words linger. "He wasn't, Rome. He wouldn't be now. I'm still trying to fit in. I'm still trying to do something he believed I wasn't meant to do. To him, I was born for something bigger, better than what I was doing then and what I'm doing now."

"You *were* born for something bigger. And you'll still reach the place you want to be, even if it's not where you are now." He slid his hand over my jaw and turned me to meet his eyes.

I looked over his face, his dark eyebrows that were normally dipped in a frown, the strong jawline and his scruff. I found myself yearning to feel it over my skin again.

"If I reach that place, will you be there with me?" I murmured, not sure I wanted his answer.

He leaned in and took my mouth instead. He tasted of the only thing I ever really wanted: my own destruction and salvation twisted together in my love for him. He'd either bring me to my knees or save me from myself.

Did he feel the same about me?

We lost ourselves in one another for maybe a minute, maybe an hour.

When I finally pulled away from him, I'd decided one thing. Trust was only given when you gave a person a reason to put their faith in you. "You got seventy-two hours, Rome. I'll stay here until then."

The left side of his mouth kicked up. "You don't have much of a choice, Kate-Bait."

"I think you'll listen to me either way," I threw back, not really sure at all.

He chuckled and got to his feet, then grabbed my biceps and lifted me too. "Whatever helps you sleep better in my bed." The man winked at me like all of a sudden we were on joking terms. Rome, the underboss of America's most ruthless mafia, wanted to play.

And I couldn't hold back the smile that spread across my face, because this side of him warmed something in me that had been cold for a very long time. "Pretty sure the thing that's going to help me sleep at night is you getting me out of these zip ties." I waved them in front of us.

Towering over me, he crossed his arms in that black hoodie of his. "I don't think I will."

"Rome!" I whined.

Then I saw his eyes track down my body, and it immediately heated. I searched his face and saw him lick those soft lips. My gaze turned greedy. The sweatshirt material covered the tattoos I was obsessed with but not the contour of his muscles. It stretched over his biceps like the seams were about to break. Rome could never get something baggy over those muscles. He was too big, big in all the right places.

I took a step back when he took one forward. "Maybe I need to take advantage of the position I have you in for tonight."

I lifted my chin. "Maybe keeping me tied up will get me to the high I've been searching for. I can't seem to hit it lately."

He shook his head. "Baiting and taunting me, huh?"

"I'm not doing anything of the sort." I turned away from him and sashayed around the room in the dress I knew he loved seeing on me even if he hated any other man seeing me in it. "I'm just speaking the truth."

"You know damn well I get you off every single time I touch you."

My nipples tightened at the deep timbre of his voice. "Is that so?" He came toward me, and I backed up against the wall. "What if I'm faking it?"

He pushed his body up against me, and his length against my stomach alone had me whimpering. "You couldn't fake with me if you tried. I'm the detonator to your bomb, woman. You ignite every single time, and I love watching you explode in beautiful chaos around me."

"Light me up, Rome. I better feel the damn fireworks."

His hands went to the sweetheart line of my dress. Before I could protest, he ripped it down the middle. The dress tore down to the skirt and left my chest exposed to him. "I'm going to burn this material," he mumbled almost to himself before he took one of my breasts in his mouth. He sucked so hard, I had to swing my arms up over his head to rest on his shoulders so I wouldn't collapse from the pleasure and pain of him.

"Rome," I panted, "I'm here all night, you know, and the next night and, well, seventy-two whole hours."

He licked up the swell of my breast, and I shivered. "I need to be working."

"Work on me." I held his gaze for a second before he shook his head and kissed me again.

I lifted my arms back over his head and to his front, then yanked his black sweatshirt up and ran my hands over his abs. I wrapped one leg around his hip so I could get him closer to my core, where I wanted him always. I wanted to be connected to him forever on another level, away from the mess the world pushed upon us.

I shoved his hoodie over his head when he pulled away long enough for me to do so. Then we were back on each other, out of control, lost in our own little panic room. We may have both been broken, shattered apart by what the world had done to us, but our fragments were beautiful flying around in that room together.

My hands trailed down to slide into the waistband of his pants, but he grabbed my wrists and slammed them up over my head. "I want to see you first. Don't act this time. Show me if I can't get you to orgasm."

His other hand went under the skirt that was still bunched around my hips. My leg was wrapped around his waist, but my body immediately gave in to riding his fingers as they slid into my slick center.

"Jesus, Rome." I breathed his name, not sure I could hold out long. My body was a victim to everything he did to me, a prisoner to his touch and an addict to his attention.

His chin scruff scraped at my neck as he bit the sensitive spots and then licked them better. He pressed his thumb against my clit and said low into my ear, "Show me you can't, baby. Show me I'm nothing to you."

My head slammed back into the drywall as the violence of my orgasm overtook me. My pussy tightened around his fingers, and he swore over and over as I rode his hand hard, milking every ounce of the feeling I got from him. He crashed into my lips and finally let go of my wrists above my head. I brought them down hard on his neck, hoping for just the right angle and momentum.

The zip ties snapped off from the force, and he chuckled into our kiss. "Always a warrior, Cleo."

I bit his lip and yanked at his hair, wrapping my other leg around him. His hand immediately went to my ass so he could carry me to the bed. We fell into it, equally ravenous for each other now.

"I want you in me," I panted as I scooted up the bed and shoved the remains of the dress off me.

"I'm not here to disappoint, Katalina." He followed me up the bed as he got rid of his pants. Then he moved between my legs. "This is my place now, got it?"

I smiled at his possessiveness. "Only yours?"

"Damn right." He didn't enter me gently. Like a thunderbolt, he crashed into me, reminding me that he had the strength to break me.

I took just as good as he gave when I spun him so he was on the bottom and I was on top. My hands on his chest, I rode him. "And this is my place, right?"

"It's your home, baby. I'm always your home."

His words shot through my heart, through my soul. Like lightning in the darkest night, he lit me up for that moment.

And during that whole night of lovemaking, I embraced the fact that our lightning may only strike once. I had to capture the beauty of it before it disappeared.

CHAPTER 26
ROME

I LEFT HER TO get breakfast, to get my bearings, and to get intel on the fact that I was sleeping with the heiress to the Russian mob.

Cade had already pulled intel from Georgie's phone, and he called both Bastian and I about it that morning. "Well, there's a lot more information than I wanted in here."

Bastian grumbled into the phone, surely tired from lack of sleep. "Is there information on where the fuck Katie's at?"

"We've got everyone out looking," I said, lying through my teeth. I hadn't looked at all last night.

"Dimitri took her. It's obvious from the communications," Cade announced. "I've got— I think we need to meet to discuss this."

Cade was always worried about tapped phones. We were intelligent enough to have people within the FBI bury our conversations. We switched out phones too. Still, you could never be too careful, and I was sure Cade had the information

I needed, information that would start a war I wasn't sure I was ready to participate in.

I found myself wishing I could keep that girl in my panic room for more than seventy-two hours.

She'd trusted me with her life this time, given me her freedom for long enough that I questioned my place in all this. For the first time since losing my unborn child and taking my father's life, I wanted to put something before the family.

I was about to do whatever I needed to in order to save her.

"I'll meet you both at my club." It would be the most secure option.

"I'm already here with Dante," Cade mumbled, and then my line went dead.

Our new boss would have to decide if he could trust this lone wolf because, after the information Cade was about to share, I would have to share something about Katalina.

I parked underground, below the large new skyscraper that housed my club, Stonewood Enterprises, and other real estate the family had acquired. The building rivaled the tallest in the city and made a statement to all.

I swiped my key card and entered an elevator with marbled tiling. It shot straight to the exclusive club doors and opened to all the luxury this city had to offer. Velvet seating trimmed with gold flanked bars that shimmered with gold molding.

I'd dressed in the traditional Italian attire of slacks and loafers. The shoes clipped across the floor as I stalked toward the table of men I called family.

Dante's arms spread across the back of the booth, while Bastian had pulled over one of the lounge chairs. He had two men behind him, security that always trailed him now that Mario had flown to New York. Cade was on a laptop across from Dante.

It wasn't lost on me that no one else was in the club area. The music still played quietly, but my bartenders were gone and the staff that normally buzzed about the patrons was nonexistent. Across from Bastian, one other chair sat empty.

He pointed. "Take a seat, brother."

The monster that had been quiet for a little while now stirred.

When Bastian saw me scan the two men behind him, he said, "I hope it doesn't come to that. Should I be concerned that it will?"

I didn't answer him. I couldn't honestly tell him one way or the other yet. I kicked the chair to the side and sat down. "I'm here for Cade's information, not to share mine."

"You're here to do what I say," Bastian replied so fast, his voice whipped through the air and everyone jumped to his attention.

Good, Bastian was starting to learn how to hold the reins of his power.

He would need to. And I wanted that for him, for us all as a family, as long as we could get through this first.

"What is it you're saying I do then, Bastian?" I leaned back in my seat, put my hands in my pockets, and let my legs fall open. I wasn't here to fight. Not yet, at least.

"Tell me where Katie is."

I didn't look toward Dante, but I was sure he'd figured out by now that I'd been the one to knock him unconscious. He knew those drugs as well as I did, and we were some of the only people who had access to them.

"So, you know what I know, then?" I looked to Cade, and he winced like he was trying his best to stay quiet and not override his brother.

"We know enough," said Bastian. "You took her last night. I don't know if that was to save her from us, to save her from them, or to dispose of her as a complication to the family, which she inevitably will be if she's still alive. Where do your loyalties lie?" Bastian asked, narrowing his eyes at me.

"Where they need to lie," I replied, not at all in the mood to defend my actions.

One of the men behind Bastian snarled as if I should be shaking and begging already. From the bulge at his side, I knew he had extra magazines from the glock he was probably hiding in his bulky jacket coat pocket. He was too big to know how to use his body. He'd be all force and try to swing his gun as a last-ditch effort.

Guy Two was more reserved, hadn't cracked an expression, hadn't glanced my way at all. He seemed far away, so far away I kept my attention on his behavior. He jerked when he heard movement to his left and looked like a man ready to jump at a pin dropping. I'd seen the look hundreds of times now, and I'd killed about the same amount of people for that reason.

He was a mole.

I'd take his life by the end of our meeting. I was sure of it.

"You can't know priorities because you don't have all the information. I'm the only one privy to all that," Bastian said through a sigh.

I shook my head at him. Bastian was still struggling with his father handing over the family to him. "An underboss can have all that information too. Cade has most of it already with what he pulls for you."

"The family never worked that way," Bastian countered, like he couldn't burden us all with what we knew already.

"Our family—between Cade, you, and me—always did, man. You know it, I know it, and he knows it too." I nodded at Cade.

"You shouldn't have taken her without consulting us, then, Rome." Bastian pinched the bridge of his nose. "How do I explain that to everyone? You keep acting without my consent."

"You don't, because you don't need to explain to anyone anymore."

"I did, and I still do. My father—" Bastian stopped. He knew his father shouldn't be a part of this at all. "It doesn't matter. I need to keep this family in line."

His resolve to finally set an example had Dante, Cade, and his muscle on the edge of their seats. We wanted to see if he'd make the call. It was the right decision.

And today, with all my pent-up adrenaline, I was itching for it too. "If I can make one request?"

He waved me on, not looking up from the demons he was battling.

"I want the man on your left first."

Bastian's head shot up, and he glared at me. He thought I was taunting him, thought I was asserting that I could beat his men one by one. He didn't know there was a mole among us.

He probably didn't know that I could beat them all too.

I didn't care about my life. I only cared about surviving for others. When the wind shifted and I became a monster and a killer, it wasn't about points being proven or saving my own soul—it was about taking away the threat.

Bastian shifted in his seat. The only sound in the club was the soft music pumping around us.

His left hand lifted, and one forward motion of his pointer finger had our mole descending upon me.

He moved much quicker than a man of plain muscle. He had training, the type of training that makes you light on your feet, that focuses on fluid motion, and I could tell immediately that, when he aimed at my gut, it would hurt more than most.

He was ready to use my momentum against me, but I didn't bend over in pain. I stood from my chair instead. He backed up and swung around to hit me with a kick that would bring me to my knees. If I fell to them, the torture would begin. That's when he'd make an example of me.

I took the hit but met his fighting style with my own. I pulled him to me and plowed my fist into his jaw. I could work with momentum too. I'd learned enough fight styles under my father's tuition to know how to toy with anyone.

I took sick pleasure in it now. I needed to let off steam, needed to center myself, needed to let the animal out to play. We danced a bit more. He got a hook to my face, and I spat the blood on his shirt. I twisted his arm as I caught another punch, and he flew down to swipe my legs out from under me.

No one said a thing. The sound of bodies breaking down and two men trying to rip one another apart mixed with the music overhead.

We grappled on the floor. He got a hold of my throat and, thinking he had me, smiled as he squeezed hard enough for me to lose my breath. The look in a man's eyes when he's about to take a life can show you exactly what terror he can inflict upon the world. This one was sick, joyous, thirsty for any and all blood to be spilled by his own hands.

I smiled back. A killer to a killer. One monster to another.

His smile disappeared when he saw that my monster was meaner than his. He'd forgotten that at the end of the day, strength sometimes overpowered the fancy footwork. I pried his hands off, snapping two of his fingers in the process. He screamed out like he'd never experienced a damn broken bone before.

The well-trained ones were always screamers. They'd been taught in a gym, where no one ever beat them enough to understand real pain.

I glanced at my family. Cade and Dante were smiling like they'd known all along I was about to give them a show, but my eyes fell to Bastian's. "I'm the underboss, but I protect this family like you. He's a mole. Let's work together, huh? Let me have him, and we'll figure the rest out."

I gave him the last call, stepped to the side and let him rule. There would be times I wouldn't back down, and one of those times would be with Katalina. But here, we needed to find a balance.

He breathed in deep like we'd found a middle ground finally and nodded his head.

"My blood is your blood. You bleed, I bleed, brother," I said to him. I meant those words for the men sitting around me. I meant them for the family.

I turned to the man crawling away from me and stalked forward. "You with Dimitri?"

He spit and swore at me in Russian. It was all the answer we needed.

I was happy I got to tear apart someone who'd threatened us. I jerked his arm out from under him and turned him back to face me. I kicked him hard in the nose, and the blood poured from it as he screamed. I took both his ears in my hands and bashed his head against the tile.

Over and over again.

His eyes rolled with the first hit. The second and third, he lost consciousness. I felt the skull give on the fourth blow. The satisfying crunch loosened the muscles in me, relaxed my soul, and calmed the monster. He'd had his fill for the day.

Dante was shaking his head. "That's a damn mess, even for you." He pointed to the blood pouring from the mole's skull and at the blood on my shirt.

"I needed it," I admitted as I came back to sit in my chair.

Cade was calling a cleaning crew and waving the boys out of the booth so he could get on with handling the mess.

"I could tell." Dante chuckled and cracked his knuckles. Like me, he had his own demons that had to be silenced every now and then. I could tell our fight had made him itch.

I shook my head and shrugged at Bastian. "I saw him lean a little too much toward his ear. He's got a bug in there, I guarantee it."

The man left standing by his side dug around in the dead guy's ears and held up a small device.

"He'd been vetted so many damn times." Bastian turned to his other muscle. "Don't fuck me. Or we'll fuck you."

The man nodded and held his hands up. "I'm here for the family only."

He was. I'd known him long enough to be sure of it. But we went through new soldiers for our family quickly. Soldiers were untrained, always considering their options, and people's loyalties shifted more than they should have in this city. My father had been the perfect example.

Bastian turned back to me. "You going to answer my first question? Where's Katie?"

"Depends on what you plan on doing with her."

"She's been with us a long time, Rome."

"So had that guy." I motioned toward the battered corpse. "Now he's dead."

"It's funny. I considered that you might have already killed her. I should be able to know what you're going to do." He twisted the ring on his hand as he shook his head.

"Your father didn't know what my father would do all the time, either, Bastian. It makes you human, not unprepared to rule this city." The words made everyone stiffen, but they had to be said. "I took my father's life so that our family could live on. I'll stand by your side and do what's right for the family always."

"What's right, then? Should we kill her?" he asked, holding each of our gazes. He didn't know this time.

I didn't know the answer either.

I just knew I wouldn't let it happen.

"I can't do that," I said. "Won't let anyone else do it."

"So you'll choose her over the family?"

"She is my family. And I'm hers."

"More than this one?" he whispered.

"More than any one," I replied, ready for the truth to penetrate, to tear us apart if need be. If this was to be a fight, I wanted it to be a fair one.

"So we back you, then. We fight for her and see where she ends up." Bastian stood and motioned at Cade. "Tell Rome what you found."

Cade turned his computer toward me. It showed Katie's family tree. Katalina was the daughter of Anastasia, Dimitri's sister. She'd died years ago, after a supposed deal gone wrong. I knew it'd been a bloody mess that her father always regretted, but now I questioned the story. Her brother took over when their father got dementia. Dimitri reigned while his father, Ivan, deteriorated in a nice house right outside of the city.

Just one night ago, Katalina had shaken hands with her own blood. Had she felt an instant connection?

Would she finally feel like she belonged somewhere? Would she abandon us for them?

"Do we know why they wanted to kidnap her?" I asked, my mind already running away with the possibilities of losing her.

"Her grandfather wants a reunion of sorts. We're not sure if her uncle will accept her or kill her. Right now, it seems they want her alive and are happy to accept her under their wing."

"And if she wants to go?" I asked.

Bastian looked toward the ceiling. "That girl is going to be the death of us all. I can't let her, Rome. You know I can't."

"How much does Mario know?"

Dante and Cade looked out the window immediately.

Bastian met my gaze. "Not a damn thing. Or maybe everything. He doesn't know what we know. He doesn't know they're looking for her, but he may know she's Russian blood. My father was always..."

"Too good to Katalina," I finished for him and stood up. I needed to get back to her. I needed to clear my head. "I need a week with her. She needs to come to terms with what we all are to her before she chooses her fate."

"We don't have a week." Bastian's hand flew down on the table. "This is going to be difficult enough without you asking for extra time to fuck her."

"You know damn well I'm not fucking her on our family's time. I could do that with anyone. If anything, she's fucking me, and I'm trying to scramble through the shitstorm of feelings we have for each other. She needs to choose us, Bastian. She's our girl; she belongs with us. We have to make her see that."

"I'm aware. I'm also aware that the bratva are going to be up our asses because she disappeared into the thick of the night. They'll sweep my place, everyone's place, and then they'll figure out we're hiding her. She's a convoluted complication now. Are we torturing her or protecting her from them? They'll find either of those things a slight to their family."

"So what?" I shrugged.

"So I don't need a fucking war on my hands!" He raised his voice and got in my face.

"You're the head of the most powerful mob family in the country, most likely the world. Undoubtedly, you will someday have a war on your hands, Bastian. Let's have it be one that's worth it. The bratva are nowhere near as organized as we are."

Cade perked up, ready with stats. "He's right. They're organizing slowly. They've grown over the past decade in terms of government allies. Small gangs around the city have teamed up with them also. But we're the Armanellis, Bastian. We got this."

"I want to rule without fear and bloodshed."

"The mafia doesn't get that luxury," interjected Dante.

"I need a week," I said.

Bastian scratched his forehead. "Fine. Let the bloodbath begin."

CHAPTER 27

KATIE

H E'D LEFT A note for me that morning.
Notes weren't my thing.
Not anymore.

I'd only ever gotten two. One from Rome telling me he'd never write me again—which was ironic now that I held another one of his notes in my hand—and the other...

The other one was from the only other person I'd ever loved. It was a bad one, a deadly one. One that made me want to lie down and die with him.

My mood soured. The man better wake me up next time he was going to leave me for hours on end.

Plus, the note wasn't even good. There weren't any hearts or balloons or our names scribbled next to each other.

> *I'll be back in a couple hours. The cabinet next to the bookshelf has food.*

Rome

PS Do you think Cleopatra was ever kidnapped?

PPS Books written by Poe are on that shelf if you want to read.

By food, he meant granola bars and apple juice. My stomach growled in protest when I'd eaten three and still felt starved.

When I heard footsteps in the hallway, I sat up in the bed. I chucked one of the bars at his head as he walked in.

"What the fuck, Katie?" He swerved to try and balance the tray he had in his hands.

"That better be something better than the shit you left me," I said, wiggling a little too excitedly at seeing him with food. I needed real nourishment after the night we'd had together. Plus, I'd been left by myself for hours, naked in a bed that smelled like him. I'd had a bit too much fun with that, honestly.

He set the tray down on the nightstand. "I cooked you macaroni and chicken. You're welcome. Because I don't cook."

I kept the sheet close to my body as I stretched for some of the food. He sat on the edge of the bed and surveyed me.

"Um..." I started. "Did you season it?"

"Season what? The macaroni?" he asked, one brow lifted.

I groaned and fell back into the pillows. "I'm starving, Rome. Bastian used to cook me gourmet meals, and now I'm being subjected to this?"

"That's good food, woman. I cook just as good as Bastian. Try it."

I scooped up one spoonful of macaroni and almost choked when it hit my mouth. I tucked the sheet farther under my arms to cover the fact that I hadn't got dressed yet, which was through no fault of my own. Rome had left me with a ripped dress and nothing else. "So, I appreciate you making me macaroni and cheese, Rome, I really do. But this isn't edible!"

"Are you kidding me?" He looked so offended I almost took back what I'd said.

Then I glanced down at the slop in the bowl. The cheese had curdled around crunchy noodles, and the butter hadn't completely melted. I tried not to laugh at his poor attempt to cater to me while I was essentially his prisoner. "So far, I've got no clothes and the worst food on the planet. And I'm confined to a secret room. Should we do a comparison between you and Bastian now?"

"Compare me to all the men you want, baby." He stood up and stalked toward the door. "I know how to make you scream in the dark of the night. There's no comparison to that."

My pussy clenched at his words. I immediately wanted to call him back to the bed, tell him to forget the food and forget my complaining. Instead, I held my ground. "They say food is the way to a man's heart. You should consider that advice for women too."

"You're still as high up on your pedestal as Cleopatra would be even when confined to this damn room."

At the mention of Cleopatra, I rubbed my hand over my neckline. "I don't have my necklace," I murmured. It'd become a sort of emblem to who I was, to who I could be, to who Rome imagined me to be.

He huffed and then stormed out of the room, slamming the door behind him. I heard the loud thwack of the deadbolt locking.

I sat there, no clothes on, completely turned on, with a plate of inedible food.

None of my needs had been met.

Fucker.

I rolled to the side to place the food back on the nightstand and wondered if Bastian and the boys had started the hunt for me. Did they already know Rome was keeping me here? And why was I the center of everyone's attention?

I was just the bait.

I'd pulled enough intel on the government and the bratva for them to want me dead, though.

A few minutes later, Rome swung open the door and entered with large T-shirts and athletic drawstring shorts. He threw them on the bed. "You're starving, and I'm starved for you. Get dressed before I take advantage of you without letting you get any nourishment."

I glared at him. "I like being naked."

"You like being a brat," he threw back and turned to leave again. "Get dressed."

"For what?" I countered but scrambled across the bed to pull a T-shirt on. I left the shorts untouched. "I'm not going anywhere. And where are you going? I'm bored as hell in here."

He growled. "I'm getting you edible food."

The door slammed shut again. I got out of bed and ran to the bathroom. I pulled my hair up into a bun and splashed some water on my face. I guess this would have to suffice because I didn't have access to makeup and hair creams. I rummaged through his drawers and found deodorant and a toothbrush. I used them both in the hopes I could remain somewhat presentable for the next two days.

I smirked at the fact that I wasn't at all dolled up for him, wasn't putting on a show for him, and still he was running back and forth for me.

Being a prisoner had its perks, I guess.

When I finally reentered the room, he'd placed our food on the carpet and was lying on his side across the floor, staring at me in the bathroom door. "Fuck me," he groaned and wiped a hand over his face.

I sat down cross-legged across from him and looked in the brown paper bag. "What are you moaning about over there?"

He rolled onto his back and extended a closed fist to me, lifting his eyebrows. I put out my hand and he dropped my necklace into it. "Went and got it."

I stared at the gold in my hand as my heart seized at his gesture.

"Don't get emotional on me now, Kate-Bait." He said softly and when I looked at him, he was smiling. It stretched across his face, and the deep chocolate brown of his eyes sparkled.

"Thank you."

"Yeah, yeah. Now, let's move on. I'm trying to focus on food but all I want to eat is you, in my shirt, right now. Clothes were supposed to help." I glanced down and saw his cock was standing at attention underneath his sweats. I pulled his white tee between my legs, but it wasn't really any use. I crawled on all fours around our food. His gaze was locked to me. I arched my back and made each movement languid. I felt myself get wetter and wetter. By the time I reached his side, I was ready for him.

We didn't say one word to each other. He'd put his hands behind his head and stared up at me, like he was prepared to sit back and watch.

I wanted him to.

I lifted his shirt just a bit around my hips and straddled him. I shoved his pants down and let the length spring free.

No prep was needed for either of us. I dropped down on him hard, and we both gasped. My hands went to his neck for leverage. He flexed under me, meeting me stroke for stroke.

I squeezed harder and harder as I rode him faster and faster. He grabbed my hips and rammed me down on him over and over again. Later, I'd see the bruises where his fingers had imprinted on me.

Fast, hard, and untamed, I took the orgasm I needed. I dominated him and it. I loosened my hands and let air back in his lungs as I hit my high. My pussy convulsed around him as he gulped in a breath, and he came in me on his next thrust.

I crumbled around him, knowing this home on top of him, around him, with him in me, was the only place I'd ever really need to be.

He smoothed my hair up toward my bun and sucked on my neck, murmuring, "I'm scared I might want to be a prisoner in here with you forever."

I smiled against him. "You'd get nervous sleeping next to me."

He stiffened like my comment hurt him. "Why would you think that?"

I pulled back from him, slid off, and went to the bathroom to clean up. "Rome, you don't trust anyone with your life. I bet you never sleep next to women."

The idea of him next to another woman sliced through me. I reached for the matte black handle of the shower, and immediately, hot water from a large round showerhead fell like rain into the open tiled area. I didn't give myself time to enjoy the luxury of it all. I threw the shirt to the side and jumped right under the water, closing my eyes to let it run over me. I wanted it to wash away the reminder that outside of these walls, Rome wasn't as accessible to me and much more accessible to other women. They were less complicated, less tied to the family.

"I don't sleep next to women because I'm not fucking other women." He stepped in behind me and pulled me against his stomach. His hand went straight to my breast like he couldn't keep from touching me. "You're the only one I'm thinking about, so you're the only one I'm fucking. We were past others after Bastian. Right?"

I moaned when he pinched my nipple and whispered, "Yes."

"Don't you realize the pull you have on me?"

My head fell back as he massaged my nipple. "We don't have to indulge it."

"This isn't indulgence. It's obsession, Katalina. It's you consuming me. It's you bound to me. It's your face on my mind since the first moment I saw you."

248

He turned us toward the vanity and mirror. It was fogging up, but I saw his massive body behind mine, how his tattooed arms wrapped around me, how he focused on only me.

I looked up at him. "You've haunted me as much as I haunted you, Rome. You've been in the worst of my dreams and nightmares."

"Then, I better find a way to make it into the best of them too, huh?" His head dipped down to bite my neck.

His hand trailed down my stomach and slid right into my pussy. The water droplets seared our skin with heat, the steam invaded our lungs, and my panting could be heard all around us. He hooked one of my legs up around his arm so that his fingers fucking me were bared to us both in the mirror.

"Fucking beautiful," he murmured into my hair. "Fucking mine."

I came at his words, at seeing myself so open and free and in complete ecstasy in his arms.

He let me ride it out and then got to his knees. He hooked my leg on his shoulder and told me to hop up.

"Rome, I don't think I can keep going."

"Baby, look at yourself in that mirror. You can do whatever you set your mind to." Then his mouth was on me, and I held on for dear life. He ate me out like he was ravenous, and I like to think that appetite was for only me.

CHAPTER 28

ROME

WE'D EATEN AND she'd slept next to me for hours. I'd slept too. Like a fucking baby who'd been crying for weeks and was finally in a safe enough place to close its eyes.

It could have been that I'd locked the panic room. It could have been that I'd locked her in the panic room with me. Or it could have been that she was the only person I trusted to be by my side when I slept.

All of the above. Maybe.

I rolled to the side of the bed to get the notepad from the drawer, trying not to wake her.

Her raspy voice blurted out, "Don't leave a note. I hate them."

"What's there to hate?" I pulled a pen out and started to write in an effort to get her worked up. "You used to write me."

"And you never wrote back. I only ever got one letter from you." My heart, the one I never felt when I took a man's life, seemed to stir and then drop to the pit of my stomach at the sound of her voice shaking with her explanation. "The only other note I ever got was my dad's suicide note."

I swore and stuffed the notepad as far back into the night-stand drawer as I could before I turned to her. "Katalina, I didn't know…"

"How could you?" She shrugged, a defense mechanism. Was her heart just as dead as mine because she'd turned away from her emotions to survive?

"Because you could have told me sooner. Or I should have asked sooner. Someone should have been there—"

"There was no one to be there, Rome." She sat up and swung her legs over the side of the bed, then searched for a T-shirt on the ground. We'd left the room a mess of clothing and food as we took advantage of our world away from the world. "The state helped place me, and I had some money saved for a small ceremony for my dad, but who would I have invited to mourn with me?"

The silence stretched between us because I didn't know what to say.

"I survived, right?" She lifted her arm. "You survive because if you don't, you die."

"Do you still have it?"

"Have what?"

"The note." I knew she did, knew she'd have reread it like she'd reread the research for her father's condition over and over again. Those pages had been worn out, tired of her scrutiny. She'd have done the same to his words, tortured herself.

"Sure." The shrug came again. "I know it by heart now." She let the words flow out like a recited poem. She choked on *I choose death so you can live.*

"You're enough, you know? He would have thought that. He always thought that. I saw the way he looked at you when we were there that night. He loved you like the stars love the moon, Katalina. He looked at you like a father should his daughter."

252

She shook her head. "He loved the idea of me, but he wouldn't love this. He wouldn't love what I'm doing. I had a dream with Bastian for a reason, to make him proud, to make myself proud. I don't really belong with any of you, Rome. I'll never be blood, but I could be something more to others, to girls who need someone to stand up for them—you've said that yourself more than once."

"I was antagonizing you." I tried to backtrack.

"You were right though. I'm never going to fit by anyone's side. Not with the Armanellis and not with you either." She pulled my shirt on abruptly and went to grab some of the shorts she'd ignored since I'd brought them in.

I grabbed them away. "I agree with everything you're saying. I agree with your father too. You're bigger than just being at someone's side. Cleopatra ruled an empire because she wasn't comfortable only standing beside someone. She climbed over everyone, was a damn triumph because she wouldn't let another triumph over her. You're the same."

"Maybe. Maybe not." Turning on her heel, she started to pace back and forth. "I'm not going to do anything in this room. I know that. You know that too. You need to—"

"I need to tell you what I know." I held up a hand when she opened her mouth to agree with me. "I'm going to. All of us are going to."

"All of you?" Her voice rose. "Bastian knows?"

"Bastian, Cade, Dante. We know."

"Mario?" She whispered his name like she was sacred.

I worried about the way he'd looked at her all these years now, worried he'd been much more involved than he should have been. "I'm figuring that out."

"Figuring what out?" she screamed and pulled at her curls. The swells under my white T-shirt rose and fell rapidly with her fast breaths, her frustration showing.

"Being kept in the dark isn't fun, but you don't have a choice. It's for your safety at this point."

"I don't want to be saved, Rome." She turned to the wall and pounded on it. "I've learned I can only save myself. I want to save myself always. I don't need someone else to do it."

"You said seventy-two hours, then you can roam my place for a week. We still want you lying low, though."

"This is bullshit," she blurted out. "I don't get why I can't know if everyone else does."

"We need this time," I repeated, knowing I could lose her to her real blood, knowing that for once an influence greater than the pull of our mafia family could take her away. "I need you to trust me." If she trusted me, I could trust myself enough to know I wouldn't lose her.

But I felt us slipping through my fingers.

Like trying to close up a wound, the blood kept pouring out.

If she bled, I would bleed. If she died, we all would.

I was sure of it.

CHAPTER 29

KATIE

I COULDN'T KEEP TRUSTING them. And yet the only place I felt home was with this man between my legs, and he was keeping me from the world.

We couldn't go on like this.

My father's note echoed over and over in my mind. I was made for more than just hiding in the shadows, letting others take control. I'd embedded myself deep inside this family so that I could be a true part of it, not a pawn.

Staring into the eyes of the man I thought I loved felt like war against my own mind. The longer I sat there going over all my days with the family, the more I wanted to demand answers.

Yet Rome didn't ask me for anything. He didn't ask anyone in the family for anything, really. He executed his job like I did mine. We'd been the same for a long time.

"I want gourmet food and you to read me Poe until you lose your voice."

He eyed me curiously.

"I should be able to sneak around your house at least. If Bastian and them already know, what's the harm? You guys can keep the Russian mob out of here. And I want to get some clothes."

"I'm agreeing to everything but the last thing. You don't need clothes."

"Bring me more clean shirts, then."

"Done." He grabbed a book from the shelf and wrapped his arm around my waist before he lifted me and carried me back to the bed.

I snuggled into the crook of his arm. It might have been selfish and totally stupid, but I wanted these last couple of days with him. I wanted him to myself in our little panic room. "I'm probably going to regret agreeing to this."

"If you do, we'll have had this at least." He held up Poe. When he turned to a page and started reading, I got lost in the story.

Darkness and death were obsessions of the author, and maybe that's why we both gravitated toward him. I looked at Rome and his strong jawline as he read. He glanced at me, and his smirk warmed my body. In a different life, maybe we could have been the perfect couple.

When he finished the story, he grumbled, "I think Poe killed people."

"Like you?"

"Somehow. He writes like he knows."

"Do you ever wonder what it would be like if you hadn't ever killed anyone?"

His lip pulled back, and he grunted. "Not really. I was born for it. My soul was never really quiet. I was an anxious kid and always had tendencies."

"Like killing baby animals?" I lifted my eyebrows in mock horror.

He chuckled at me. "No, crazy woman. What the hell? I just liked finality. I wanted an end to everything. I wanted puzzles complete, shows to come to their end, and people to finish everything they started. It led to me wanting to complete business for the family, and that was ultimately taking lives and tying up loose ends."

"Hmm. Do you think we'll be a loose end?"

"One way or the other." He picked at the fuzz on the blanket I'd wrapped around me while he'd been reading. "I think we'll figure out how to end us if that's the case, though. It'll probably be explosive."

"Why do you say that?"

"I killed my father. Not everyday someone gets to say that. I'm the monster, Katalina. It's what I always was. And you're Cleo. What we have will always be explosive, it always was."

"I wasn't always Cleo, and you weren't always this way. We were all kids once."

He shook his head. "My father didn't have time for a kid. I grew up the moment I was in his care."

"I'm sorry," I said because I at least got the love from my dad and wouldn't have traded it for anything else in the world.

"No reason to be. He raised me to compartmentalize and be perfect for the job I do now for the family. I learned his mean streak was predictable, and I trusted that in him. Until I couldn't. Then, with his betrayal, he taught me to trust no one."

"Is that why you've been circling me for years instead of giving in to us?"

He shrugged. "Maybe. Maybe I'm scared of what the monster will do to you ... or what the monster in me will do *for* you."

"The monster in you *saved* me," I murmured, remembering the day he showed up at Marvin's, how my heart swelled, how I tried my best not to care, and how I cried silently that night when he told me he couldn't take me in.

"I'm starting to think my monster loves you." I held my breath at his words. "And I'm scared at some point I won't be able to control it."

"Then I guess our end will definitely be catastrophic." The words were ominous, but I smiled at him because I'd lay down destruction at this point to be with him.

"Best way to go out." He winked at me and then dove for my mouth. I giggled and let him have me.

Those were the days I would long for later on.

Rome got more lenient with my stay hour after hour, and I came out of his panic room the next day. We cooked together—terribly, but still together. We laughed together, moved and lived in harmony together.

Hope and happiness blossomed in me when I ignored the glaring issues we were facing. I kept myself cut off from the world. I didn't ask for a phone, didn't attempt to turn on the TV or contact my friends through the internet.

I was isolated with the man I knew I loved for those few days in an ignorant, stupid bliss. I shouldn't have been so blind, and I shouldn't have turned the other way.

I regretted those days and longed for them all the same.

CHAPTER 30

KATIE

"YOU'RE KIDDING ME, right?"

"What do you mean?" I tightened my ponytail. Earlier today, I'd gotten so bored, I'd disguised myself well enough that I could go to a little shop around the corner. Rome hadn't exactly said I could leave his place, but he had said he was finally taking me out tonight.

That called for celebration. The closest store was eccentric, and I was all about it. They had knockoff clothes and second-hand items, but it was someplace to go where I knew I wouldn't be seen.

"We're not going anywhere with you dressed like that." He pointed at me accusingly, as if my outfit was completely ridiculous.

I had to admit, it was different. The latex fit every nook and cranny of my body like a glove. I was actually surprised it wasn't custom made for me. To say I was proud of the rare find was an understatement. "This is perfectly legit for whatever we have to do tonight. I'm wearing combat boots and a dark outfit. It's the best way to hide in the shadows."

"You're wearing a fucking dominatrix outfit. If you're trying to bait me, you're failing. You're so far from getting your way, you don't even know."

I scoffed at his words, even though my stomach clenched at the slight stabbing pain of knowing I hadn't turned him on.

I popped a hip out and looked at him in the mirror. "My outfit works. Either like it or don't, but this is how I'm dressing."

"Why are you so difficult?" He pinched the bridge of his nose as I got on my coat.

"My coat covers most of my outfit anyway. Jesus. Can I have a little fun? I've been cooped up in here for two fucking weeks doing nothing."

"You were doing the same damn thing at Bastian's."

"Bastian's was planned. I was able to move freely around his penthouse. We went on scheduled excursions. You went shopping with me!"

"You didn't leave that penthouse much at all."

"What? Did you track me while I was there?"

"Of course I tracked you," he shot back, not at all apologetic for his actions. "It's my job."

"Whatever. It doesn't matter. This is different!" I threw up my hands and then stormed past him, done with the conversation and wanting to get on with the night.

He stomped out after me. "You're something, you know that?"

"What a compliment," I grumbled as he checked a few of the locks and the security system he had in place.

Then we were walking in sync toward his garage. He stepped in front of me as we turned corners to make sure no one was watching us, and then he cut the lights to the garage as we made our way over to a black SUV with tinted windows.

He opened my door and grabbed me under my shoulder to hoist me in, probably a little more aggressively than necessary.

Still, his touch shot through me, and I gasped at feeling his strong grip after knowing exactly how our touches exploded together.

He slammed the door as I cut my gaze to him and licked my lips.

Fuck, he was in a mood.

How was it that he wanted nothing to do with me right now, but I wanted everything to do with him?

He drove the back alleys in silence and checked his rearview mirror constantly. The night sky was muted by the city lights, the buildings glittering with their manmade brightness.

"You ever think the country might be the best place to be?"

"Why? The city all of a sudden too much for you?"

I sighed. I was tired of sparring with him.

We drove over a bridge, and the car rattled as the tires bounced off the metal. "I think the city can be too much for anyone. It wants our blood, and I'm not sure we'll have any left to give once we've been drained of it."

He glanced at me, his dark eyes suddenly not so empty of emotion. His tattooed arm flexed as he gripped the steering wheel. "No city is going to drain you of your blood, Katalina."

"It feels like you're all hiding this huge secret, and it might be that. Honestly, it wouldn't be the worst way to go."

"It's also not the way you will go. You're stronger than that. We're stronger than that."

I nodded, letting his words sink in.

"Your blood is my blood, Kate-Bait. You die, I die." His hands white-knuckled the steering wheel, and he didn't look at me as he spoke. His jaw clenched, like he was trying to hold back whatever he was feeling.

He pulled over in a dark alley, and when his head whipped my way, I saw the need finally, the hunger I'd seen the last time he touched me. I saw the Rome I'd missed for the past hour, the one I thought might have only been a dream or a nightmare.

I quivered under his stare, my core aching for anything he might give me in those moments his gaze roamed over me. "Maybe my blood isn't, though. Maybe this family isn't mine to—"

His hand flew off the steering wheel and went straight to my neck. He yanked me forward so I was just inches from his lips, feeling his hot breath on my cheek as he said, "There's no arguing your place. Your blood is mine. We bleed together, woman. Always. Remember that."

He devoured my mouth and bit down painfully on my bottom lip. He wanted to taste blood, and I moaned when I realized that was his intention. I could submit to this man. I knew that even if he was inflicting this little bit of pain, he would never take it far enough to truly break me any more than I'd already been broken.

I unbuckled my seat belt and climbed over the console to straddle him.

The latex of my outfit squeaked as I did, and Rome burst out laughing midway into our kiss.

"Are you kidding me?" I shoved him in the chest and glared at him. "Don't fuck this up by laughing."

He laughed harder, and I caught the side of him no one ever saw. Rome never really laughed, not like this. He'd momentarily lost the dark side of himself—the empty, hollowing side that sucked at your soul when he looked at you—and appeared like a genuinely carefree guy in his twenties.

The family had painted him as a killer and an angry, ruthless one at that. Even the villain in the story had dimensions that were pure and innocent. A villain is molded and shaped over time by the torture they have to endure. I wondered what Rome would have been like had he never been born into the mafia. I liked to think his laugh would have been contagious, that he would have gotten everything he wanted, lived the life he wanted.

I didn't believe in happy endings, but I could wish for them in the dark, hidden corners of my mind.

"Are you about done?" I grumbled as I straddled him.

He wiped at nonexistent tears just to be a dick. "It goes to show that outfit is good for nothing."

"Except that I'm on something hard, and I'm sure it isn't your Glock. So my outfit's good for something."

"I'm rock solid because you're in front of me, woman. It's been that way since the day I laid eyes on your little ass. Not because you're wearing a second skin."

I ground my teeth together.

"How hot are you in that thing, anyway?" He raised an eyebrow as if he wanted to continue his stupid joke about my attire.

I gripped the front zipper and bit my bottom lip. If I couldn't seduce Rome while I sat on top of him and make him forget about my outfit, I'd lost my touch. "It *is* getting hot in here."

Slowly, I started to pull the zip down. The sparkle in Rome's eyes died, and the hunger in them grew. He shifted so I could feel his length up against my pussy, and I moaned as the zipper traveled tooth by tooth down my body.

Rome sucked in a breath as it passed my chest. "Fuck. You're not wearing a damn thing under there, are you?"

I stopped right at my hips and leaned forward. I threaded my fingers through his hair to pull him close and whisper, "I don't ever wear anything under my clothes when I'm with you."

"Because you want to feel like you might be taken by me?"

We stared at each other as I gave a tiny shrug. The side of his lip turned up, like he was getting used to my noncommittal answers.

My hand drifted to his zipper and shoved it down quick. His cock sprung free, and I whimpered as I gripped it, seeing that he'd worn nothing under his jeans either.

I stroked up and down his length, not once but twice, before I tipped the head of him onto the line of zipper teeth right over my pussy. "Feel that?"

His groan was guttural and his eyes dropped closed while he let me play with the one part of him I wanted in me at that very second.

"The zipper goes all the way down and around." Rome's eyes shot open as he understood my meaning. "Very easy access for both of us."

"Unzip it, Bait," he commanded.

I shook my head and rubbed a thumb over the pre-cum at the tip of his dick.

His jaw clenched. "You love the control, don't you?" He glared at me.

"I love what I can get from you, sure." I rode my pussy over him this time, dry humping right where I needed, and shifted my other hand up to my breast to start to get myself off.

Rome watched for a minute, letting me ride him just the way I was. His breathing sped up, his stare on me narrowed, and I felt his thighs start to clench with each roll of my hips.

My breath caught as I climbed toward my climax. I closed my eyes and arched to get there, riding him quicker and panting out little moans, when suddenly Rome's calloused hands flew into the top of my jumpsuit and yanked it down around my arms, trapping me.

He shoved my hips back away from him and ground out, "You want to fuck, you fuck with me. I'm not here to ride for your pleasure only, Bait. I'm getting mine too."

With that, he dragged his fingertip down the center of me, all the way to the zipper. He pushed it farther until it rolled over my clit. He stopped so that just that hot button was exposed. "Want to get off before I fuck you into oblivion?"

I sucked on my teeth, pissed he'd stopped my show of getting off just to take control for himself. I also bucked back so hard that my body just missed pressing on the horn for everyone in Chicago to hear when he rolled his thumb over that sweet spot.

"Hurry up and get on with it then," I said, trying my best to be irritated.

He chuckled. "Ask nicely, Katalina."

I wanted to punch him. Then I wanted to get on my knees and suck him dry. Something about him taking control of me shook me to my core. He was the only one who could, though I never wanted to let him know it.

I sighed heavily and rolled my eyes so hard, I'm sure he saw only the whites. "Don't you know by now that I'm not nice?"

"You're nice for me. You always will be. Deep down, somewhere where you aren't broken, you still long for acceptance, for love. You want to be nice, Katalina. So be it."

My stomach twisted, and my heart galloped in my chest. Rome pushed my boundaries, scaled the wall, and swam through the moat around my fortress. He wanted inside my soul, and he wanted to move past the broken edges of it to where he thought I was still whole.

"What if I'm broken everywhere?" I whispered. Most days I felt that way. I'd died with my father, and now I was this shell of a human, not really connected to anyone, striving to be a part of a family I wasn't sure I could ever truly fit into.

His hand slid to my chest. He rubbed over my heart like he could soothe the fast beats. "Then you've survived, and you take your broken pieces, turn them to what you need them to be, and live with it, Bait. You were always a survivor. And you've always been the best at it."

Maybe my shaking my head pushed him over the edge, maybe he saw the doubt in my eyes, maybe he was just done talking, but he didn't give me the chance to contradict him.

He pushed the zipper down just enough and plowed into me, not hesitating over the repercussions.

I didn't stop him either. I took what I wanted, riding him like I deserved every part of him in me. I yanked his dark waves of hair so hard he groaned as my nails clawed his scalp. He bit my lips and then ripped his mouth away so he could bite and suck my neck. The marks would be brutal, bruised, and red tomorrow. Rome wasn't going easy on me.

I wasn't going easy on him either.

We wanted a piece of each other. Even if it was broken, jagged, and dangerous.

Maybe we were past everything else. Right now, it was just the two of us, in that car, in the city, under the building lights that kept us alive, that drowned out the total darkness but muted the light of the stars. Our natural light, the one that brightened even the darkest soul, had been extinguished.

Chicago wanted to show how it owned us, how it molded us into who we were that night.

I thought I could navigate it all just fine. I thought I had this city by the balls. All these men, my relationship with Rome, all this mafia—I thought I had a handle on it.

I was wrong.

CHAPTER 31

ROME

HER PUSSY CLENCHED down on me like a Venus flytrap. It almost reached the point of pain, it was so tight. It squeezed like I was its last lifeline.

Any man would have felt that way with their hands around her tiny waist, thrusting up into her like they had the ability to split her in two. Her nails scraped at my back, her teeth dug into my neck, and I knew she drew blood in some places. She was leaving her marks on my tattoos, and she was probably doing it on purpose.

The sick thing was that I wanted her to. Katalina was more of a permanent mark on my body than any of the tattoos could ever be.

She sped up our tempo as I rubbed her clit and bit down on one of her nipples. She moaned my name like I was the only man she'd ever longed for.

I knew I wasn't.

I thrust into her harder, faster, rougher. I wanted to make my mark this time, or maybe get my fix.

I wasn't sure anymore.

But as she orgasmed on my dick, I remembered why I couldn't leave this woman behind, couldn't get enough of her. Her venom spread through the SUV like an airborne toxin as I met her with my own high. I moaned her name and cradled her to my chest when she slumped against it. Her vulnerability seeped into my soul.

I smoothed her caramel curls; I whispered sweet nothings in her ear. "God, you feel good. I fucking missed my home."

"It's only been a few hours."

"A few hours too long," I said, resting my forehead against hers. It wasn't nothing I was whispering—it was everything. Every moment that passed, I realized I wanted her unleashed beside me.

Her venom was everywhere, and I sucked it up like it was water and I was stranded in a desert.

I wanted her poison.

She sighed in my arms, and I worried for the millionth time over these past few days if we would be able to survive the storm ahead.

And would it be our storm or the city's? Because we were just as volatile and just as deadly.

A tapping on our window had us both jumping.

She froze when she saw a police officer. "Fuck," she swore, long and low, as she scrambled off me and started zipping up.

"It's fine. He can't see in," I mumbled, readjusting my still wet dick and trying to shake the fog.

"Roll the window down, Rome! What are you doing?!" she screeched as she wiped at her lips.

I hit the button, and the cop leaned forward, his blue eyes piercing everything he could as quickly as he could. When his gaze found Katalina, I waited a beat to see if he'd find his footing, to see if he'd drop his stare.

I cleared my throat. "Sir, there a problem?"

He didn't glance my way. "License and registration."

Fine. We were playing it this way. I reached into the compartment and pulled it out. He'd know soon enough he was wading into water he didn't want to be in.

"You know it's a very dark alley you're both idling in tonight, miss? Any extracurricular activity going on?" One eyebrow lifted as he waited for an answer from Katie.

Her slate eyes cut to him, and her jaw hardened at his insinuation. "Are you assuming something, officer?"

"Should I be?" He sucked on his front teeth.

"Do yourself a favor," I said. "Check my license and registration."

He eyed us back and forth. "Don't think I will," he mumbled, but the man did something stupid. He pulled his gun like it was protocol. "Step out of the car, miss."

Katie's eyes widened right before they narrowed. I saw the fear followed up by the determination.

That woman. She was a phenomenon. I couldn't tell if she was scared for my life or her own, but her resolve hardened as she stared at the barrel of the gun.

"Officer," I said quietly, "holster your weapon. Check my registration. I don't want more blood spilled this week."

My words held enough warning that he glared at me in question. "More blood? Are you drunk?"

"I'm tired. That's about it. If you want to go this route, I'll most likely be more tired from killing you, but I'll do it. Don't make me." I sighed, really not wanting to beg the man for his own life. "Please."

He took a step back, as if it finally occurred to him that this might not be a good idea. He stalked away, my license in hand.

"We need to go, Rome," Katie whispered.

"What for?" I shrugged and leaned back on my headrest to shut my eyes for a second. This night was becoming more ridiculous every moment.

"I'm not fucking this dumbass cop because he thinks I'm a prostitute and wants to get his rocks off in a dark alley. If you think I'll stoop to that level, then I—"

"Don't ever repeat those words." I got in her face quicker than I should have. She didn't recoil at all though. Not like a victim of abuse, not like I'd seen others do. For some reason, Katie didn't have a preservation instinct with me and it scared me a little to realize it.

"Well, why are we sitting here then? He's going to shoot you or have me fuck him."

"He'll do neither."

"You realize I'm a mixed woman in a dark alley dressed like a hooker, and a cop with a loaded gun is asking me to step out of the car, right?" The hitch in her voice had me searching past the stone of her eyes, looking for the hint of fear. "I'm not scared, Rome. I'm pissed. I shouldn't have to be scared, nor should any woman. The imbalance in power is what makes this all so sickening. No woman should have to be nervous when she's stopped by a cop in the middle of the night."

"But most are?" As the words left my mouth, I realized how stupid they were. "Of course they are. Jesus."

"So drive." She pointed forward, night completely forgotten, and rightfully so.

Except Mr. Cop was back already. "Um, I'm so sorry, sir. So sorry to have wasted your time. I apologize." The man pointed to Katie, but his eyes were downcast.

"Seriously?" she whispered.

I knew our licenses were marked. Armanellis were rarely pulled over, and when we were, we didn't get tickets.

"Officer, tell the lady you apologize for any disrespect too." I couldn't help myself. Katie shoved me as if I was taking it too far. So I took it one step further. "And when you apologize, look her in the eyes and mean it. Be the man your other officers expect you to be. Don't terrorize women."

He looked her straight in the eyes and mumbled so many apologies, I had to cut him off and tell him to leave us to our alley.

As he drove away, Katie watched him go, then punched me in the arm. "You had that up your sleeve this whole time?"

"I don't use it on command, woman. We don't ever want them to pull our licenses."

"I'm telling Bastian I want one."

"You don't need one."

"I definitely need one." She readjusted the latex on her body. "I'm in a systemically racist, patriarchal society. Literally every woman should have one."

I stared at her in her fiery rage, ready to school anyone who countered her argument. "You're fucking beautiful. And one day—not today, but one day soon—I might have to tell you I love you and watch the chaos that ensues."

"Why does it have to be chaos?"

"Because I'm the protector of the mob. I can't have distractions."

"I'm a distraction then?" she asked, head tilted with pain in her eyes.

"You're the biggest distraction because I may put you before everything, even the family."

She nodded and turned to look out toward the brick walls steeped in darkness. After a moment, she whispered, "Thank you." She cleared her throat and dragged one finger along the windowpane. "You didn't have to make the cop say sorry. I appreciate it."

I wanted to tell her that's how life should be, that a man should stand by his woman.

But I couldn't rightfully claim to be her man until I came clean about the secret we all knew.

Her head fell back on her headrest as she sighed, ran her hand over her face, and then chuckled as she looked up toward the car's sunroof. "Honestly, I sort of want to ride you like a horse all over again after that display of chivalry. Is that what I just witnessed?"

"You witnessed a real man, Kate-Bait."

"Real men take me out, Rome." She winked at me. "We going to your club or what?"

I intended to take her there, but Cade had texted that we needed Georgie's laptop. I pulled away from the alley and took two more turns.

"What are we doing here?" she whispered like we were still being watched.

"I have to get something from Georgie's place."

"He's got security and—"

"I'm well aware of his layout, Kate-Bait." I cursed my bad idea. We should never have left my place, not when I was always supposed to be available to the family.

"I'm going with." She grabbed her coat.

The hell she was. "No." I shook my head, my voice low and final.

"I'm not staying in the car after what just happened, Rome. Not an option."

I swore under my breath and glanced down the alley, but I already knew I wouldn't leave her. I didn't know who would be around after what we'd encountered. This night was going to shit, especially since I hadn't told Bastian, Cade, or Dante to have us watched, because she wasn't supposed to be out of the damn apartment in the first place. "Wear that in with the hood up. I don't need cameras catching our identities."

Her hands were already placing the hood on her head. It cloaked her face in such a way that the city lights danced over her strong bone structure. I glanced away to scan the perimeter and remind myself that we were targets at all times, that I couldn't have my dick control the situation tonight.

At least, not anymore.

"Let's go," I grumbled as we swung open our doors. We moved into the shadows quickly, where Katie didn't have to be told to follow close behind me. She let me lead without question, like she knew our places in this.

I wondered if she knew her place with me when it came to our personal relationship. Because I was starting to think I needed to know it more than ever before. Starting to think we needed to lay some boundaries.

Bombs needed to be secured.

"He shouldn't be home," I whispered once we were in the elevator. "Be quiet in the hall. I'll pick the lock, and we'll move in and get out."

She nodded and whispered back, "There's a security system right when you walk in. I have the code."

Who knew she'd be handy? We moved well together down the hall and into the apartment when I got the door open. She went straight to his bedside where the laptop sat in a drawer. We were about to get out of there with no issues when we heard a key in the lock.

"I got this," she whispered as she shoved me into the closet. "Let me handle it."

I shook my head that it wasn't a good idea, but she'd already spun around to stand in front of the door.

Fuck me.

She tried for nice; I heard her pleading with him that she'd missed him, that everything was a misunderstanding.

But Georgie had smartened up. He was done falling for her. "You think you can keep lying to me and playing with my emotions, girl? Your mom was just as much of a bitch right before we killed her."

He'd gone off in an emotional rage and thrown out the one thing I had needed to tell her.

"What?" Katie whispered, but the sound wasn't meek. It flew from her mouth like a demon ready to wreak havoc.

I was across the room, hidden in that closet, but my body felt hers. The way she punctuated the T, the way the air whooshed from her lungs and then hung there. The room was pregnant with her pain and anger.

I winced at my missed opportunity to be the one to tell her.

"Your mother had her little side piece." There was a pause. "Dougie. Douglass, to be exact. What a proud name for a proud man. I remember your dad's way, how he walked around with his head held higher than God, like he thought he could tame her, like he thought their love would transcend her bloodline. Pride had him cutting lawns, breaking his back like his fathers before him. And for what? You?"

"Georgie, my dad—"

"Oh, baby. Don't look like that. I didn't know much of you then. And you had me fooled real good up until a little while ago. Damn, I almost thought I loved you. Maybe it was my love for your mother. She was hypnotizing, I tell you. And I may not have got a taste of her, but I like to think you tasted just as—"

I lunged for the closet door just as I heard the guttural sound leave Katie's mouth. As I whipped it open, her arm was swinging so swiftly around, I knew Georgie would be too slow to stop her momentum. The small knife she must have hidden on herself was pointed directly at his throat.

He saw it too late, tried to dodge, but she outmaneuvered him like she did most people in her life.

The knife punctured the side of his neck, hitting the arteries and larynx. Georgie's eyes widened, and the gun I didn't know he was holding clattered to the ground as he grabbed at his stab wound.

Katie wasn't done, though. She twisted and then shoved the knife away from her, slicing his back.

He mouthed "Katie" as they stared at one another.

"Oh, no, Georgie. You of all people seem to know that my real name is Katalina. Let it be the last name you say as you bleed out on the floor. I wonder if you'll like the taste of my name on your lips mixed with your blood as you choke on it."

"Fuck, woman." I grabbed her wrist and pried the knife from her hands. "We were just supposed to get the laptop."

Eyes of gray mist filled with questions and pain glanced up at me. "Did you know?"

I took a breath, pulling my phone from my pocket. "Doesn't matter now, does it?"

"It does. You knew. You all knew, and you didn't tell me."

I threw her knife just out of reach from Georgie and turned to dial Dante's number. "We need a cleanup at Georgie's."

"A cleanup? We don't got shit on the schedule. I'm in the middle of—"

"This time Katie hit Georgie. I got her here. We need a cleanup. Now."

"Fuck, man. Bastian know?"

"I guess I'll be the one telling him."

"Maybe call Mario first."

"Mario's not the one we answer to anymore."

"Don't be a fool, Rome. You and Katie answer to no one. That's the problem. It's about to be our whole family's problem." The line went dead.

We stared at Georgie. His voice was gone as he writhed on the ground, struggling to breathe.

"I'm certain he deserves more pain than this, but I don't enjoy seeing anyone grapple for one last breath. Is there a way to...?" Her voice trailed off as she lifted a shaky hand to her mouth.

I nodded without needing her to finish. I knelt in front of him and snapped his neck swiftly.

Katie hissed at the sound, and her chin shuddered. One lone tear rolled down her cheek. "I'm not sad to have lost him or that I took his life. I'm just..." She let out a breath and closed her eyes. More tears escaped, and I wondered if there was a way to capture them in a jar, sell them to the highest bidder. Katie didn't cry.

The Katie I knew didn't care enough to cry, not about a single thing.

"I'm just more lost than I ever thought I could be, and I've always been okay with that, been okay with being empty. Now, there's you. And I figured that was good, right? We were doing good in your apartment, Rome."

"We are good, Katalina."

"No! No. This is all a lie." She motioned between us. "You built this on a lie, Rome. And now, I'm mad and empty all over again, except that this asshole plants a seed of purpose here." She pounded her chest. "My heart all of sudden doesn't feel so lost. It feels full. Full of anger and revenge and longing to know what the hell happened to my mother, to my father, to get the real story beneath it all."

"Katie, stay fucking lost," I growled. "We can be happy with that."

"It'd be easier that way. But we're just scraping by, Rome. What's a life without a purpose?"

"A carefree one?" I tried.

She shook her head and went to pick up her knife.

"You need to get rid of that knife, not keep it."

"It's mine. It doesn't really matter anyway. I'm done hiding."

"Katie, you're staying with me. We'll figure things out—"

She spun around and pointed the blade my way. "I'm staying where I want. I'm going out in the light of day. I'm tired of this bullshit. You'll help me, and so will the family. If you won't, I'll climb over both you and Bastian, or—"

"Or what?"

"Or I'll die trying. My blood is your blood, right? You're either with me or you're against me, Rome."

The line had been drawn, and she stood there with blood splattered on her neck, red dots around the gold Cleopatra necklace she wore, the one I'd fetched for her because she couldn't bear to be without it. She'd become her now. I knew it. It was her time. And my time to stand by her.

I stalked up to her and took her mouth in mine. I tasted her power and gave her my surrender.

After this, I wanted to help her. After this, I was taking her.

Katalina, in the light and the darkest of the dark, was mine.

And there went that bomb.

Tick, tock.

Boom.

CHAPTER 32

KATIE

MAYBE I SHOULD have been concerned about the red stains on my hands as Dante filed in with their cleanup crew. I'd seen a few of them before, but they were nameless associates of our family, ones I'd probably never see again unless they proved their worth.

Had I proved my worth tonight or lost it all? And what was there to prove to a family that wasn't mine? If Georgie was right, if he wasn't lying, I belonged on the other side of the tracks.

My heart didn't rush when Rome mumbled that Bastian would be furious. We stood at the elevator doors, Rome with his hat on and my hood back up for no good reason. The cleanup crew would be calling the police later tonight to have them wipe the cameras.

In this city, we were protected.

As the elevator door pinged, Rome walked in and then turned to me, black fire licking through his eyes. "Get in the elevator, Katalina."

He'd almost told me he loved me in that car, and I'd been ready to drive off into the sunset with him. Now, could I love him knowing he'd kept it all from me?

I stepped forward, staring at my heels clicking on the marble flooring. "You called me that for how long knowing the name was Russian?"

His full lips folded into his mouth as if he held back pain. Or secrets. I wasn't sure anymore. "It wasn't like that. I needed to be sure."

"Or you needed to figure out your angle. Like a kill, there always has to be a set end with you." I threw the words out fast, ready for a reaction.

His jaw ticked, but he didn't unleash the way I thought he would. "You're mad. I'm tired. We just took a life. Let's calm down and figure out how we are going to tell the family."

"We?" I guffawed and stumbled back onto the elevator railing. "Was it *we* when you held the information hostage? When you didn't tell me a damn thing?"

He sighed as if he was going to respond.

I didn't let him. "No. This is on me. I'll take the fall, and I'll tell anyone who wants to know why I did what I did."

"No, you won't," Rome whispered, but then he slammed his hand into the wall behind me, close to my face. "Don't you understand?"

I searched his eyes and found the fear that snaked its way through me. It had crept in as Georgie said the words about my mother. It flowed through me and spread so fast that I almost choked on it.

I'd been protected because I was a part of the family.

But tonight, I'd officially become their enemy instead.

"Of course you understand," he said, his deep vibrato rumbling over me in anguish. It warmed and chilled me to the bone all at once. He breathed me in, his body only centimeters apart from mine. "You've been my downfall for a long time,

Kate-Bait. Now, you're the whole family's. What am I going to do with you?"

"It's most likely your job to kill me." I slid my hand to the back of his head and pulled him in to kiss me. I tasted the mouth that haunted my nightmares and filled my dreams. I wanted to feel his tongue over mine once more, to indulge in my favorite thing one last time. But then I let the anger take over; I pushed the fear down and away along with him. "I can't kiss you right now."

"Fair enough." He sighed and pulled his phone out. After a minute, I heard Bastian's muffled voice. He must have already heard the news from the crew. Rome stared at me as he said into the phone, "I didn't have control of this situation. No one controls her."

"I'm right here," I mumbled but thought better of arguing with them when Rome stabbed the elevator button harder than necessary.

"We planned to eliminate him anyway...I know it's not according to the appropriate plan, Bastian. You want to lock her up forever? It's the only way to contain a feral animal."

"Oh, for fuck's sake." I sighed and combed a hand through my hair as I stared at myself in the mirrored elevator walls. My waves had lost their luster and bounce. The splatters of blood over my collarbone looked decorative, like freckles that belonged there. Maybe I'd always had it in me to do what I'd done; maybe blood on my hands was in my biological makeup.

"If we want to have the whole damn family come, then we should drive out to Heathen's. We don't need eyes on all of us gathering in the city after what just happened," Rome growled. "I'll have Cole close down the place. It shouldn't be that busy there. I'll be at the bar in an hour."

Rome motioned for me to step forward as the elevator doors opened into the underground parking structure. We wove through cars and shadows and then up a flight of stairs to the alley.

Rome stabbed the end button on his phone and then stalked in front of me as we approached his truck. I didn't question how he surveyed the area, because I knew he'd been trained to. Didn't he know I was capable of that too though? I'd looked out for myself for long enough to know where to step in the shadows, how to be quiet in them.

When I reached for my door, he shoved my hand out of the way and yanked it open himself. He grabbed my elbow before he let me get in. "Don't try to take control of the situation tonight."

"You can't take control of the mob," I retorted. "They infest the bones of a city, spread like a cancer, and never die. We're uncontrollable."

"You know what I mean," Rome said into my hair, his eyes closed like his frustration would be gone if he could just not see me.

"I know you want me to do something I'm not capable of doing." I ripped my arm out of his grip and slammed the door hard in his face.

Everyone wanted to tell me what to do, who to be, how to bait, how to do my job. I'd done it for them for years. I'd showed I was more than capable, and still I was told over and over again what to do.

Would it have been that way if I'd been raised with my mother?

Rome started the truck, and I gripped his muscular arm as a new thought shot through me. "I need to go home first."

"Home?" Rome asked, an eyebrow raised.

I ground my teeth. I didn't want to tell him his place was starting to feel like mine, that I enjoyed being cooped up with him, especially when I got a foot massage while I read him Edgar Allan Poe on the couch.

"Your home, Rome." I rolled my eyes. "And give me your phone. I'm calling all the men over."

"We should talk about it first."

"Like you talked about how Georgie knew my dad?"

When he sighed in defeat, I grabbed his phone and shot out a group text to Dante, Cade, and Bastian that we were headed home, to be there in twenty. No excuses.

My heart pounded fast and loud, like it finally had something to beat for. The only other thing that stirred it like this was Rome, and when I looked at him now, I wanted to scream.

They'd all hid more than enough from me over the years. Mario had let me sit in on some meetings but never all the important ones.

I'd been a tool, not a member.

I'd been just a woman to them, and I was suddenly very aware that I didn't want to be that anymore.

Fitting in with them wasn't my future. They hadn't allowed it, and now I saw how stupid my dream to be one of them had always been.

Rome parked the car under his apartment, and we took the elevator up to his floor. "What do you need from me, Katalina? You want me to back you when we walk in there?"

"Do what you've always done." My voice came out foreign to me, cool and distant. "Be a part of the family."

He grabbed my arm to stop me from walking to his door. "I've never been a part of the family. I'm their killer. I'm the cousin, not the brother. I have a purpose like everyone else. Without that purpose, you die."

"What's *mi famiglia*, then, huh?" Shoving at his chest, I glared at him, tears springing to my eyes. "Where do we belong without it? One foot in with the family means we got no feet in. We either are or aren't."

"We belong with the people we end up loving. You make your own family. You fit in there."

"Well, it'll be interesting to find out if my own family, the ones that made me, let me belong there, then."

I shoved him back, but he didn't let me go. His hand on my arm didn't budge, and my adrenaline spiked so fast, my hand flew to the blade under my arm and held it to his throat. He'd seen the knife coming and already tilted his head. He probably could have pulled it from my grasp before it made it to his neck.

I lifted a brow and whispered, "You're coddling me? Letting me put a knife to your neck? You think that's going to make me think twice about my actions tonight?"

"I'm giving you a right to express your emotions. You deserve that."

I shoved the edge into him, and he winced as blood dripped from the cut. His tattoo would be cut because of me, scarred by my anger. "I have a right whether you or anyone else gives me one, Rome." I shoved away and took my knife with me.

When I turned the doorknob to his place, it gave way. Bastian and the boys were there already.

Walking in, I knew I looked a mess. Cade's mouth dropped along with his phone, and Dante swore, immediately getting up to come to my side. He slid the knife from my hands and wrapped me in his arms.

I didn't return the hug. I stared at the Armanelli family's king.

Bastian's gaze was as unwavering as mine. "Katalina."

"Bastian," I replied in the same tone.

Two leaders, enemies, captains of an army, studied each other before they fought. Some could sit down and enjoy a meal together, talk over their options and even decide on a fair fight.

Bastian scrutinized me like I was a new formidable opponent. Before, he'd hugged me hello, held me on his arm, and let me into his home. He'd cooked me dinner, left me unattended with his trust, poked a finger into the holes of my socks.

Now, his attention never strayed from me. I wasn't a beautiful, useful tool to him anymore but a threat. For the first time, I witnessed a respect and fear that my bloodline must have inspired in him.

Very few had ever looked past my beauty. It was what I flaunted, what I knew how to exaggerate. Tonight, every single one of them would witness my mind instead, would realize I'd been a part of their mafia as more than just bait.

Dante whispered in my ear, "We practiced for this. Remember?"

Every time he'd beaten me to the ground on those practice mats at the gym, he'd held out his hand. "Each of these losses prepare you for the one thing you have to learn. Every fall makes you stronger than the one who's never fallen before. Get back up, face them again, and beat them."

As Dante stepped around me toward the sink to wash my knife, I took a breath and pointed at Bastian. "Your father used to ask me questions every now and then. He'd whisper them to me at a meeting he'd let me attend, ask me over the phone with Jimmy. Do you think Mario kept me around just to tempt other men, find information on them for the family?"

"No one kept you around for that, Katie," Bastian replied, folding his hands together over his lap. That gold ring shined on his finger, mocking me with what it represented. Only a few of the top family members wore one. All the men in the room had them on.

Not me.

"Let's all sit down and talk." Bastian motioned toward Rome's couch where Cade sat, looking completely out of his element. He'd put away the technology that was normally an extension of his arm and gave us his full attention. Dante stood by me, like he'd be on my side no matter what.

I felt Rome's hand on the small of my back, maybe for support or maybe to keep me close enough to know my next move.

Bastian pointed to the chair across from him, a lone one with metal arms but leather upholstery. The metal wouldn't scrape against any cement if I pulled it toward me before I sat. The leather wouldn't feel as uncomfortable as a folding chair. The interrogation probably wouldn't be as intense either.

Still, I wouldn't be in the hot seat tonight.

I hadn't done anything wrong.

"I'm not sitting down." I brushed away Rome's hand from my back. "You all take a seat, huh? You answer the questions tonight, not me."

Delivering the command and telling them exactly what was on my mind liberated me. Freedom is powered by purpose and a relentless drive to overcome your captor. I'd been captive to the family's idea of me for too long; I'd given in to the idea that I was less than I was. Buried deep down inside me, the quiet rumble of injustice turned loud and threatening. Why had no man put me on the pedestal I deserved? Why had each one taken advantage of the person who had no one after her father died?

I started to believe in myself and in my revenge in those moments. Suddenly, my life demanded I respect myself first, respect what I'd been through, and make everyone else respect me too. I realized I'd missed that part for so long. If I couldn't respect myself, then I wouldn't gain the respect of others.

The surge of anger, of anguish, of desperation I should have felt all these years in so many bad situations pulsed through me. For so long, I'd shrugged it off, I'd kept moving, I'd walked on.

I'd closed myself off to feeling a damn thing.

I smiled at my newfound emotions. They were demonic, demanding, and cruel. Respect could be earned, but it could be taken too. I'd do whatever needed to be done.

The world had made me this way.

I was ready to show it exactly the woman it created.

CHAPTER 33

ROME

MEN AREN'T BUILT like women. Or at least, not like Katalina.

We could never read emotions as well, navigate a room as well, or know someone else's next move like her. She didn't play chess. She dominated it. It was like sitting across from your opponent and realizing they had all queens lined up instead of pawns.

The fight wasn't fair.

We all knew that. Bastian most of all. He knew he was surrounded by family that was supposed to protect him but that would protect her instead. She'd outmaneuvered him and the family with a love she didn't even express.

Dante trained her, and Cade talked with her when he wouldn't open his mouth to anyone. And I slept next to her like a cub trusting a lioness.

We respected Bastian as the king of the family.

But we loved Katalina.

In the family, men aren't supposed to get close to any woman unless we claim them as our untouchable. None of us had claimed her; none of us had claimed anyone. We'd all been without that love, sailing through life completely oblivious to the absence of it. Then, like a colossal tidal wave, she crashed down onto our boat and we couldn't escape. Maybe we wanted it so badly—to be loved and to love in return—that we welcomed it. I don't know. The only thing I knew for sure, though, was that once a person felt love, the absence of it was all-consuming.

Once the love was there, people lived for it, died for it, and killed for it.

These men, they'd kill for her. They'd murder their king if they had to.

"Seems I'm in the hot seat, then, no?" Bastian shifted in his chair without peering around to look at his closest allies. He'd pinpointed the threat in the room.

Katalina stood like a dominatrix over him, looking down on him like he was beneath her. "You make the rules. You're the boss, Bastian. You own this city and everything in it. Including the hot seat, tonight. You know my place in the Russian bratva, no?"

Bastian licked his lips but didn't answer.

"You all know my place, right? You all wear that ring on your finger like you're brothers with no secrets."

"Katalina, the ring isn't anything against you," I murmured.

Her gaze slashed to me, and her steel-gray eyes narrowed. "It means everything. It means you've officially had a place at the top of this family for as long as you've worn it. And for you, even before then, because your blood bleeds the same DNA as theirs."

"Family ties only solidify responsibility. Not trust or respect. The ring is for the men of the family. It's just a tradition carried on—" Bastian tried to explain.

"Does tradition make something right, Bastian? Tradition was men before women, tradition was my skin in the fields, beaten and bloody, working for men who thought they owned us. Your tradition has set in stone the impossibility for a woman to stand just as tall as a man in this family. It's made me a pawn and a tool. Disposal never suited my character."

"No one was trying to use you. I was ready and willing to have you on my arm—"

"By your side, as an extension of you. I would be owned by you, not respected." She spun around the room, and her hair whipped around with the same fury we all felt coming from inside her. "Can't you all see? You're pacifying me when you should be just as angry at the inequality." Her gray eyes glistened like smooth stones wet from a fresh rain—hard, cold, beautiful, and unbreakable. I started toward her, but she held up her hand. "I want you all to let me go," she whispered, staring out the window into the dark abyss of our city. "If you truly want to understand and to make this right, you'll let me go and let the bratva have me."

"Are you out of your mind?" I roared.

Bastian jumped from his chair. "Absolutely not."

She stalked up to him and shoved him in the chest. "Why? Tell me. Are you scared I'll share the family's secrets, or are you scared to lose me as part of the family?" She paused, long enough for him to answer. When he didn't, she smiled, but it didn't reach her eyes. "Did you know I had Russian blood in me? Before Rome found out, did you and Cade know? Mario has always known everything. Telling his sons—"

"I didn't know, Katie. I swear." Bastian held a hand to his chest like her accusation hurt him, but we'd all wondered it. I'd mulled it over and still had my ideas about Mario's involvement.

Cade piped up. "I never thought to do the digging until now. We did it a long time ago when Jimmy first brought you in, but there was nothing then. I remember thinking you were just some ...well, anyway, I didn't know. As for Bastian, Dad shares more with him." He shrugged, almost unaware that he had put Bastian back under the gun.

Bastian looked around the room, sweat beading his brow. He yanked at the collar of his shirt. "You guys know I wouldn't have hidden that. This is my family, but us, in this room, we're a unit. I would have..."

"You would have what?" She egged him on when his voice trailed off. "Done exactly what you did now? Asked me to be on your arm? Embedded me in this family?"

"My father could have killed you," Bastian shot back.

Dante tensed, and I'd had enough. "You're out of line, fucker," he said.

"Me?" Bastian slammed his hand into his chest. "Katie knows me!"

She shrugged like she didn't. "I've had a lot of men in my arms, Bastian. I wouldn't say I knew all of them that well."

"Woman, I swear to Christ." He stepped toward her, but Dante got in between them as I stepped in front of her. "You're all kidding me, right? I take control of the damn city, and you question what I know about the one fucking woman we all have ties to. I love her."

An uncontrolled rumble rolled out my chest.

"Not like that, you dumbass." Bastian glared my way. "I love that she's a part of this unit. I love that she is who she is. With you. I don't want things to change just because we know her bloodline."

Would it change now? It would have to. Katalina had morphed into a fireball, ready to tear apart the city to find the answers she wanted.

"I trusted you all for so long." Her voice was just above a whisper, and we all leaned in to hear exactly what she had to say. "I gave up my confidence in my ability to earn a seat at the table over and over again for this family. I've lain on my back and taken men for you. I've sold my soul." Her voice cracked, but she cleared her throat and carried on. "I won't do it anymore."

"We never wanted that for you," Bastian started.

"Let me go. Let them have me," she said again.

"For what?" Bastian whispered. "They have no organization. They're ruthless and lack morals. They don't want you for anything but to use as a weapon against us. They'll end up killing you."

"Some would say the same about your father," she shot back. "And now you."

"But you know deep down that's not true. I'm not my father. Woman, if I'd known you felt this way for so long, I'd have changed something. You never said—"

"It's not my responsibility to educate you on who's deserving, Bastian. You and your father and the whole family should have seen that. Now, I want the opportunity to figure this out on my own, to find my own answers, to see what could belong to me, to us."

I stepped toward her, reaching for her hand. She yanked it away as if I'd burn her. "Katalina. Cleo, this isn't a fight you need to have. Don't do this alone."

"I have to." She licked her lips and scanned all of me, like she was taking me in for the last time, like she was memorizing me. "Call him, Bastian."

She disappeared down my hallway, and we all stared after her. From the sound of drawers being opened and bottles clinking around, she was changing and packing.

Would she forgive me if I dragged her back to the panic room and locked the door?

I considered if it was worth it, if I'd rather have a shell of her than nothing at all, because walking into the enemy's arms...that was just asking to disappear forever.

She breezed back in with a duffel bag over her bare shoulder. Her signature cut-off shirt was back on, and her ripped jeans hung low at her hips. It was like the traffic and wind outside stopped. We all stood there, four men about to get on their knees and beg her. We would have made a perfect picture, all the men in love with Katalina. None of us moved an inch either, like we didn't want her to jump away from us.

My cousin, the man who was supposed to protect every single person in this family, did the one thing that could make my heart stop. He slid his hand into his suit pocket and pulled out his phone.

My blood turned cold, but I swore I could hear it pumping furiously through my veins. It felt like a sea had rushed into my heart and messed up all the chambers. Every part of my body was breaking, malfunctioning, failing. I couldn't take in air. I could barely stand.

"Katalina will be in front of Rome's apartment. She'd like you to come get her." He hung up without listening to Dimitri's response.

She backed away toward the door. "You follow me, you don't let them have me, you ruin this for me, and I'll tear this family apart by tearing myself apart first."

She spun around, grabbed her knife off the counter, and walked out, slamming the door behind her.

We all stood there, stock still, so silent we could hear the traffic out in the night. We all knew the truth.

She'd turned the tables, and her words rang true.

If Katalina ripped herself apart, if she came back harmed, we'd blame one another.

I'd kill for her, die for her. I only wanted to live for her. The men in that room were the same. We waited with baited breath to see if Katalina would succeed in running into the lion's den and then coming home to us all without our help.

I fell to my knees and let the damn tears roll down my face. Dante and Bastian laid a hand on each of my shoulders.

I knew that it might be the last time I ever saw her breathing, alive and well. And even if I did, I knew she'd never come back the same.

The monster in me stirred. The beast had fallen in love with her, had made a comfortable place to hole up in while she silenced all the noise that used to aggravate him. Without her, my mind and body screamed. The demons ricocheted around in me, trying to find a way out. The monster wanted answers and names and heads rolling. Anyone who knew, anyone who even looked sideways at how we'd come to know her, had a price to pay.

And payment was overdue.

THE END

Katie and Rome's happily ever after is coming!
Read **Love of a Queen** today.

Subscribe to Shain Rose's newsletter to be the
first to know about all things Shain Rose:

shainrose.com/newsletter

Keep in touch by joining
Shain Rose's Lovers of Love Facebook Group:

facebook.com/groups/shainroseslovers

ALSO BY
SHAIN ROSE

Meet the Billionaire Stonewood Brothers

INEVITABLE

A second chance romance that spans childhood to adulthood. When Jax saves Aubrey from a fire her father started, will they be able to overcome the trauma and focus on their love for one another?

REVERIE

An angsty, enemies-to-lovers standalone romance where opposites definitely attract. When Jett acquires Vick's company, everyone is wondering if they have what it takes to survive the tension in the office.

THRIVE

A captivating friends-to-lovers small town romance where Mikka and Jay will have to face their dark pasts while indulging in small town delights.

ACKNOWLEDGEMENTS

To my hubs, you get me. I couldn't ask for a better half.

To my kids, please stop being no help. You're killing my vibe...and I love you. ALWAYS.

To my family, I couldn't ask for a better one.

To my readers, none of this would be here without you.

THANK YOU!

ABOUT
SHAIN ROSE

Shain Rose writes romance with an edge. Her books are filled with angst, steam, and emotional rollercoasters that lead to happily ever afters.

She lives where the weather is always changing with a family that she hopes will never change. When she isn't writing, she's reading and loving life.

FACEBOOK PAGE:
facebook.com/author.shainrose/

BOOKBUB PAGE
bookbub.com/authors/shain-rose

TIKTOK:
tiktok.com/ZMJcuQP8Q

GOODREADS PAGE:
goodreads.com/shainrose

INSTAGRAM:
instagram.com/author.shainrose/

WEBSITE:
shainrose.com

Made in the USA
Columbia, SC
29 April 2024

35050557R00172